Everyone is wan praise for *Death* and Ian Moore

"A joyous read!"

—Alan Carr

"A writer of immense wit and charm."

—Paul Sinha

"A very funny page-turner. Fantastique!"

—Adam Kay

"Ian is one of my favorite writers; this is hilarious and a great mystery too."

—Janey Godley

"Good food and a laugh-out-loud mystery. What more could anyone want in these dark times."

—Mark Billingham

"Like going on a joyous romp through the Loire Valley with Agatha Christie, P. G. Wodehouse, and M. C. Beaton. A delight."

—C. K. McDonnell

"Ian Moore is a brilliant, funny writer who perfectly captures the foibles of rural France, but judging by this book I will never be visiting his bed and breakfast."

—Josh Widdicombe

"Beautifully done. Very funny indeed. I can't imagine how one plots something like that. Tremendous work."

—Miles Jupp

"I'm so punchdrunk from the sheer entertainment of it I've got a sore jaw. Encore!"

—Matt Forde

"This is like two great books in one, a tricksy whodunnit, and a really, really funny story."

—Jason Manford

"Such a brilliant read, smart, funny, and his sharp writing captures the nuances of 'Anglo-French' relations beautifully."

—Zoe Lyons

"This book is a fun and funny read and I'm very much looking forward to the next one."

—Ian Stone

"Funny, pacey, and very entertaining."

—Robin Ince

Also by Ian Moore

Death and Croissants

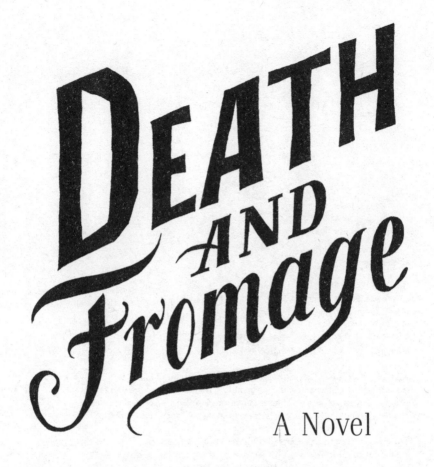

A Novel

IAN MOORE

Poisoned Pen
PRESS

Published by Poisoned Pen Press, an imprint of Sourcebooks
P.O. Box 4410, Naperville, Illinois 60567-4410
(630) 961-3900
sourcebooks.com

Originally published as *Death and Fromage* in 2022 in Great Britain by Farrago, an
imprint of Duckworth Books Ltd. This edition issued based on the hardcover edition
published in 2022 in Great Britain by Farrago, an imprint of Duckworth Books Ltd.

Cataloging-in-Publication Data is on file with the Library of Congress.

Printed and bound in the United States of America.
VP 10 9 8 7 6 5 4 3 2 1

For my dad, who taught me the love of film.

1

Richard Ainsworth was out of his depth and out of his comfort zone. Also, if he carried on drinking this excellent sauvignon blanc at his current rate, he'd likely be out of his box too. A tasting menu soirée to celebrate the opening of Les Gens Qui Mangent restaurant, coinciding with the promised return of Valérie d'Orçay, had seemed too good to be true. And so it had proved. So, now Richard sat conspicuously alone at a table for two, surrounded by every local bigwig within a fifty-kilometer radius in the Follet Valley looking like a man who has had—as Humphrey Bogart put it so eloquently in *Casablanca*—"his insides kicked out."

He tried to refrain from taking another sip of wine, avoiding eye contact with the gleaming crystal glass for a moment before giving in to its charms with a "what the hell?" shrug. Immediately a waiter was on him, quicker than a wasp at a picnic, filling his glass while wearing a look on his face that managed to be both obsequious and contemptuous at the same time. *A Parisian waiter*, thought Richard, trained in the secret art of slick silver service delivered with an impenetrable, almost phosphorous resentment.

"A turp-urp, monsieur?" asked the weaselly little man without looking down. His attempt at English proved the Parisian credentials beyond doubt, the "I'm better than you" one-upmanship the clincher, a pro brought into town for the fancy opening night.

"Oh go on then." Richard's joviality was forced. Also he'd wanted to reply in French, just to let the man know he wasn't to be pushed around, but his instinct was to reply in English, as every damn Parisian-trained waiter knew. How had he even known that he was English? It wasn't as if Richard went about the place with a bowler hat on his head and a pot of tea at his side. He'd even made a huge effort with the language since he'd moved to France and was just the right side of fluent, knowing that a full-blown multilinguist is never quite trusted, especially an English one, and jokey translating was always a good conversational icebreaker anyway. Sometimes he even pretended to know less than he actually did just to get things started. Maybe it was his suit, not worn for years and the cut of which was, he'd been told, very English. He'd had no idea whether it was meant as a compliment or not, and had preferred not to pursue it. English "style" was very much admired by the French, but he wasn't sure that a Debenhams off-the-rack counted. Normally his clothes were standard middle-aged fare: smart without being flashy, maybe a snagged pull in a sweater away from the dreaded "He's let himself go" that the newly single man of a certain age should fear. But tonight, he'd even ditched the string around his neck that held his reading glasses and which stopped him from losing them. Inevitably he now lost them on a boringly regular basis, but it had been at Valérie's suggestion, so he thought it a small price to pay.

Richard suspected that it wasn't necessarily his appearance that gave his Englishness away, but a vibe, a sensibility, a very definable quality that made him different from all the French people in the room. It was an awkwardness of the high-end cuisine restaurant environment that betrayed his roots; whereas the French accepted it naturally and behaved as if it were their birthright, Richard felt out of place, unworthy of his surroundings almost, an imposter about to be unmasked. Put bluntly, Richard's Englishness stood out like a battered sausage on a bed of gratin dauphinois.

That said, he thoroughly enjoyed his life in the wider Loire Valley and his role as an exotic-ish foreigner in its quiet, slow-paced world. One of the locals, the rather giddy Jeanine, who ran the *boulangerie* in town, said that he looked a bit like the Earl of Grantham from *Downton Abbey*, which he'd never seen. Since then, however, he'd always tried to affect a stately manner when shopping for his daily baguette, which if he was honest was quite tiring and not his style at all, more used as he was to a kind of endearingly polite befuddlement. He just felt out of sorts this evening, that was all; something was missing. Of course, it was obvious to everyone what that was, as the place opposite him, with its gleaming cutlery and empty plate, screamed, "He's been stood up." *Dammit!* he thought, nearly breaking the stem of his delicate wine glass. When would the pitifully few women in his life, which at the moment amounted to three, including an estranged wife, a demanding daughter, and his missing dining companion...when would they stop taking him at his word and start reading between the bloody lines? He hadn't been publicly effusive when Valérie had said she was coming to stay, but he'd hardly worn the granite coldness of a statue either. He thought you were supposed to play it cool.

"Another turp-urp, monsieur?"

Richard tensed, ready again with a French comeback for the limpet-like man, then his shoulders slumped and he said a hollow, "Really, already? Well, why not?"

The waiter held the bottle at the base and expertly twisted it as he poured the wine into Richard's glass. Placing the Pouilly-Fumé back in its ice bucket and wrapping the serving cloth around its long neck, he nodded his head smartly to one side, practically clicked his heels, and with small, delicate steps weaved his way back through the tables in search of someone else to bully. Richard sat looking morosely at the bottle, a Didier Dagueneau no less, which at least cheered him up. There were worse ways to be stood up, and he should be proud that his standing locally was such that he had been invited in the first place. He decided to forsake the Bogart angry snarl at the non-appearance of Ingrid Bergman and switch instead to Cary Grant's lighter, roll-with-the-punches touch that broke hearts in *An Affair to Remember* when Deborah Kerr failed to appear at their rendez-vous at the Empire State Building. It comforted him briefly: Richard once again, as he had done since his teenage years, finding solace and escape from reality in golden-age Hollywood cinema. He decided that he may as well enjoy himself.

The tasting menu had thus far been pretty good. He'd lost count of the number of courses, possibly eight, maybe more, a dizzying food circus of pan-fried scallops, quail eggs, ginger-infused *pois gourmand* sorbet served as a starter, kiwi granita as a palate cleanser, *raviolis de joue de veau avec soubise à l'oignon* as the main course... Richard was no expert; he usually approached fine dining of this caliber with a trepidation bordering on fear, so he had no idea if it was Michelin standard or not. What he did know was that even after eight courses—or was it nine?—he was nowhere near full. In fact, he thought guiltily, trying to suppress his Englishness, he was quite peckish.

"Monsieur?" The waiter was back, his nose so high in the air it risked getting stuck in one of the ceiling air ducts that had been left uncovered, as seemed the modern way with restaurant design, all pipes and tubes. The Pompidou Center had an awful lot to answer for. "We are about to offer ze dessert, would monsieur like ze red wine or to stay wiz ze white?"

Richard knew a trap when he saw one. "I believe the dessert is goat's cheese based?"

"Monsieur is correct." His nostril twitched.

"Then I shall stick with this excellent sauvignon blanc, thank you, as nature intended," he added grandly and in French.

The waiter arched an eyebrow, clicked his fingers for some reason, like a discontented flamenco dancer, and slid off.

The small victory cheered Richard up no end, as small victories always did. He often reasoned that small victories were the very essence of life, the *moteur,* as the French would say. If life was a war and defeat therefore inevitable, small victories along the way gave at least the impression that it may be a close-run thing. He also, now that the wine had properly kicked in, regarded Valérie's no-show as a small victory, though he realized that was putting a spin on things that even a seasoned politician would be proud of. He knew that she would have loved the evening, basked in it, and been the center of attention. Her elegance, poise, and beauty would have been the envy of every other woman in the room, while the men would not have taken their eyes off her. Also, thanks to her profession, with one perfectly executed, balletic roundhouse kick she could have broken the waiter's brass neck. Ah well. He took another sip of the wine, then topped his glass up himself. Another minor triumph.

"Richard?" He looked up guiltily as he placed the bottle back in the wine bucket, suspecting security were on him for breaking some wine code.

"Yes? Ah, Noel." He relaxed. Noel Mabit was an odd little man, dressed almost like a waiter himself, which was quite un-French, as they prefer informality in a formal setting. Noel leaned over Richard, his hands clasped together. Richard couldn't put his finger on what he didn't like about Noel; nobody could, even the long-suffering Madame Mabit, who often referred to him as her appendix, in that she wouldn't miss him if he were gone. He was just always there. He was on every committee, at every function, like a small-town minister without portfolio, cajoling others to get involved while not seeming to *actually* do anything himself.

"Richard, I'm so sorry to disturb you." He made an obvious glance to what should have been Valérie's chair opposite. "Have you met Monsieur Auguste Tatillon?" He indicated the figure behind him.

Richard had not met Monsieur Auguste Tatillon but he had certainly heard of him. His reputation as one of the more acerbic restaurant critics in France meant that he loomed over the culinary world like a dark cloud, all-powerful and capable of utter destruction. His word meant the difference between success and failure. As one chef not known for his deference to any living being had put it, his pen was sharper than a Japanese kitchen knife. Tatillon hovered behind Noel, looking bored, his lips pursed, his eyes cold.

"We haven't had the pleasure." Richard stood and offered his hand to the critic, who was taller than he'd realized and slim, bordering on skinny, looking rather like he could do with a decent meal.

"Delighted," mewed Tatillon, though he looked anything but.

"Monsieur Tatillon now has business here in Saint-Sauver tomorrow and wishes to stay the night," Noel gushed. "I suggested your charming bed and breakfast, Richard. I assume you have space..." He couldn't help waving a hand toward the empty chair. Richard's B&B, though he preferred the French term *chambre d'hôte*, was what had given him his standing in the community in the first place, and for that he was grateful, but he didn't like late bookings, as they represented a change of plan, which he was never quite comfortable with. On the other hand, it was quite clear that Valérie, who had booked the last free room of the three he had, wasn't coming, and it would be a feather in his cap to have the famous Auguste Tatillon staying at Les Vignes, even if it would put inordinate pressure on the quality of his morning croissants.

"Of course," he said, "I'd be honored."

Noel clapped his hands with glee. "Monsieur is most kind," said Tatillon with a pained expression, making it sound like Richard had just punctured his eardrum with a fish knife. He moved off back to his own table.

"How marvelous!" Noel couldn't contain himself. "Auguste Tatillon! Staying here in Saint-Sauver! You won't let us down, will you, Richard?"

Richard ignored the "us." "Is he more important than Sébastien Grosmallard then, this critic?"

"Who?" Noel's eyes followed Tatillon as he glided through the tables as if on roller skates.

"Sébastien Grosmallard, Noel. Our celebrated three-starred Michelin chef. Our host." The lights dimmed. "And here he is now."

One of the doors to the kitchen opened, spraying light into the dimmed room. From the bright light a shadow emerged; the enormous bulk of the fiery Sébastien Grosmallard, the enfant terrible of French cuisine, now more middle-aged *terrible* than he'd care to admit, but still the brilliant scourge of the culinary establishment. He stepped forward through the door and the restaurant lights were turned up slightly. He was in his chef's whites, the cross-buttoned tunic undone at the top and struggling to stay closed further down. He had sweat on his brow, his shoulder-length curly hair was stuck to his forehead, and he looked exhausted. In his right hand was a plate, which he held aloft, and under his left arm was a smaller man, who he was practically carrying.

The room applauded, and so did Richard. It was quite the entrance—very Grosmallard, people would say. The applause died down and Grosmallard nodded his thanks.

"*Mesdames et messieurs,*" he boomed, his deep, sonorous voice almost echoing off the exposed pipes, "I have come home!" The applause started again and he held his left arm aloft, dropping the smaller man on his feet. He waited for the applause to die down again. "This"—he held the plate aloft—"is the dish that made my name! *Parfait de fromage de chèvre de Grosmallard!*" He bowed to more applause as the restaurant lights flashed full-beam and suddenly the place was awash with waiters and waitresses who'd maneuvered into position during the gloom, placing the celebrated dish in front of each guest. "Only this time," shouted Grosmallard over the din, "it is made by my son, Antonin!" He hauled Antonin back under his arm, but most people were staring in wonder at the majesty in front of them. To describe it as a parfait of goat's cheese was underselling it.

On the white plate was indeed a parfait of goat's cheese, egg shaped and smooth as marble. Beside it was a small beetroot-and-raspberry tart; nasturtium flowers lay across the tart, as delicate as snowflakes. But the theatricality of the final touch, the central eye-catching drama of the dish, was the red-berry coulis accompanying the two other elements and which lay beneath both. It was on the plate as a perfect handprint, a perfect blood-red handprint. It was magnificent.

Everybody sat down to eat and a silence fell over the room. It was awe, mostly. Richard was no fan per se of food as art, but this was a stunning piece of work, even if it did remind him of the real bloodied handprint on his B&B wall that had first introduced him to Valérie. He didn't know where to start; it felt a shame to ruin such a tableau, and he could sense others had the same apprehension, before a collective deep breath and "Geronimo!" had everyone diving in. Then he quickly noticed something else: the atmosphere in the room had changed. There were murmurings, discontented murmurings, that came first from Tatillon's table, and then the chatter, not positive, began to increase in volume.

"He has changed the recipe!" one excited diner yelled.

"It's sacrilege!" screamed another. Richard even though he saw one woman faint.

Suddenly, anger and pandemonium were everywhere, before being halted by a bloodcurdling scream that came from the kitchen and traveled through the pipes until the noise not only filled the room but surrounded it, a primeval howl.

"You've killed me!" went the painful roar. "You. Have. Killed. Me!"

Richard picked up his wine shakily and was just about to take a drink when it was taken from his hand.

"Have I missed anything?" asked Valérie, before taking a gentle sip, the wine and the lights catching the gleam in her eye.

2

The diners drifted slowly out of the now somber restaurant and away into the car park. Their low whispers may have bordered on silence, but spoke volumes. There was a time for gossip and speculation but this wasn't it; this would shake the town to its core. Richard noticed that Noel Mabit was lingering, presumably to offer his services in the aftermath, but nobody wanted to talk to him. The staff were clearing up, trying not to make too much noise; even Richard's nemesis waiter looked shocked. He saw Auguste Tatillon waiting for him by the door, a small, elegant leather case in his hand. He'd have resembled an evacuee if it wasn't for the detached, high-handed air; the cold look on his face was that of a stern teacher let down by a star pupil.

The look on Valérie's face wasn't much warmer. "This is ridiculous!" she kept saying. "Honestly, French men!" Then she looked at Richard and revised the opinion to "Men!" in general. Richard, rendered slightly fuzzy around the edges by too much high-quality sauvignon blanc, didn't have the faintest idea what he'd done to deserve the rebuke, but seeing as that pretty much described his adult life, he was able to find a kind of comfort in it.

"So what happened to your car?" he asked, trying to get off the subject of his vague culpability.

"I don't know," she replied dismissively. "I stopped to let Passepartout have a little walk and the thing would not start again after that. I had to wait to be towed here." As usual they switched between English and French, but Valérie's French accent in her reply was made stronger by her irritation.

Richard had forgotten about Passepartout, Valérie's pampered Chihuahua, who went everywhere with her, and who permanently eyed Richard with a haughty suspicion, not unlike waiters and food critics. "So where is Passepartout now?"

"He is in your car—"

Richard made to interrupt.

"Yes, Richard, I broke into your car. It was very easy to do. I don't know why you bother locking it." She was losing patience. "Oh, this is ridiculous!" she said for the umpteenth time. "All over some silly cheese." A passing diner heard her words and looked at Valérie like she had just blasphemed. *This is France*, said the look, *there's no such thing as "silly cheese."*

The muted atmosphere was broken by another howl from the kitchen, almost shaking the saloon-style doors that mostly hid what was going on inside. Then the door swung open violently, almost smashing into the wall behind it and narrowly missing a plate-laden waitress in the process. Once again the imposing figure of Sébastien Grosmallard filled the doorway; he looked like a bull ready to gore anything that stood in his way. His eyes were a fiery red, almost as if he'd been weeping, and he held a bottle of wine in his left hand. "I am ruined!" he screamed, though it was more of a throaty roar. "Ruined!" He slowly surveyed the room, looking for a target.

"Monsieur Ainsworth?" It was Auguste Tatillon, tapping on Richard's shoulder, still with the snooty look on his face, but with half a fearful eye on Grosmallard still snorting on the other side of the restaurant. "Can I suggest we depart? Monsieur Grosmallard has a fiery temper, a scandal to deal with, and an intense hatred of the humble critic."

"Yes, yes of course," Richard said hurriedly, himself unable to take his eyes off the famous chef flailing around in the doorway like King Kong at the top of the Empire State Building. "Can I introduce you to—"

"In your car, most certainly—sorry, madame, but can we go please?" He started to move toward the exit with Richard following him before turning back, noticing that Valérie hadn't moved. She was unimpressed by Grosmallard's antics and looked like she was perfectly willing to tell him so, a slight smile on her face, her eyes almost pitying what she regarded as the pathetic creature in front of her, the wounded beast.

"Men!" she said again, loud enough for Grosmallard to hear, though he was too wrapped up in his own desolation to register it. Richard went back, took her gently by the elbow, gently enough not to awaken her martial arts skills, and guided her toward the door and a waiting, visibly shaken Auguste Tatillon.

The night air was still warm, but the purity of it hit Richard immediately and he felt a little more woozy than he had done in the restaurant. "The car's over here," he said in a determined fashion, so that the others wouldn't know. He'd parked it facing the road so that nobody would see that he'd planned to sleep in it, at least until the wine wore off.

"No, it's not, Richard, I moved it. I didn't want Passepartout disturbed." She put her arm in his and led him and the following Tatillon in the opposite direction. Richard caught Tatillon's eye and offered his best Gallic shrug, acknowledging he was not in any way in charge. "I'll drive, I think," Valérie said, brooking no argument.

Moments later they were leaving the car park, with Valérie cursing the ancient gear mechanism of Richard's battered 2CV. Tatillon was slumped down, as much as his height would allow, in the front seat, with Richard relegated to the inadequate and uncomfortable back seat next to Passepartout, who, as usual, didn't look pleased to be sharing the same space.

"Grosmallard doesn't know where you live, does he?" Tatillon asked, trying, but failing, to hide the anxiety in his voice. The man looked terrified, thought Richard, a long way from the ice-cold destroyer of reputations who struck fear into even the most famous culinary maestros; he was literally shaking now.

"No, I don't think so." He was absolutely certain that Sébastien Grosmallard had no idea who most of the local guests were, never mind Richard Ainsworth, and certainly not where he lived, but a little projected self-importance didn't hurt once in a while. "Are you really so worried about him?" Richard went to put a reassuring hand on the critic's shoulder; unfortunately, he did so just as Valérie took a corner slightly too fast, causing the car to lean to the right. Richard narrowly missed Tatillon's shoulder, grabbing the crown of his head instead and, to his horror, completely dislodging the man's toupee. He immediately sat back, embarrassed, but the hairpiece had stuck to his hand. Shaking it, trying to get it off, he excited Passepartout, who regarded the thing as a slightly smaller rival and started barking at it, snarling as he did so. To avoid the dogfight, Richard managed to throw the toupee back into the front, where it stuck to the inside of the passenger half of the windshield. It looked disturbingly like road-kill, and it left an uncomfortable silence. Even Passepartout buried his head deep into his expensive travel cot. Very slowly, Tatillon peeled the false hair off the windshield, looked at it, and sighed with resignation. He looked human for the first time since Richard had set eyes on him.

"Maybe now," Tatillon said slowly, the grandeur and clipped consonants gone, "even if Grosmallard knows where you live, he won't recognize me."

"Men!" Valérie said again, though this time with far less venom. "You look better without it anyway, I have to say," she added in a detached way.

Tatillon smoothed the piece in his hands, which to Richard looked like he was stroking a guinea pig. "Thank you, madame." Tatillon sounded weary. "I am inclined to agree with you, but it's my cloak, if you like, my disguise. With this on, I am Auguste Tatillon"—he went back to the clipped, scornful voice—"fearsome restaurant critic." Then he looked out of the passenger window, catching his own reflection. "Without it, I don't have to pretend," he added quietly and with a touch of melodrama.

Well, this is awkward, thought Richard. He sensed that Valérie was itching to continue her onslaught against men and, no doubt, their absurd vanity. It was something he wouldn't necessarily disagree with, but he felt a change of subject might clear the air.

"You should have sent me a message," he said, "when your car broke down. I could have come to get you." If he'd been entirely sober he might have detected a sudden frost in the car. "I wasn't exactly enjoying myself, eating on my own. I don't know how you do it, Monsieur Tatillon. I felt very self-conscious..."

Tatillon turned his head, about to reply, but was interrupted. "I sent six SMS messages, Richard, and I left two voicemails. I think you were enjoying yourself just fine."

So that was it. Men had let her down, or *man* in this instance, Richard specifically representing the gender.

"He wouldn't have received them anyway," Tatillon mumbled, still looking dolefully out of the window. "Grosmallard hates social media, so he pays for expensive jammers to be installed in his restaurants."

"Oh," Valérie said, a hint of contrition possibly hidden in there somewhere.

"I rather admire that." Richard broke the short silence again.

Tatillon stopped moping in the window and turned to the others. "Grosmallard's greatest dishes are all about flavor in the first instance, and of course that's right, but also it's the drama of the presentation. The theatrical, the visual. Which is why he hates cell phones. If everyone can see a picture on Instagram, the drama is lost, the shock disappears." He was warming to his subject now and showing a genuine passion beyond the usual icy superiority. "At its best, Grosmallard's food is sublime, but also, also, his dishes tell a story beyond the genius of the flavor!"

"I read that somewhere!" Richard said, caught up in the moment.

"I wrote it," Tatillon declared, some vestige of pomposity still lurking even without his wig.

"I see. So what was wrong with tonight's dessert? Why the kerfuffle? It looked stunning to me."

Tatillon shook his head sadly. "The drama was there, for sure, but the flavor...it was not."

"I liked it."

"Even the parfait?"

"Yes," Richard answered nervously, feeling like he was failing a test.

"But the goat's cheese..."

"Yes?"

"It was vegan goat's cheese!" The man could barely contain his anger. "To declare that you have 'come home,' then insult your home with fake cheese!" He spat these last two words. "Vegan goat's cheese has neither the flavor nor the consistency for a restaurant, a Michelin-class restaurant. It is a bland imposter."

"I see." He didn't.

"We were promised a return to glory after all these years; instead we got a..." He seemed lost for words. "We got a joke, a comedy, a farce!"

Richard didn't think it was going to be an entirely support-ive review that Tatillon would be putting in, and after seeing Grosmallard's reaction that evening, he wouldn't want to be around when Grosmallard read it. He thought about trying to defend the man, but he couldn't offer any expertise. He was rescued by his phone catching up with Valérie's messages and firing out various dif-ferent tones, one of which he didn't recognize.

"That was my phone," Valérie said, bringing the car to a halt at Richard's gate. They all got out, Richard with some difficulty, while Tatillon took his case from the boot and Valérie produced a small overnight bag from under Passepartout's cot. "I left my luggage in my car," she said. "We can go back tomorrow." Something told Richard that she was going to go back anyway, but he put it to the back of his mind as it suddenly struck him that he had given her room to Tatillon in a fit of pique.

"Right-o," he said, trying to buy himself some thinking time as to where to put her.

"That's a shame." Valérie's face was lit up while she looked at her phone. "My rendezvous is canceled tomorrow. Unfortunately, the owner has died. That is a shame; he seemed very nice on the telephone."

"The owner? Are you, er, you know...?" Richard was trying to control himself.

"Yes, I am house-hunting." It was stated coldly, almost like a press release, and he caught her eye, but he could read nothing into it. "I need to get out of Paris." There was another awkward silence, which Valérie broke. "Poor Monsieur Ménard," she said gently.

"Ménard? Did you say Ménard?" Tatillon was lingering by the gate, waiting for someone to open it.

"Yes, it seems he died this evening." Valérie picked up Passepartout's bag and gave it to Richard.

"It is probably just as well," the critic said sarcastically. "He was Sébastien Grosmallard's cheese supplier."

3

Richard stood behind the breakfast bar as usual, making himself look busy. If old films were his escape, then standing in the kitchen of his bed and breakfast, either leaning on the heavy oak surface like a Tudor innkeeper or pretending to wipe away a non-existent coffee ring, was where he could get some thinking done. It gave him the air of being there without being there. On hand for any customer demands should they arise, but with a look on his face hopefully distant enough to make the guest think twice about making any. Breakfast was nearly over anyway, which was just as well, as he had a lot on his mind.

He had a good group of guests at the moment, not as demanding as they could sometimes be. There was the gay couple, who had been up early wanting to fit as many chateaux as possible into their day. Two very good looking men in their early thirties, Messieurs Jean and Olivier Fontaine, who, when Richard went off to feed his hens, a moment he reserved for really deep thought, had cleared their table and washed their dishes. Periodically he read about guesthouse owners who refused to accommodate gay couples on some archaic principle or other and he just didn't get it. In his experience, gay couples always left their rooms neat, tidy, and absolutely spotless. If he thought there was a market solely for the pink euro in the Follet Valley, frankly he'd jump at the chance. Young heterosexual couples were different. Usually in the early stages of a relationship, the male part often feeling the need to beat his chest and complain about something in alpha-male fashion while the female part, to her credit, looked slightly embarrassed. Plus, younger straight men always had absurd Arctic-explorer beards these days, which meant blocked sinks and therefore the unending ire of the formidable Madame Tablier, his *femme de ménage* and a cross between a hard-edged woman of the soil and a nightclub bouncer.

Families were the most difficult guests, though. Out of the corner of his eye he watched the family at the table in the corner. Like so many others, a working couple who rarely saw each other, down from Paris for the week with their children, who they saw even less. Richard found it painful to watch families who didn't know each other pressure themselves into some sort of cohesive unit for a couple of days. Madame Tablier wasn't keen on families either. Families meant children, and children meant crumbs on her pristine tiled floors or fingerprints on walls. She appeared now through the double doors, clanking her old metal bucket as she did so, a thunderous look on her face as though she'd been detailed to mop up a particularly debauched music festival. The mother of the family, a heavily made-up, petite woman with a blonde bob, said, "Bonjour," as did her husband, a balding man with the collar on his generic rugby shirt turned up. They both looked at their children, a boy and a girl, smartly dressed, hair still wet but combed, and both with chocolate spread smeared around their mouths. The children ignored their parents.

"What do we say, children?" asked the mother. The look on her face suggested that the nanny would be getting the sack the minute they got home.

"*Bonjour*, madame," the children said in unison.

"Huh? Oh, yes." Madame Tablier was momentarily caught off guard. "Bonjour. Now make sure you don't drop anything on the floor." She made off for the narrow staircase but only got a couple of steps before she reversed to let Auguste Tatillon pass her. She didn't look impressed and clanked off up the stairs.

Tatillon was once more bewigged, and with it came the nose in the air, which Richard was now convinced was less supercilious posturing and more balancing his hairpiece at an angle to stop it sliding off. Tatillon approached the breakfast bar, once again gliding across the floor as he had in the restaurant the night before.

"Morning, Monsieur Tatillon, I hope you slept well." They were always the first words Richard said to any guest in the morning, sometimes more than once, small talk not being his thing.

"Well, I was up late, obviously, writing my piece on Grosmallard."

"Ah, did it go well?"

"As well as an obituary can," he said ominously. "Though perhaps that's now in bad taste; one can never be sure these days." He leaned in closer. "About, er, last night, monsieur..." He trailed off and pointed toward the ceiling, and Richard looked upward, following his long, bony forefinger.

"About last night?" Then he realized that Tatillon was pointing at his hair. "Oh, oh, I see. Oh no. Your secret's safe with me. Discretion is my middle name."

"And discretion"—Tatillon couldn't have gotten much closer—"is it also the middle name of your wife?"

My wife? thought Richard. What on earth did the long-distance Clare have to do with anything? Then it clicked, and he couldn't help blushing. "Oh," he said, "Madame d'Orçay, you mean, she's... erm, she's an old family friend, so to speak."

Tatillon leaned back, a predatory twinkle in his eye, reminding Richard of Shere Khan in *The Jungle Book*. "How interesting," he purred, practically licking his lips.

Richard ignored it. "Now for breakfast, monsieur. I have a selection of breads and some fresh croissants. It's not often we have a famous restaurant critic staying with us... I've also prepared"—he bent down and opened the oven door, producing a warm plate covered with a metal cloche—"an oven-baked, freshly foraged mushroom stuffed with free-range scrambled egg, all on a bed of smashed balsamic tomato and topped with fresh chives." He pulled off the cloche with the panache of a seasoned magician. "Voilà!" he said in triumph.

"Yes." Tatillon leaned in close again, another secret to be shared. "Do you have any Nutella?" he whispered. "I can't get enough of the stuff; I adore it. Just some Nutella on toast, thank you." He turned to make his way to his table, then half-turned back. "Not your wife, you say? Odd—you bicker as though married."

Richard put the cloche gently back on the plate, ignoring the jealous looks from the Parisian family as he did so. I suppose they did, he thought—bicker like they were married, that is. Valérie had been particularly irritable when she'd finally arrived, but then her car had broken down so she had every right to be. And as for the carry-on with Grosmallard, just because his famous dessert was served with vegan cheese, surely it wasn't the end of the world? Obviously, Richard knew very well the general French attitude to vegan food; it was a bit like the British attitude to watching people add milk to tea before the hot water. We know it goes on, but we don't want it here, thank you very much. But then Fabrice Ménard, the cheese supplier, the much-vaunted cheese supplier at that, had died. It seemed an odd coincidence, but also it might be totally innocent. He vaguely knew Ménard, and despite the enormous success of his business, even internationally, he'd always seemed a timid little man, quite weak physically too.

He had explained this to Valérie the night before when she'd shown him the text she'd received. It was from Hugo Ménard, the son:

Property no longer available. My father is dead we're no longer forced to sell. H. MÉNARD

Even to Richard, this was a message that invited a lot of questions rather than closing the subject. Firstly, it was sent with unseemly haste, but also, and maybe Richard was reading too much into it, it appeared to suggest that Ménard senior hadn't known about the imminent sale of property on his own land. And "no longer forced to sell"—his was a thriving business, the king of the cheesemakers in the valley of the goat's cheese. It was certainly intriguing, and Richard knew Valérie well enough to know that she wasn't going to let it go at that. He also knew that he'd be roped in too, that he'd kick and buck against being roped in, that he'd make a reluctant show of giving in to Valérie, but that, not so very deep down, he bloody loved it. It was why he hadn't slept. That and the fact that Valérie d'Orçay was asleep in the next room, in his daughter's bed, and that she was house-hunting in the area.

The Parisian family got up from their table, the children receiving yet another admonishment, this time for scraping their chairs rather than lifting them. As soon as they'd gone, Richard took the breakfast plate back out of the oven. If no one else wanted it, then he may as well eat it instead. He removed the cloche, this time with no flourish at all, his efforts wasted.

"Oh, Richard!" Valérie had, as ever, opened the door without him noticing. "Is that for me? It looks delicious. Morning, monsieur." She nodded to Tatillon, whose mouth was agape, a piece of chocolate-smeared toast halfway toward it, as she walked past him to another table. She had gone full Audrey Hepburn this morning. She was wearing black capri pants, black ballet shoes, and an oversize Breton jumper. Her sunglasses were perched on the top of her head, neatly nestled into a loose hair bun, and over her arm was a straw bag containing Passepartout, the ultimate accessory. The chocolate toast still hovered comically close to Tatillon's mouth as she passed. If it had been a cartoon, his toupee would have risen and spun round.

He regained his composure slowly as Richard served Valérie the cooked breakfast. "I'll join you in a minute," he said, loud enough for Tatillon to hear. "I'll just put some more coffee on."

"Could I have a bowl of water for Passepartout as well, please?"

"Coming right up." Long gone were the days when Richard had tried to tell Valérie that pet dogs weren't welcome in the breakfast salon, or in the bedrooms either for that matter, but Valérie had just looked at him like she understood perfectly well what the rules were but that Passepartout wasn't a pet dog, he was part of the family, and therefore the rules didn't apply. It was one of many battles that had been fought and in which Valérie's immovable take on logic had won the day. As Richard's father had impressed on him, though, it wasn't the winning that counted, it was the taking part. Even if defeat was inevitable.

Tatillon rose languidly from his table and covered the plate with his napkin. He made his way slowly toward Valérie, making sure he caught Richard's eye as he did so. "Madame, you look enchanting this morning," he schmoozed.

"Thank you," she replied as only a woman who hears this all the time can.

"Madame, I am invited to another restaurant nearby for dinner this evening. Alas, it's all work, work, work! However, I would be delighted if you were to join me. One hopes it will be more successful than last night."

Valérie beamed up at Tatillon. "It would be a pleasure, monsieur, thank you." She looked at her watch, while Tatillon turned to Richard, a look of victory on his face. "Are we free for dinner, Richard?" she said, hidden from view as Richard watched the man's face fall.

"Yes, I think so. That's very good of you, monsieur. Will you be reviewing?" he asked, making no effort to hide his own look of triumph.

"Yes," the man replied flatly and turned toward the stairs. "I shall see you both this evening then." He didn't bother to hide his irritation.

"Shall I bring some Nutella?" Richard whispered as Tatillon climbed up to his room.

Valérie looked up. "What did you say?"

"Nothing," he replied, sitting down with two coffees.

Madame Tablier clanked back down the stairs, her eyes immediately locking on Passepartout. "Oh, so you're back, are you?" Her eyes narrowed. "I didn't notice any dog hair in the rooms."

"Bonjour, madame." Valérie rose and kissed her on both cheeks, utterly disarming the woman. "I slept in the house last night…"

"In my daughter's room," Richard added immediately.

"Hmmm, more funny goings-on, I reckon, like last time. Anyway, I don't like that bloke I just met on the stairs, leaving chocolate fingerprints on my banisters…" She continued muttering to herself as she went outside.

"Now, Richard," Valérie said with sudden urgency, "I've decided to go to the Ménard property anyway." He went as if to interrupt. "There's no point in arguing with me. I don't like the tone of the text I received."

"Or the speed of it."

"Or the speed of it, exactly, Richard."

"So, you want to see for yourself."

"So, I want to see for myself. Oh."

"Are you going to say you didn't see the text, then?"

She looked down at her breakfast. "Unfortunately, I replied. I said how sorry I was and so on."

"Ah. So, you can't just turn up, then?" They sat in silence for a few seconds, Valérie picking at her food.

"Listen," Richard said calmly, "I spoke to Ménard a few weeks ago. We talked about him supplying me with his fancy yogurts…"

"And?" There was a flash of excitement in her eyes.

"And nothing really, it was just one of those polite aperitif conversations. Nothing came of it." She looked disappointed. "But," he began, then asked hurriedly, "they've never met you, right?"

"No, never."

"Well, as we're passing that way anyway to pick your car up, I could just pop in, ask if he's given it any more thought..." He took a triumphant swig of coffee that was far too hot for swigging.

"Oh, Richard!" she exclaimed, putting her fork down. "Brilliant!"

4

The excitement fizzed off Valérie like static electricity. If she'd been subdued and short-tempered the night before, that had only lasted until she received the news of Fabrice Ménard's death. Put together with the vegan goat's cheese scandal at the restaurant, she had immediately jumped to the conclusion of what used to be called foul play. Her almost childish need for adventure was very appealing to Richard, despite his being almost the exact opposite and proudly so. She sensed intrigue and excitement and was behaving like a child on the first day of the summer holidays. Of course, as an apparently much sought-after bounty hunter, the thrill of the chase was literally her lifeblood; she needed it like an addict needs a high, though Richard knew that this particular adventure was, like Ménard himself, doomed to be short lived. He felt slightly guilty about keeping it to himself for now, but it was well known locally that Fabrice Ménard had a heart condition. Richard, like the lion in *The Wizard of Oz*, didn't have the courage to tell her.

"Did you sleep well?" was all he could think to ask as he drove along the same country road they'd taken the night before, only this time with Richard's more studied caution.

"What? Oh yes, yes we did, thank you." Passepartout appeared to nod in agreement from the back seat. "You should have told me that you were fully booked, though, Richard. We could have found somewhere else..."

"Oh no!" He realized immediately that his reply sounded more panicked than suave, the effect exaggerated as he took his eyes off the road and the car leaned into the same bend as it had the night before. "I wouldn't hear of it," he added in his best David-Niven-under-fire voice while righting the car.

Valérie giggled. "What a silly man," she said, causing Richard to blush. "Why do men wear wigs anyway?"

Relieved to realize he wasn't the silly man in question, Richard gave it some thought. "Denial, I suppose," he said. "It's not something I've ever had to worry about." He realized he was fishing for a compliment like every other middle-aged man in the world, and silently admonished himself.

"You have fine hair, Richard. It would not suit you to be bald. Some men it does, however." That would do. "No, I think it's that they are hiding something, maybe even hiding from themselves. That man is a different person with his hair on; he finds it empowering." She paused, mulling it over. "Like when some women enlarge their bosom, is it for other people or for themselves that they do that? Both, I think." Richard quickly dismissed the idea of returning a similar compliment and concentrated instead on the road ahead.

"I'm surprised I didn't notice it earlier," he mused, barely audible above the noisy engine. "They normally stand out, things like that, usually quite obvious. His wig, I mean, not the, er..." Valérie seemed not to hear him. "Do you think they're like dentures? The glue loses its effectiveness toward the end of the day, something like that?"

"I wonder if he put his hair back on to write his review," she asked, thinking aloud. "I would bet that he did." She bent down to retrieve her enormous cell phone from her bag, and after a minute or two she found what she'd been looking for. "Auguste Tatillon, connoisseur. France's foremost authority on culinary excellence. Silly man."

"Well, that's critics for you." Richard had known many in his career as a film historian. Some were genuine enthusiasts; some were like vultures sitting in the darkness, hoping for failure because they preyed on bad news like a carcass. They behaved as though they had the wisdom of Solomon, but Richard had found them generally preening and joyless. Personally, he had never seen a film without *some* merit in it, and that's just how he liked things.

"Yes, his latest review is up," Valérie said, her excitement returning. "Les Gens Qui Mangent, Saint-Sauveur." She paused. "Oh dear."

"What?"

"Its title is 'The King is Dead, But Was He Ever Alive?'"

"Ouch. That seems in poor taste, considering." Richard winced.

Valérie began reading to herself.

"Well?" Richard asked.

"Oh, I'm sorry. OK." She cleared her throat. "'I was running late for my train. As usual, la Gare Montparnasse was awash with the flotsam and jetsam of a city gone to seed.' He thinks he's Victor Hugo. 'I had no time for a sit-down lunch at my usual brasserie in the 14th arrondissement and instead bought a pre-packaged sandwich on the station concourse. It was a ham baguette, a simple *jambon beurre*.

Alas, the bread was flaccid, the ham an insult, the poor pig having died in vain, and the butter no better than curdled milk.'"

"Do you think he has to review every meal he has? That must be very tiring."

"Do you want to hear the next sentence?" Valérie asked, clearly building up to something.

"Go on."

"'It was still the best meal I had that day.'"

"Harsh, that."

Valérie continued, "'The food of a great chef, of any chef, of anyone who prepares a meal for others, is a reflection of their personality—an extension of their character. It is their soul that they arrange on a plate; they lay bare the very heart of their existence, the very core of their being. It is therefore with sadness that I declare that Sébastien Grosmallard is no longer the enfant terrible of French cuisine, merely terrible. A husk of a man with no life force within, a zombie chef. His star does not wane but burns out with violence, destroying other stars that would shine in the process...'"

Richard shook his head. "Well, he did tell me it was an obituary."

"It's worse than that."

"I thought the meal was rather good. The champagne-seared scallops with asparagus were..."

"'...like beach pebbles after an environmental disaster.'"

"Oh. Well, the veal cheek ravioli..."

"Was 'so undercooked, the cheek still ran with the tears of maternal separation.'"

"Blimey. And the onion *soubise*?"

"'Like the contents of an oil crank.'"

Richard stayed silent for a minute, taking it in. "Well, like I say, I thought it was all rather good."

"Yes, Richard, but you are English," Valérie said emphatically, as if that automatically rendered his opinion null and void.

"Meaning what?" He couldn't hide the hurt.

"Meaning that you see food differently, that is all. Food to the French is an event, a diversion; it's an art. Food to the English is fuel—you fill up, you carry on. That is all."

Richard wished he had an argument against this. It was a stereotype and it was changing, or at least British pubs were now called gastropubs if they served a carvery with *jus* rather than gravy. He remembered as a young man his grandad walking out on a pub lunch because the chips with his fish and chips were, according to a chalkboard menu, "fried three times." "I'm not paying for old chips," he'd stormed. "It's food mucked about with."

"Well," Richard said sullenly, "it was bloody good fuel last night."

They sat in silence again for a moment, Richard feeling slightly wounded as if he bore responsibility for his nation's cooking heritage, and Valérie having no idea Richard was smarting.

"Interesting..." she said slowly, without going any further.

"What is?" he snapped eventually.

"The dessert, the source of all that ridiculous pantomime when I arrived..."

"I dread to think what he wrote of that!"

"He says that it rescued the evening," she said with surprise.

"Really? I'd bet Grosmallard would argue that point."

"Ah, no. Excuse me, I hadn't finished the sentence. Shall I read it?"

"If you think my culinary faculties are up to understanding it."

"What are you talking about, Richard?"

"Nothing. Go ahead."

She cleared her throat again. "'So we limped toward the end, like marathon runners, the pain unbearable. The dessert was to be the dish that once made him the talk of the gastronomic world, that is to say, France.'"

Richard tutted loudly.

"'The *parfait de fromage de chèvre de Grosmallard*, as he calls it now. And here, at last, was a flame.'"

"Well, that sounds positive."

"'An old flame...'"

"Ah."

"'It was a reminder of ancient glory, a monument to his past, like the Colosseum or the Parthenon; interesting, but a ruin all the same. A well-trodden tourist spot that no longer has the pull it once had. My first thought was that Grosmallard should have left it in the past rather than reawaken happier memories for his guests, but then a twist of genius changed my view. The "cheese" in the parfait was vegan cheese, not even real goat's cheese, on which this area thrives and of which it is so proud. Vegan goat's cheese! In the Loire Valley! Genius, I say! The evening was not about resurrecting his reputation at all. We had been duped. It was about Sébastien Grosmallard's future, and that future is clearly feeding the lunchtime office crowd with snack food fads out of a vintage van on the Place de la République. Cheap, eat-as-you-walk morsels or gullible drones who think vegan cheese will mean fewer hours preening themselves in the gym mirror. Sébastien Grosmallard has finally found his future; it is time, therefore, that we forget his past.'"

Richard whistled. "Bloody hell! And there's no mention that his son made the dessert, then?"

"No, did he?"

"That's what we were told. I'd assumed that's who he meant when he was saying, 'You've killed me.' His son."

"Or"—Valérie grabbed his arm—"he meant Ménard. The supplier of the cheese!" She couldn't contain her excitement.

"Look," he began, thinking this had gone far enough and that he didn't care to see the comedown if it went any further. "About Fabrice Ménard. He was ill, he had been for some time. A heart condition that he was being treated for. This will be natural causes, I'm afraid." He turned the car in to the parking area of Fromagerie Ménard. "Just don't get your hopes up," he added ridiculously.

She tightened her grip on his arm, digging her nails in. "Richard," she said, "look!"

Richard looked and his heart sank. The car park was full, the place a hive of activity, an ambulance, the fire brigade, and three or four police cars all parked at odd angles, suggesting urgency. Every facet of French health, safety, and security was there, even the Police Nationale, the big boys. If this was natural causes, they were quite possibly overreacting.

5

Richard swung the car round violently, almost toppling the old Citroën in his hurry to head for the exit.

"Where are you going?" Valérie hissed, but with half an eye on Passepartout's welfare.

"Well, we're not sticking around here, are we?" Richard meant it as an entirely rhetorical question, briefly forgetting that no such thing ever existed in a conversation with Valérie.

"And why not?"

"Because the place is crawling with police, obviously!"

"So?"

Richard stopped the car and looked at her. His whole life, from his schoolboy years onward, the rule had been—and he would argue that he was speaking for the majority of people here—to walk away in the opposite direction if you saw a lot of police. It might possibly be a middle-class instinct, one based on irrational guilt, but there you have it. Don't get involved, don't be seen to get involved, don't be seen.

"Well, they're busy," he said weakly.

A shadow fell on them as a milk tanker pulled into the car park. Quickly, Valérie jumped out of the car and made her way toward the factory, now hidden by the enormous lorry. "Natural causes," tutted Richard, "natural bloody causes." He caught Passepartout's face in the rearview mirror; it had "What did you expect?" written all over it. He was now in a quandary. Should he stay in the car and wait for her return or should he follow? He was essentially her cover, so he should really follow. Also, why in heaven's name were there so many police? In the two-horse race between natural causes and foul play, the latter was ahead by a good length.

"OK, kid," he said, as though Passepartout was actually Ingrid Bergman, "I'm going in." A dramatic hero's exit marred only by his swift return to leave the windows open for the unimpressed Chihuahua.

He couldn't see Valérie, so he had a decision to make. He didn't want to look like he was snooping but he didn't want to appear so nonchalant as to attract attention either, so he decided to stick with the yogurt cover and head for the sales office. Despite the amount of uniformed people milling about, it was quiet as everyone calmly went about their business. The sun bounced off the two enormous fermentation tanks which stood next to a one-story corrugated building. If it wasn't for the activity of the authorities, it could be any other normal summer's day; the driver of the tanker was having his delivery signed for by an employee in white overalls, white boots, and a white hairnet. Whatever had happened to poor Fabrice Ménard, life and cheese went on.

There was no sign of Valérie as he opened the sales room door. In fact, the room was empty, with no one at the reception desk. Often

Ménard's wife, Elisabeth, would sit in on reception when she wasn't at their main shop in town. The business had grown enormously in the last fifteen years, along with their international reputation, but they were still, at heart anyway, a small family concern, and they had liked to keep it that way. The door behind the reception desk was open and Richard could see more uniforms, more white-coated employees, and a few others in the same outfit as the cheesemakers except that their overalls were light blue. *Forensics*, he thought. *What has been going on?*

"Can I help you, monsieur?"

Richard spun around. In the doorway was a stocky man with the sun behind him. He stepped forward, and though he wasn't smiling, he didn't look aggressive either; there was an air of world-weariness, fatigue perhaps. His suit was slightly too big for him, crumpled and dark blue, and his worn, light-brown suede shoes didn't match the suit at all. His white shirt had the top button undone and a loosened, striped, and stained tie hung limply from the curled collar. His dark hair was parted neatly at the side, and his slightly overgrown mustache had bits of croissant in it. The effect was of a man down at heel, maybe even one who'd given up, and his sad, brown eyes confirmed it.

"I am commissaire Henri LaPierre. You are?" He held out his hand, but with no warmth whatsoever.

"Yogurt." Richard panicked.

Most people would possibly react to such a startling non-sequitur but LaPierre didn't flinch. "I see," he sighed. "Not my department, I'm afraid."

Richard gathered some composure from somewhere and apologized. "I'm sorry," he began, "I was a bit thrown by all the, er, the activity. I'm Richard Ainsworth; I run a *chambre d'hôte* nearby."

"Hence the yogurt," confirmed LaPierre as he produced a greasy paper bag from his jacket pocket and took another bite of croissant. "I apologize, but I have not had breakfast yet. You are English?"

"Yes," Richard replied a little too cheerfully. "My surname gives it away, I suppose."

"That and your accent, yes." LaPierre was still unsmiling, so Richard didn't know if it was a joke, as his accent sometimes was, or a criticism, which was the same. "Did you know Monsieur Ménard?"

"Fabrice? Yes, not terribly well but well enough to talk to occasionally. Has something happened to him?" he added innocently.

"Indeed it has, Monsieur Ainsworth—are you squeamish?" He didn't wait for an answer. "No, then follow me please."

Richard followed the commissaire through the reception area. He didn't like this one little bit. There's an English attitude toward French policemen that is utterly reliant on the image of Inspector Clouseau, and with his mustache, LaPierre conjured up that image. But that was as far as it went. LaPierre was more your dogged cop, incorruptible, a terrier who would never let go until he... Richard shook his head. *Concentrate, man,* he told himself, *you're not an undercover PI on a job for a dame, you're here to inquire after organic goat's milk yogurt.*

"When you say squeamish?" he asked nervously. "What do you mean? What's happened?"

"I am afraid to tell you that Fabrice Ménard took his own life this morning." He stopped and turned to Richard.

"Really?"

"You look surprised, monsieur," he said quickly.

"Well yes, I am."

"Why?"

"Why? Well, I thought it was his heart..."

"But you are not surprised that he is dead. I ask myself why?"

Richard could feel himself beginning to sweat. "Well, I guessed by all the activity that something serious had happened."

LaPierre's eyes narrowed.

"Also..."

"Yes, monsieur?"

"You just told me. In reception."

LaPierre's eyes darted from side to side. "Indeed," he said and turned around again, walking through the factory as the employees silently got on with their daily routine.

"Look," Richard said, keeping up with the smaller man, "when I say I'm not squeamish, I'd rather not see the body if that's OK with you. It's really none of my business."

LaPierre stopped again. "The body is long gone; it was found late last night. No, I meant that you need a strong stomach."

"It sounds terrible." Richard was seriously regretting coming up here with Valérie, and where was she anyway? He took a deep breath as they exited the double doors at the back and went into an older, smaller building. Whatever horror he was about to see, he was determined to get through it.

"It's the goats, monsieur," said a shaken LaPierre. "I cannot stand the smell; they make me feel nauseous." He certainly looked a bit green as he held a grubby handkerchief over his nose and pointed to a dozen or so bleating goats in a pen.

"Is that it?" Richard asked incredulously.

"It is enough!"

Maybe he's not as dogged as I thought, Richard mused. He looked around the building. The goat pen was off to one side with a connecting door to the field outside, though they were being fed by a white-coated employee, who also wore a face mask. There were fridges and gleaming marble tables and an old fermentation tank on a much smaller scale to the ones adjoining the main factory. It looked no bigger than a large house furnace.

"This must be where it all started," he said, and it did have the feel of a working museum.

"This is also where it all ended," LaPierre said through his handkerchief. "As I said, he was found late last night, head first in that tank thing there."

"The fermentation tank," Richard added, trying to be helpful.

"You seem to know an awful lot about it, monsieur." LaPierre's eyes narrowed again.

"I like goat's cheese," Richard muttered defensively.

"His feet were sticking out of the top; that's how he was found, by his son."

They both fell silent as the image ghosted itself into the room. It was certainly an awful way to go, drowned by soon-to-be goat's cheese. Also, and Richard felt guilty for thinking it, really quite absurd. "How do you know it was suicide, though?"

"He left a note. He climbed those ladders there." He pointed to a set of small steps, which hardly constituted a ladder. "He laid down his wallet and his wedding ring and a simple note." The policeman produced a small notebook of his own and read aloud, "I betrayed you. I cannot do this anymore."

"Is that it?"

"Yes. Then he must have climbed in, head first. *Fin*," he added unnecessarily.

"I betrayed you..." Richard wondered aloud. "I suppose he means what happened at the restaurant, with the vegan cheese substitute, I mean."

LaPierre turned slowly toward him. "You know about that?"

"Well," Richard stammered, "I was there."

"You were there?"

"Yes."

"Who with?"

"I was alone, actually."

"You were there, but you were alone?"

"Yes. I was stood up, if you must know."

LaPierre relaxed; seemingly he knew all about that kind of experience. He shrugged.

"Monsieur le Commissaire?" The voice came from behind Richard and he turned to see Elisabeth Ménard standing in the doorway. Madame Ménard was tall, slightly taller than her husband had been, and handsome too. She had always maintained that just because she was a farmer's wife, a goat owner, and a cheesemaker, it did not mean she could not dress as elegantly as she wished, reportedly spending a fortune in the process. Her dyed blonde hair was subtle rather than showy, but her makeup showed that she had been crying, and crying a lot.

"Madame," LaPierre replied.

"Madame Ménard," Richard interrupted, "I am so sorry to hear about Fabrice. It must be a terrible shock."

She looked at him as if trying to place him, then smiled weakly, nodding as she did so. "Monsieur le Commissaire," she repeated, "I feel stronger now if you would like to conduct your interview again."

"Of course, madame," he said as she turned away. He gave Richard a look that suggested they had more to discuss but that now wasn't the time. "Monsieur Ainsworth." He sniffed. "Do you have a business card, or something with your number on it, please?"

"Yes, of course." Richard fumbled about in his jacket pockets.

"You there!" The policeman was addressing the employee still feeding the goats. "Can you show this gentleman back to the car park, please. Don't let him touch anything. Good day, monsieur!"

Richard felt slightly insulted by the thought that he might touch anything. Did the policeman really think he'd try to nab a few yogurts on his way out? He followed the employee back through the factory, then the reception area, and into the car park. The employee kept walking, obviously taking the role seriously enough to make sure Richard left the property.

Then the employee suddenly turned on him, pulling off their mask and hairnet. "I did not stand you up!" the "employee" said defiantly. "I told you, my car broke down."

6

Richard parked his car in frosty silence back at the deserted Les Gens Qui Mangent restaurant. In his sideview mirrors he could still see the fermentation tanks of Fromagerie Ménard no more than a couple of hundred meters away, and as he reversed into the space next to Valérie's sports car, he could also see Valérie pouting in the passenger seat.

"I didn't say you stood me up," Richard argued as he pulled on the handbrake and turned the engine off.

"Yes, you did. I heard you." He wasn't getting on very well.

"All right, I did say you stood me up, but I was just making small talk, you know, bonding."

"Bonding?" She looked at him dubiously.

"Well, you know? I was trying to..." He tailed off. There was silence for a moment. "I mean technically, you did...because you, er, you weren't there." She gave him a filthy look. "Anyway," he said hurriedly, "so it's suicide, then, and not a heart condition. He took the vegan thing pretty badly, it seems."

"I don't believe it," she said simply.

"What don't you believe? Suicide? Why ever not? He was suffering from poor health, he was involved in a cheese-related scandal, which doesn't sound much, but round here...well." She didn't look convinced. "He may even have had debts—why else sell one of the houses on the farm?"

This brought Valérie out of her sulk. "Richard, of course, the house sale! I've only dealt with the son, Hugo. Why did he let me know so quickly? His father's body must still have been warm."

"Especially in an antique fermentation tank." Richard had forgotten that his particular brand of finely honed British sarcasm just bounced off Valérie like a rubber dart. "Sorry," he said meekly.

Valérie ignored the comment and the apology. "That's right, the fermentation tank. It doesn't make sense; why do it like that? His feet would have been sticking out of the top! So melodramatic. Richard, we must find out the time of death."

Richard sighed. "So you don't believe it was suicide, then?"

"No," she said very definitely, "and neither does Commissaire Henri LaPierre."

"What on earth makes you think that?"

"Because he was so suspicious of you. Why be suspicious of anyone if it's suicide? You already have your killer."

"Suspicious of me! What do you mean, suspicious of me?"

"You were at the restaurant, alone." She gave him a look of faux apology. "You were at the *fromagerie* alone, too. He thinks that you are sniffing about. Naturally he asks himself why, so yes, he has his eye on you, I think. As a suspect."

"As a suspect!" he cried. "In a suicide? You were the one

impersonating a cheesemaker, not me—there's probably a law against that around here! Anyway, he has the suicide note."

"What did it say, this note?"

"It said, 'I betrayed you. I cannot do this anymore.'"

"It's time everybody knew," she added definitely.

"What are you talking about?"

Valérie produced a torn scrap of paper from her pocket, the same as the paper LaPierre had held.

"'I betrayed you. I cannot do this anymore. It's time everybody knew.'" She had a look of triumph on her face.

"Where did you find that?" Richard asked, impressed.

"It was under the goats' straw. Somebody, the murderer I think, had the whole note, tore the last sentence off, and, in a panic, threw it to the goats, expecting them to eat it. They did not." She finished the sentence like a lawyer with a defeated witness.

Richard thought about this. "But why? There is no murderer." He didn't sound convinced. "Even with the last sentence, it would still be a decent suicide note. If you see what I mean? It doesn't prove it's not suicide."

"Yes, but it invites questions that the murderer doesn't want asked!" She was enjoying this enormously, Richard could tell. "Richard!" She grabbed his arm suddenly and pointed toward the restaurant. "Look!"

The front door had opened violently and was still swinging on its hinges. Through it came the thin figure of Antonin Grosmallard, followed closely by a redheaded woman wearing glasses and carrying some files. There was obviously a dispute going on.

"Who are they, Richard?"

"Well, that's Antonin. Grosmallard's son; he was involved in the dessert, according to the presentation."

"And the girl?"

Richard looked more closely. "I'm not sure," he said. "Maybe it's Grosmallard's daughter, Karine. I've not met her before."

"She's very pretty," Valérie said decisively, a simple fact offered up without jealousy or side.

"I suppose so," Richard answered stealthily, having learned long ago to keep his opinions on women away from other women. In the end it didn't matter, as she wasn't listening anyway and was already out of the car and crossing the car park toward the arguing figures on the other side. *Let her go*, thought Richard, who needed some time to think.

He leaned his head against the driver's window and looked at Valérie's car sitting smartly next to his own. What was the exact car again? A 1979 Renault Alpine A310, V6 engine, she'd said. It looked sleek, stylish, beautiful even, possibly dangerous, and was the kind of bright yellow that got you noticed. It reflected Valérie perfectly, as much as the 2CV, his own piece of motor nostalgia, was Richard to a tee: battered, muddy in color, worn and rusted around the edges, largely impractical, certainly reliable, and, for people like Valérie, easily broken into. He noticed her car keys sticking out of the top of her bag, then looked at Valérie, now chatting with the Grosmallard children. Then he looked at Passepartout, who had a suspicious look on his face.

Richard couldn't put his finger on why he didn't entirely trust Valérie. It was partly her profession—he assumed that the job of bounty hunter necessarily required a certain amount of false front—but also he couldn't quite believe that she'd taken an interest in him; though to his disappointment, her interest had proved to be purely platonic. In essence, his slight mistrust of Valérie was because of a lack of confidence in himself, and maybe it was time to do something about that. Taking a look at her car might be a good start, if indeed it needed looking at. He'd found her so practical at everything he'd seen her do that it was difficult to see car mechanics being beyond her. Unless of course she was delayed by something else and had tampered with the car, like the nuns in *The Sound of Music* who had removed the distributor cap to disable the German soldiers' car. He hoped that wasn't the case, if only because he didn't know what a distributor cap was, where it would be, or what it should do. He didn't even know if the engine was at the front or the back of a 1979 Renault Alpine A310.

He decided to google it on his phone, and found out that it was at the back. He also found out that it was the same engine used in a DMC DeLorean, which he knew was the car used in *Back to the Future* as a time machine. This was perfect cover, then, if she found him tampering with it. He picked up Valérie's keys, careful to avoid Passepartout's eye as he did so.

Sitting in the driver's side, comfortably hugged by the bucket seat, he felt something he rarely felt: power. He wasn't "into" cars as some people are, but sitting there in a sports car felt markedly different to sitting in his own, and he could see why some men's first midlife crisis port of call was a sleek sports car. Fumbling around under the steering wheel, he searched for the hood switch, and after a while found it. He went out to the front of the car and pulled up the hood, if that's what it was called. Quickly, he cursed himself for forgetting that the engine was at the back and was about to close the trunk. There was a large case, as Valérie had said there would be, and the jack equipment was strewn across the empty space. Only it wasn't a jack. And Richard had watched *The Day of the Jackal* often enough to know exactly what it was. He slammed the trunk shut and got back into the driver's seat. This time, though, he didn't bother to look for the trunk switch, or engine lid, or whatever these things were called. He put the key in the ignition and turned it.

There was a low rumbling sound after Richard turned the key and the engine started up first time. He didn't feel so powerful anymore.

Valérie opened the door, a big smile on her face. "Oh Richard, it started first time! You are clever!"

He smiled weakly.

"Now," she continued, "that was very interesting. I feel very sorry for them both. Sébastien Grosmallard sounds like a monster to me— the boy is very obviously terrified of him."

"And the daughter, I assume that was Karine, then?"

"Yes, she's very striking. She worships her father. She's the one who persuaded him to open the restaurant in the first place; without her, the great Grosmallard would just be 'lending his name to in-flight menus,' according to her brother. Although he was quick to add that that was his father's fear, not his own opinion. I think this has hurt them all, but maybe those two more than the 'genius.'" She exaggerated the last word, leaving Richard in no doubt as to her feelings about the great Grosmallard. "Anyway," she carried on, her excitement only heightened by the information she'd gleaned. "You are clever, Richard. I didn't know you knew about cars. I'll see you back at the house."

"I need to get some things in town first," he said, trying hard to match her mood.

"No problem." She beamed. "I'll meet you there."

He nodded, got out of the car, and got back into his own. She roared off and Richard followed slowly. He felt markedly different in his own car, less powerful, less in control. A feeling that wasn't helped by the fact that he was essentially now also acting as her Chihuahua's chauffeur.

7

The he evening sun shone warmly in the Val de Follet and onto the glass doors of the restaurant as Richard, Valérie, and a fully wigged Auguste Tatillon waited to be shown to their table. The first thing that Richard noticed about this restaurant was how different it was to Les Gens Qui Mangent. Whereas the decor at Grosmallard's place had a kind of forced, old-fashioned, modernity, Garçon! felt more relaxed. The style might have been more old school, a cross between art deco and American diner, but the effect was less austere than Grosmallard's brushed metal pipes and direct lighting. Even the serving staff were less formal. They still wore the inevitable black trousers and white shirts, but the collars were open and the ties loose, a deliberate adjustment of tradition that allowed the diners to loosen up a little too. The complete opposite, then, to the previous night's waiting staff and their prison-guard hostility.

Tatillon had been difficult to evaluate on the short trip over, not that Richard had tried that hard to engage him. At times the critic behaved like the critic, with a patronizing grand edge to his voice, before realizing not only that Richard and Valérie were his invited dinner companions—well, Valérie was, at least—but that they had both seen him without his hairpiece, his shield, in place. They'd been party to the softer underbelly of the demon reviewer, so his aloof act didn't work on them; it just created an awkward silence. Despite that, Richard couldn't help but be impressed by the man's toupee. It was utterly seamless and must have cost him a fortune, though of course restaurant lighting would be a big help to the follically challenged. Richard also had to privately admit that they were lucky to have gotten to the restaurant at all, as Valérie's car had had difficulty starting. He might have done her an injustice on that score.

The three of them were shown to a table in a darker corner of the restaurant, a table for four, where Tatillon maneuvered Valérie onto a chair by the wall before sliding into the space next to her. Richard tensed, expecting a reaction from Valérie, but quickly realized that she must be tacitly agreeing to the seating arrangement or the famous critic would likely be eating any *menu dégustation* through a straw. Richard sat opposite Valérie and she gave him a reassuring smile to let him know she was in control of the situation. If it was a situation; Richard wasn't entirely sure.

They ordered drinks and sat in silence waiting for them to arrive, which thankfully didn't take very long. The waitress put them on the table gently before scuttling off without taking any food orders; they hadn't even been given a menu.

"Forgive me," Tatillon said, as if there were a choice, "but I have already ordered for us." He continued to scan the room as though any interior design faux pas might affect the flavor of the entrées, but seemed on the face of it satisfied, leaving his tiny notebook, placed very deliberately to the side of the knives, blank for the moment.

There was also a sense of excitement about the man, though whether as a genuine devotee of food, restaurants, and the French gastronomic world or as a lover of the power he wielded within, it was difficult to tell.

"Well, I must say, it feels very different to the place we ate in last night," Richard said, breaking what was becoming yet another awkward silence. "Cheers," he added, raising his small glass of muscat.

"Of course," Tatillon snorted, as if talking to an idiot, and then softening as he realized again that the act didn't work with these two. "They are almost two different worlds, eras certainly. Guy Garçon, the wunderkind of French cuisine, is the future. Sébastien Grosmallard is, alas, the past."

"It seems a very brutal world, Monsieur Tatillon." Valérie didn't seem impressed.

"Please, call me Auguste," dripped Tatillon, reminding Richard of the cartoon character Pepé Le Pew. "It is a brutal world, Valérie— may I call you that?" He didn't wait for an answer. "Heroes come and heroes go; it is like a battle, an odyssey."

"There are no heroines then?" she replied coldly.

"But I thought Grosmallard was the enfant terrible of cooking?" Richard immediately regretted his choice of the word "cooking" before noticing the wincing effect it had on Tatillon, and so made a mental note to use it more often.

"He is. So is Guy Garçon! They both are." He was giving this Garçon chap quite the buildup.

"Can they both be enfants terrible?" Valérie added mischievously. "And across different eras?"

"Indeed. Sébastien Grosmallard is an enfant terrible for the establishment. His food is—was—cheeky, playful, precocious, but *within* accepted rules."

"And Guy Garçon?" Richard was pleased to see that Valérie, not noted for always seeing the nuance of conversation, looked nevertheless as though she were on the same wavelength as Richard, namely that this was all poppycock.

"Guy Garçon is an enfant terrible, but, *anti*-establishment. His creations *break* the accepted rules!"

"In a cheeky, playful, precocious way?" Richard asked.

"Precisely." Tatillon sounded like he'd outwitted a mastermind of debate and Richard caught Valérie's eye roll to signal something stronger than poppycock. "He is like a graffiti artist spraying slang on the walls of the Académie Française but...but...in beautiful calligraphy!" He seemed very pleased with his simile and wrote it down in his notepad. Richard considered it nonsense. The Académie Française, the feared intellectual defenders of the French language, were like an ancient realm of knights, and anyone approaching their walls with a can of spray paint was likely to be guillotined before the lid came off.

"Well, I've seen him on television." Richard was keen to show any knowledge he had. "And he seems very enthusiastic."

"Pah, television!" Tatillon didn't just spit the word, but ejected it as though it had been released by the Heimlich maneuver. "That is child's play, snack food for the masses. He does it to sell his chain of restaurants, that is all. A necessary evil."

"And Monsieur Grosmallard has his range of airline food. Is that also a necessary evil?" Valérie asked with apparent innocence.

"It is..." Then he smiled to himself. "It is terminal!" He wrote that down too.

"So, messieurs et madame." It was the waitress with their food. *"Croque garçon de pâtes à la truffe du poste?"* she asked, leaving Richard and Valérie looking blank.

"For monsieur," Tatillon said, indicating Richard.

"Brochette d'huîtres et litchis en couronne d'épines avec crème de cresson?"

"Madame."

"And finally, *vol-au-vent aux cuisses de grenouille, gambas sirènes, et jus de girolles.*" She placed this expertly in front of Tatillon, whose nose was in full sniff-the-ceiling mode. Richard also couldn't help noticing that he'd saved the most elaborate dish for himself. The vol-au-vent was the centerpiece, with muscled frogs' legs protruding out of the top as though diving into a lagoon. The *gambas sirènes* were king prawns with the fantails left on to look like diving mermaids, but epicene king prawn mermaids, presumably, partly submerged in a creamy sauce. It looked like a painting, a story hidden in it somewhere, Richard guessed, but he wasn't sure what. Tatillon sniffed at it, and his eyes glowed with delight.

Valérie's dish, the *brochette d'huîtres et litchis en couronne d'épines avec crème de cresson*, was just as theatrical. The cress soup was laid out thinly in a shallow bowl where, in the middle, were three intertwined rosemary stick brochettes—two of oyster, one of lychee—all made into circlets and piled on top of each other to look like a crown of thorns. A few pomegranate seeds had been added, presumably as drops of blood.

Richard, on the other hand, felt like he'd been given a poor deal. The *croque garçon de pâtes à la truffe du poste* looked like a fancy reworking of a croque monsieur, just a blousy cheese and ham toastie with another pun on the chef's name and some truffle shavings. The "sandwich" was a large ravioli covered in bread-crumbs and somehow inflated to look like a stuffed rectangular envelope, an effect enhanced by a small square of cured meat acting as a stamp in the corner. The truffle shavings were, he conceded, cleverly added to look like a written address. Richard pierced the envelope and the unctuous, steaming cheese oozed out with tiny lardons of spiced chorizo in it looking like lava rocks in a volcanic flow. It was, nevertheless, impressive, though compared with the other two he felt moodily like he'd been given something from the children's menu. And God knows what his old grandad would have thought of all this.

Without ceremony, they began eating. Richard burnt his tongue on the cheese first, so casually filled a glass of water from the carafe. Valérie didn't seem to know where to start; the crown of thorns were an artistic achievement no doubt, but were unapproachable as food from almost any angle. Tatillon, however, was chewing on a frog's leg, tears in his eyes, presumably at having to break up the sensual mermaid scene on his plate, but Richard couldn't help noticing that he was still chewing on the same frog's leg five minutes later. He was no expert, as Valérie had pointed out, but he knew that wasn't a good sign.

"Madame, may I swap plates now?" he asked with his working pomp. "It is important that I taste all of the dishes."

Valérie had managed to prise some of the crown apart, which meant that not only was the original effect lost, but it now looked like a winter hedgerow in a swamp, and she seemed relieved to be rid of it. Nobody asked for a taste of Richard's posh cheese on toast.

Conversation was limited during the eating, naturally. Richard's view was that the presentation couldn't be faulted on any level, but that the food itself wasn't great. He had a feeling that Valérie felt the same way, but Tatillon was harder to read; he wore a poker face, which was presumably all part of his professional demeanor. Their dishes were taken away and glasses refilled while their host made scant notes.

"The crown of thorns was interesting, don't you think?" Tatillon didn't direct his question specifically at either of them, making it almost rhetorical, which was confirmed by his answering it and writing some notes as he did so. "He was Grosmallard's talented protégé, you know? Uneasy is the head that wears the crown, he's saying."

"The king is dead, long live the king? That sort of thing?" Richard threw in.

"Something like that. I believe he's uncomfortable with his new, elevated status—and who he has deposed. As a chef, he can only express his emotion, his turmoil, his sorrow, even, through the genius of his food."

It was difficult to know what to say after that summation. Neither of the other two had known that Grosmallard had trained Garçon, and it certainly made the decision to open new restaurants at the same time and in the same small town look bizarre to say the least. It actually looked aggressive, like rutting stags pounding at each other. Richard felt Valérie's heeled shoe brush his shin under the table to catch his attention; her eyes were wide open at this new information. *Garçon and Grosmallard, eh?* she was saying in her not-so-subtle way.

"Don't you agree, madame?" Tatillon leaned in closer to Valérie.

"Oysters leave me cold." She didn't take her eyes off Richard, and spoke in a voice that even Tatillon could tell was tinged with a warning.

The main course took much the same route. Valérie was served *croustillants de tête de veau à la mangue, baptisée de sauce gribiche*, which, despite being a baptized calf's head, looked delicate, but was, she complained, "too salty." Auguste Tatillon had *pascade au boudin noir et pommes en sauce bordelaise*, which sounded straightforward enough—black pudding and apple on a kind of pancake, served with a red wine gravy—but was presented something akin to a revenge Valentine's card. The black pudding was cut into heart shapes but broken, with the sauce dripping from them. Richard had what amounted to swanky fish and chips, *Fûtreau d'anguille au vin blanc* served with *beignets de fleurs de courgettes*. Again, the presentation won hands down in the battle with taste, with his eels made to look like fûtreaus, the ancient wooden boats of the Loire river, and the fried courgette flowers inserted as sails. More children's menu stuff. He was surprised the waitress hadn't yet given him some crayons and a table mat to color in.

"Auguste! Auguste Tatillon!" A young man in chef's garb approached the table, his arms as wide as his beaming smile. "You should have told me you were coming, ah but no. You are the silent assassin! How are you, my friend?"

Tatillon stood, discreetly scanning the restaurant as he did so to confirm that heads were turned by the meeting of these two big beasts of French cuisine. He smiled demurely and held out a hand. "Monsieur Garçon, it is always such a pleasure," he said stiffly.

Garçon wagged a finger at him. "Ah, so you are working! I can tell!" He turned to Valérie and Richard. "Out of work he can be such a pussycat," he joked, extending his hand to both of them. "Madame, monsieur—Guy Garçon. Call me GG." He shook hands enthusiastically while Richard tried to work out why he pronounced it "JJ," before remembering it was one of many carefully laid traps of the French language: the "G" is pronounced "J" and vice versa. Garçon was maybe in his early thirties, with a mop of unruly hair sitting like a mushroom cloud above a warm face, but his eyes seemed slightly hidden. He was good looking, not terribly tall, and also slightly chubby, either in the process of losing weight or gaining it. A battle yet to be won or lost.

"Won't you join us, monsieur?" Valérie asked.

"That's very kind of you, madame, thank you. Just for a few minutes. I don't want to disturb the assassin here!" He said it very lightheartedly, but that it was the second time he'd used that word wasn't lost on either Valérie or Richard. He sat down next to Richard but addressed Tatillon. "I heard about last night—were you there?"

"Did you not read my review?" Tatillon seemed genuinely put out.

"I don't read reviews, Auguste, you know that." The warmth of the smile went cold very quickly.

"Yes, I was there. It was a disaster."

Garçon shook his head and looked upset. "That is a great shame," he said with emotion. "Excuse me." He turned to the others. "Sébastien Grosmallard taught me everything I know. He is a god to me." He turned back to Tatillon. "Is it true that the cheese supplier, Ménard, he took his own life? Just as poor Angélique did."

"Angélique was Grosmallard's wife, his muse if you like," Tatillon said.

"And did you know her well?"

"Yes." He sighed sadly. "She was beautiful, from old money. The daughter of a politician. Sébastien's food was like her, refined, classy, tasteful."

"And she committed suicide also?" Valérie chewed this over. "Monsieur Grosmallard can't have been an easy man to live with or work for?"

"No, madame, he was not!" He let out a hollow laugh as a memory came back to him. "I once stayed up for three days, perfecting a new dish. And it was perfect, I stand by that. Chef tasted my creation and I swear I saw tears in his eyes. I thought they were tears of joy, but no..." He shook his head gently at the memory. "He threw my dish on the floor! 'You cook like a girl!' he shouted. Ha! I didn't see him for a week after that."

"Character building is what my dad would have called it," Richard said to no one in particular and before Valérie exploded at the anecdote.

Garçon looked wistfully into the distance. "In the end, you know," he said slowly, "it's just food." Tatillon looked like he'd been electrocuted, such was the shock of the statement, but then the waitress returned and he swiftly put his game face back on.

"Desserts, madame, messieurs." Garçon got up to leave, watching his employee carefully as she served. The dishes looked stunning but—and they all knew it—very familiar. With a few minor embellishments, it was the famous Grosmallard dessert that had been hijacked the night before, the delicate parfait, the fragile tart, and the drama of the blood-red handprint. They all stared in silence.

"I couldn't help myself," muttered Garçon, on the edge of tears. "I call it *l'hommage est un plat qui se mange froid.*" And he walked slowly away.

"Homage is a dish best served cold"—and it was by far the best thing they'd eaten.

8

Richard worked out that it was exactly fifteen hours and thirty-seven minutes since they'd finished their dessert at Garçon! They had done so in a kind of awed, even numbed silence at the flavor, delicacy, and sheer effrontery of the creation. That it had rescued the meal wasn't in doubt. That it had set the cat among the proverbial pigeons even less so. Even now, as they sat outside on the *terrasse* of the Café des Tasses Cassées in the center of Saint-Sauver, they were still struggling to process the previous evening.

The sun was at its lunchtime high and the temperatures soared as the weekly market began to wind down. In the shadow of a large parasol sat Valérie, with Passepartout on her lap and Richard opposite her. He had an ice-cold pastis on the table in front of him, the rivulets of water slowly meandering down the glass, while Valérie was ignoring her Perrier, impatiently swiping at her phone instead. Richard knew she was waiting for Tatillon's review of the night before, which he'd told them was written when they'd dropped him at the station earlier. He had given nothing more away than that, preparing as he was his re-entry into Parisian society by keeping his nose so high he was in danger of falling over backward.

"Monsieur?"

Richard looked up, squinting in the sun, but could just see the silhouetted outline of a short man dressed as a waiter. He'd seen the uniform so often recently he wasn't sure if it wasn't a mirage. The waiter leaned in closer, out of the silhouette, to reveal that it was René Dupont, owner of the Café des Tasses Cassées, a man as unsuited to work in the hospitality industry as an elephant is to building model airplanes. Richard and René had known each other for nearly four years now, and René had never called Richard "monsieur."

"René?"

The man tutted, then whispered, "For crying out loud, Richard, I'm trying to go upmarket—help a guy out."

"Oh, right." Richard sat up straight. "Sorry."

"Monsieur?" René said again, this time with a slight edge. "Your lunch." He practically dropped the plate on the table, startling Passepartout into a sullen growl. "Bon appétit," he said joylessly.

"Thank you." Richard looked confused by the charade. "René," he whispered back, "why? Why the move upmarket?"

The man sighed. It was a heavy, put-upon sigh that suggested in no uncertain terms how fate had condemned him to almost Sisyphean toil. "It's these new restaurants, isn't it? What with their Michelin stars"—he shook his head sadly—"they've raised expectations around here, made everybody feel fancy and la-di-da." He leaned in closer to Richard again, looking around to make sure he wasn't overheard. "And it's not just the grub, it's the service..."

"Monsieur, could I have some salt, please?" The call came from a neighboring table, from a man wearing a cravat and a panama hat.

Slowly, René turned his head toward the perfectly polite customer. "In a minute," he snarled menacingly, "I've only got one pair of hands!" He turned back to Richard. "See what I mean? Now, enjoy your meal."

Richard stared down at a forlorn-looking cheese omelette and chips, catching Valérie's eye in the process. Her opinion of the English and their food was visibly vindicated by the tawdry, almost gray disc on the plate. It looked like a child's Frisbee left in the garden for years to fade and wither. Richard made a show of being displeased with the effort but secretly knew this was going to be the best meal he'd had in days. Simple fare that could be eaten without pretense and which didn't have to be analyzed for backstory, motive, or baggage. To eat it, he didn't have to go on a "journey," a modern turn of phrase he abhorred almost as much as "reaching out." He took a bite of the omelette and it was, fair to say, rotten to the core, and he loved every bit of it. As he ate, he realized, not for the first time, that he could never be an aristocrat, eating fine, rich food every meal of every day. Nor could he be the opposite and eat this omelette every day either. He was an everyman; he liked to mix things up, and after two days of Michelin-starred haute cuisine, nothing would go down better than a bit of good old-fashioned culinary stodge, even if it was French stodge, so stodge-lite.

Finished, he placed his cutlery on the plate, unable now to conceal just how much he'd enjoyed the bland, flavorless, rubbery indecency of the whole thing, and looked up to see both Valérie and Passepartout with their mouths open in a scene of epic disgust.

"Shall I order dessert?" he asked nonchalantly, deciding to ignore them. "We might get the hat-trick of a goat's cheese parfait and a blood-red hand!"

"Do you eat here often?" Valérie had a look on her face that suggested she may be reconsidering her friendship with Richard, who, for his part, finally fed on egg and chips, was more emboldened than before.

"Up until recently there was nowhere else," he said. "René has turned this place around."

Valérie looked stunned by this news. "It's a strange name, though, the Café des Tasses Cassées. For the countryside, I mean."

"Well yes, there's a story behind that," Richard enthused as he set about wiping his plate with a piece of baguette. "It used to be called Chez Rémi. But Remi got into some serious gambling debts, all of which were turned over to René, who was apparently something of a specialist in gambling debt collection." He didn't notice Valérie as she visibly tensed. "Just before René could collect on the debt, as in take over Chez Remi, he was put away for a couple of years…"

"Was it for crimes against food?" Valérie finally picked up her Perrier as if in triumph.

A look of confusion came over Richard. He obviously didn't know Valérie d'Orçay very well, that went without saying. They'd only had one adventure together—or was it a case? Whatever you might call it—a few weeks earlier, and she'd seemed an enthusiastically determined person who, despite clearly being an expert in guns, hand-to-hand combat, high fashion, sports cars, and the relentless pursuit of debtors, runaway husbands, and criminals, appeared to have no edge whatsoever, no acerbity. She seemed different this time, however, preoccupied to some extent, as though something was weighing her down. Richard felt after a lifetime of watching people, whether in films or in reality, that he had some insight into the human condition, but he was also very English and so, for the moment at least, decided to ignore it.

"Anyway," he continued, "Remi was supposed to run the place until René was released, but the bank foreclosed on him, took it off him, and sold it off cheap."

"I can't imagine Monsieur René being very happy about that."

"Well, quite. Some bloke from Paris bought it off the bank, changed the name to Café des Tasses Cassées, and set about making 'improvements.' Bagels, frappy-cappuccinos, sushi, that kind of thing."

"And so the custom just drifted away?" She seemed saddened by the thought.

"Oh no! They didn't turn up en masse from day one. It wasn't the food they objected to so much, it was the change of name. Remi owed almost everyone in the town; the name of the place was practically an IOU."

She smiled at this, giving Richard encouragement.

"Anyway, René came out, offered the Paris bloke—by now desperate to leave—a fraction of what he'd paid for it, which was a fraction of its worth anyhow, and took the place on."

"And Remi?"

"Working in the kitchen, paying off his debts."

She smiled again, nodding as she did so.

"And, you'll be glad to hear, they stopped doing sushi."

"I like sushi!"

"Not the way René does it, you wouldn't!"

She laughed this time and raised her face to take the full sun, her fine features, strong chin, and large sunglasses as always giving her an old-school beauty and class. "And René?" she asked slowly. "Has he given up debt collection?"

It was Richard's turn to laugh. "Ha! Worried about the competition? 'This town ain't big enough for the both of us!'" He noticed she wasn't laughing along this time. "This town ain't big enough for the both of us," he repeated limply. "Walter Huston to Gary Cooper. *The Virginian*. 1929."

"I'm thinking of retiring, Richard. It's getting too dangerous." She looked at him intently, as though seeking his advice.

"Has something happened?" He couldn't help sounding worried.

"I just made a few mistakes last time..."

"While you were away?"

"Yes. And when it was all done, I had nowhere to go. Nowhere I could really call home to go and think and be safe."

"You have no home?"

"I have an apartment in Paris but..."

"But it's not safe?" He looked around him as though everyone in the market was suddenly a potential assassin.

"It probably is now, but here is safer, I think. I know it sounds silly but they almost got to Passepartout, and you know what I thought?"

"That I could protect you both?" Richard nodded slowly, puffed up manfully by the compliment.

"Ha! No!" Valérie almost snorted Perrier out of her nose. "I thought about your hen, your dead hen."

"Oh right," Richard pretended to laugh along. "You mean Ava

Gardner, cruelly garrotted by the Sicilian mafia?" He still hadn't gotten over the incident, to be honest; that kind of thing leaves a mark on a man.

"Yes, Ava Gardner. Have you replaced her?" she added gently.

"No, not yet. These things can't be rushed into." He swirled his finger around the edge of his glass. "Look, you say you want to be safe and so on, but you still seem pretty keen on turning a suicide into a murder—that's hardly the stuff of retirement."

She leaned forward and grabbed his hand. "Oh, Richard, I still want excitement!" She stood up quickly. "Now, I have something to do while you finish your drink. I'll be back in five minutes. Passepartout is in your hands." She breezed off, apparently buoyed by the idea of murder, excitement, and the chase. After watching her disappear into the crowd, he looked at the small dog, who met his stare, not with his usual insolence for once, but with a resignation that signaled this could become a regular thing. Richard rather liked the idea.

"Cheers," he said, raising his glass.

"Talking to dogs now, are you, monsieur?" Richard looked up to see the crumpled Commissaire LaPierre standing above him, with, as if it were possible, even more crumbs attached to his shirt front.

"Commissaire, how is the investigation going?"

"How do you know it's an investigation?" He made his question sound decidedly like a threat.

"Eh?"

"When I saw you last it was a suicide, now..."

"Now?"

"Now, it's an investigation!"

"So, it was murder?"

"Obviously. Monsieur Ménard was struck from behind. The crime-scene pathologist couldn't see that until the goat's cheese was washed from the corpse."

Once again, the image left them both silent. Also, Richard thought, just how bad must a corpse smell if it had added goat's cheese crust? He hoped the pathologist had a strong stomach and that they hadn't planned cheese for lunch. He shivered at the thought.

"You do not seem surprised, Monsieur Richard Ainsworth! It is murder and you do not seem surprised. I ask myself why?"

"Well, you just told me." Richard felt like they'd been through this before but couldn't help sounding defensive anyway.

The commissaire bent down toward Richard. "I have my eye on you, monsieur. Everywhere I go, you are there." He leaned in closer. "Everywhere," he repeated.

Richard gulped. "Well, I live here."

"Hmm, we shall see," LaPierre said enigmatically. He nodded smartly at Richard, and then bizarrely also nodded at Passepartout, before tapping his nose to indicate that Richard's obvious insanity would be their secret from now on. Then he walked off into the bar to spread joy among other people minding their own business. Richard was still shaking his head a few minutes later when Valérie's chair-scraping disturbed him. She sat down hurriedly.

"Richard," she said breathlessly, "I have a present for you!"

She reached down and then put a brown cardboard box in the middle of the table. The box was taped shut but there were holes along the side. Through one of the holes Richard could see an eye; occasionally it blinked and changed angle according to jerky head movements. Then came the sound that he found the most soothing in all his generally quiet world: the low, contented *bwok* of a hen, like a slow-motion Bruce Lee. He felt quite moved by the moment.

"I think she's already laid an egg—they do that sometimes," he said quietly. "Thank you."

"And, Richard," Valérie said, ignoring the moment entirely, "Tatillon's review is out!"

9

I think I'll call her Olivia," Richard said, still peering into the box. "After Olivia de Havilland."

"That's nice," said Valérie, not listening to him. "Now, please concentrate, Richard, I'm going to read the review to you."

"She died not long ago." Now it was his turn to not listen.

"Who did?"

"Olivia de Havilland. She was a hundred and four. The last of the Hollywood greats," he said sadly, "the last connection..."

"Oh, I know that!" As usual, Valérie was making no attempt to hide her irritation. "Now, it says here..."

"Really? You've heard of Olivia de Havilland?" Richard's surprise was as genuine as her irritation. Hitherto, Valérie's knowledge of the golden age of cinema had been much like his own knowledge of Japanese kabuki theatre—a kind of vague awareness of its existence, but no data beyond that and absolutely no inclination to find any. That she not only knew of Ms. de Havilland, double Oscar winner and one of the stars of *Gone with the Wind*, but seemed genuinely hurt by his surprise at the fact left him dumbstruck. The woman really was full of contradictions.

"Of course I've heard of Olivia de Havilland!" she snapped. "She was my neighbor in Paris. I would sometimes fetch her a raspberry *millefeuille* from the patisserie on rue Bénouville." Richard was sure he could feel his jaw touching the table below him. He tried to speak, to get even a snippet of further minutiae from Valérie concerning the great woman, but no words came out. It had been his overriding ambition since he'd moved to France to meet Olivia de Havilland, but as usual his timing was out, and she'd died before he'd gotten around to it.

"Olivia de Havilland," was all he could muster by way of conversation.

"She was a very nice lady. She had a cat called Errol."

"A cat called Errol," he repeated dreamily. Then, snapping back to full consciousness, he asked, "She had a cat called Errol?"

"Yes."

"We had so much in common."

"You and the cat?"

"No! Olivia de Havilland and me. She named her animals after famous film stars too. Errol. Errol Flynn."

Valérie looked blankly back at him, which was pretty much what he'd expected.

"Well, I never," he carried on, shaking his head. "This has been quite a day; you were best friends with Olivia de Havilland and I'm a murder suspect. I'm not sure I'm built for this level of excitement you crave."

Although Richard wasn't looking at Valérie, he had his eye at one of the breathing holes on the box, looking for signs of stardust on his latest hen, when he became increasingly aware that Valérie was very much looking at him. "Who," she began slowly, "has accused you of murder?"

Richard didn't look up. "Well, he didn't say it explicitly, just that he had his eye on me." Finally, he met her stern but protective gaze, like a mother hen's. "He clearly doesn't like me, though."

"Who doesn't like you?"

"Commissaire LaPierre. I can't say I like him all that much, either. He's like one of those policemen in films, badly dressed, single, dogged, and totally incorruptible. You can always tell a corrupt copper in films; they look, I don't know, shiny." He realized that she was staring at him again, like a teacher who'd just heard a particularly poor excuse for a lack of homework.

"When did you see him?" she asked, the serious tone in her voice setting off alarm bells in Richard's head.

"Just now. When you went off to buy Olivia. He's in the bar. He told me that Ménard didn't kill himself at all but was bashed on the head."

"I knew it!" she said triumphantly, standing up as she did so. "Come on!"

"Eh? Where are we going? Also, why are we going?"

"I don't want to be overheard, Richard." She glared at a couple seated at the next table, who hadn't the faintest idea what she was talking about.

"I haven't had the bill yet, we can't just…"

"Can't you pay this René later, seeing as you know him so well?"

"Not really," he whined, though standing up as he did so. "I'm not keen on doing a runner from an underworld debt collector!"

"A *former* underworld debt collector."

"That's not really the point. And how do you know he's former? Has he left your union?" She didn't reply. "Do you know what his nickname was in Paris? 'Thumbs.' You know why? Because that's what he broke first when you didn't pay up."

This time she glared at him, a look so withering that if Valérie herself had an underworld nickname along the same lines as René, there was a strong suggestion that it might be "Testicles."

"I will come back and pay him later for you. Now, are you coming or not?"

Richard didn't feel like he had much of a choice, which was just as well, as it was choices and subsequent dithering that had meant he'd missed out on seeing the real Olivia de Havilland. He picked the avian de Havilland up and followed Valérie into the market.

Despite it being nearly lunchtime, there was still plenty of bustle in the narrow alleyways between stalls, with vendors hoping to get rid of as much fresh stock as possible. There were gaps here and there where some stalls had already packed up and left, and what could only be described as gangs of elderly women putting the world to rights and loudly listing their health complaints with relish. Their menfolk, generally in blue overalls, the countryman's proletarian uniform, stood silently a few yards away, praying that the conversation wouldn't include them at any point. They looked mostly to the ground, trying to be inconspicuous, but instinctively raised their heads as Valérie, exotic and out of place in a rural market, swished by, her loose-fitting cream trouser suit billowing like the sails of a magnificent yacht. Richard carried Olivia's box carefully in two arms and looked more like a faithful old retainer than a companion. She slowed to let him catch up with her, not taking her eyes off her phone.

"This review is fascinating, Richard," she said, no longer worried about eavesdroppers.

"Really? I'd have thought it was a foregone conclusion."

Valérie stopped walking. "How do you mean?"

"Well, it strikes me that Tatillon had made his mind up about the place before the starters arrived, probably before we'd even gotten there."

"What makes you think that?"

"I've got experience dealing with critics, and they're a bit like insurance salesmen. They all talk a good game but the vast majority are charlatans in my experience. Also, it's just about the most bribable industry on the planet, up there with Mexican police chiefs."

"Really?" Valérie had a look on her face akin to that of a child who's just realized the truth about the tooth fairy. Once again, Richard couldn't quite work her out. She was literal and, at times, unworldly to the point of innocence, yet she was also seemingly in the Premier League when it came to bounty hunting, could handle herself in hand-to-hand combat, and had hinted previously at darker arts than that.

"Yes, Garçon was right. They're like assassins," he blurted, unable to stop the train of thought. "Some of them, not all, are paid to kill. Kill a film, a play, a career."

"A chef?"

"Exactly."

"Well, he certainly doesn't kill Guy Garçon."

"Obviously. I bet the review is glowing. It will talk about the drama on the plate, each course as sumptuous as a Russian novel. The word 'delicacy' will be mentioned more than once. What won't be mentioned is that the food wasn't all that good, was it? Those frogs' legs, for instance. I've seen less muscle on an Olympic sprinter."

"Richard, you are so clever!"

Encouraged, he warmed to his task. "The assassin part will come when we get to the dessert. Now, that was magnificent; his speciality is as a patissier, obviously. It was almost like a different chef. But it would have given Tatillon the excuse to firmly put the boot in on Grosmallard. The king is dead, long live the king. He said as much himself."

Valérie shook her head at the injustice of it all. She was many things, but cynical wasn't one of them. "Auguste Tatillon suggests that it was Guy Garçon's creation all along. He started alongside Grosmallard as a pastry chef."

"That really is nasty. Do you think it could be true? Why hasn't Guy Garçon said anything before if so?"

"Maybe he was waiting for an assassin?"

They both looked at each other. "Somebody seems to be working very hard to destroy Sébastien Grosmallard," Richard mused. "And that's assuming it isn't self-sabotage, as his reputation suggests."

"But what does this have to do with Ménard? Why kill him?"

"Ménard and Grosmallard had known each other a long time, perhaps? Grosmallard said he was coming home, and the Ménards have been here for generations. Maybe he knew that Grosmallard's famous creation wasn't his own work? I don't know."

"But why switch the cheese?" She sounded exasperated.

Richard thought about this for a moment, then shook his head. "No idea. I don't think I'd have even noticed the difference if it wasn't for all the kerfuffle that blew up."

Valérie nodded slowly. "And who started this 'kerfuffle'?" she asked innocently, her heavily accented pronunciation of "kerfuffle" almost causing Richard to drop Olivia's box.

Richard smiled. "I'm pretty certain it started at Tatillon's table."

"Oh, Richard!" She couldn't contain her childlike excitement any longer. "Now we are getting somewhere!"

"Maybe we are," he said, his smile widening as he did so. "Finally," he added, hoping it sounded ambiguous.

There are many things that can put a dampener on a potentially romantic moment, if indeed it was a potentially romantic moment. But short of Pompeii-like devastation or perhaps a sniper on a grassy knoll, Madame Tablier arriving on her roaring high-cc motorbike, helmet and goggles in place making her look like Mr. Toad, would be pretty high up on the list. And not just arriving, either, but literally driving her old machine between them and stopping the engine as she did so.

"I thought I'd find you two here," she said without removing her paraphernalia. "It wasn't suicide, it was murder!"

"Oh, we know that." Valérie coughed, stepping back a little to avoid any oil getting on her clothes.

"Well, excuse me for living, I'm sure!" Madame Tablier sulked, removing her helmet. "You've also got a new booking in, for tonight. I told them you were hardly here anymore, but they wanted the room anyway."

Richard sighed heavily. The brief fleeting moment of whatever it was already seemed so far away. "OK," he moaned, "can you get the room ready, please?"

"If I must. I suppose madame won't need the room, then?"

She didn't even look at amused Valérie, just shot a thumb in her direction.

"I'm comfortable in your daughter's room, Richard, if that's OK?"

"Oh yeah?" Madame Tablier revved up her skepticism.

Valérie giggled. "I will see you later, Richard, but I think we need to get to know all the people involved. I'll think about how to do that." She strode off in the direction of the car park, the crowds parting for her as she did so.

"She did it, you know," Madame Tablier said defiantly.

"Who did? Madame d'Orçay?" He was aware of the antipathy between the two but accusing Valérie of murder was a bit strong.

"No!" She looked at him like he was an idiot. "Elisabeth Ménard! She did it."

"Really?" It was Richard's turn to be skeptical. "Why?"

"Affairs," was the simple reply. "Affairs. And lots of them."

Richard couldn't help thinking that the small—mousy almost—Fabrice Ménard was the least likely looking philanderer in Saint-Sauver, but Madame Tablier seemed utterly certain in her assessment of things. As always, when the subject of marital infidelity came up, Richard felt a pang of jealousy and excitement. When his marriage to Clare had first hit trouble, he had suggested a more "open" arrangement, which Clare had taken to with gusto and no little success while Richard had had none. He'd told Valérie this, and while adding to her low assessment of men in general. it had also taken her about three days to stop laughing.

"Fabrice Ménard." He whistled. "Well I never. It's always the quiet ones, isn't it?" he asked, not expecting a reply.

"No." The reply came anyway. "It's all of them." The following silence was predictably loaded, not least because Richard realized he could never imagine Madame Tablier in a state of romantic flux. "What's in the box?" she asked.

"A hen."

"Dinner?"

"No!"

"All right. Keep your hair on. Anyway, I'll go and get things ready." She fired up the motorbike and put her helmet back on and then said something else which he couldn't make out.

Richard looked at his watch and puffed out his cheeks. It was one o'clock. "Well, Olivia, old girl," he said, not caring if people overheard him talking to a hen, "I should have done this years ago, but can I take you for a drink?"

10

Richard sat morosely at a table at the back of the bar of the Café des Tasses Cassées. He had the room, as he liked it, with his back to the furthest corner. If anyone came in making further demands on his patience, time, and good humor with talk of death, marital affairs, or the dessert fancies of Hollywood legends, he would at least have fair warning. He felt exhausted by it all, and was sulkily mulling over what he perceived to be his terminal case of bad timing. What was that moment with Valérie, and would it happen again? Was there any way to disable Madame Tablier's motorbike? And why hadn't Valérie mentioned that she knew Olivia de Havilland before? Suicide, murder, infidelity, and none of them came as high up his list of excitement or diversion as the near miss, as he was now calling it, with Olivia de Havilland. He raised a glass of white wine to the gently clucking Olivia in the box.

"Here." It was René, and he put another glass down on the table. "It's on the house. You're becoming my best customer!" The patron smiled as warmly as he could but Richard could see why his reputation had spread fear through the bad debtors of Paris. The smile was slightly crooked and emanated from his top lip, making it look almost like a sneer. His eyes were cold too, but he and Richard had always gotten on well. They were both outsiders in the close-knit community of Saint-Sauver, and though that's where the similarity ended, it still acted as a slight bond. "Oh, and before I forget, here's your change from earlier." He reached into his apron pocket and put 75 cents on the table. "I'm a stickler for these things," he said, this time without humor.

"I didn't leave any money." Richard looked up, confused.

"No, your wife came back after you left."

"My wife?" A look of fear crossed Richard's face. "Oh, oh no. No, that's not my wife, just a friend."

"Ah, I see." He winked. "You're becoming a proper Frenchman, Richard!" Richard didn't reply. "Are you OK?"

It was a genuine question and one that Richard wished he could answer. The truth was that he was just feeling sorry for himself, which is why he was hiding in a bar and not at home being told to snap out of it by either Valérie or Madame Tablier.

"Do you ever think life moves too fast, René?"

The bar owner snorted his response. "Around here? Are you joking?"

"Well, maybe not too fast, but that nothing happens for ages, then everything happens at once."

"I don't know what you're talking about, mate. I've been here four years and Ménard being topped is the closest I've come to my old life since then. It's got the old pulse racing a bit, not that I miss it, but you know...makes a change."

"Who do you think killed him?" It was an idle question and he didn't expect a straight answer, but René was a straight-talking man so he got one anyway.

"That chef, Grosmallard. Stands to reason, doesn't it? His fancy dessert gets ruined by Ménard's fake cheese and he loses it. The amount of money it takes to open a fancy place like that too. And I heard Ménard himself was no saint."

"I heard that too."

"Well then, he had debts all over the shop, apparently. Upset some folks."

"Oh." Richard tried hard not to look surprised.

Richard's phone rang. "Uh-oh." His chin sank into his chest as he read the name of the caller. It said *Clare*. "That's my wife," he muttered.

"Well, mate"—René gave the table a quick wipe—"if you need an alibi..." He winked again and moved off.

"Clare!" Richard was definitely losing his ability to sound chirpy, and Clare was immediately having none of it.

"What's the matter? Are you drunk?"

"Absolutely not!"

"You are, aren't you?"

"Yes."

"Oh, Richard!" There was a pause, then her tone softened. "Are you drowning your sorrows?" He couldn't deny it. "Well, I have some good news for you!"

As Richard began to look to the heavens, or at least to the old-style fan on the ceiling, he noticed Hugo Ménard just sitting down at the table next to his, putting a glass of beer down in front of him. Ménard nodded solemnly at Richard.

"Good news?" Richard asked, naturally distracted.

"Yes!" Clare, misreading his tone, sounded encouraged. "We're all coming out to see you!"

Richard nodded back at young Ménard. He didn't know him well; he'd always sensed that the young man, in his mid to late twenties, wasn't very comfortable in company. He had a cold look about him anyway, with short, swept-back blond hair and an inadequate, almost anachronistic mustache. It was then that Richard noticed Antonin Grosmallard standing at the bar. He had a whisky in his hand and couldn't take his eyes off Ménard, who was returning the stare with interest and then some. The young Grosmallard was trying to intimidate like his father would but had neither the stature nor the dark menace to pull it off.

"Bloody hell," said Richard, moving Olivia carefully to one side, out of the firing line.

"Richard?" Clare was taken aback by the effect of her statement. "Is that a good 'bloody hell' or a bad 'bloody hell'?"

Only vaguely able to concentrate, Richard's honest assessment of both the phone call and the classic Western-style standoff in front of him was, "It's difficult to say at the moment. It could go either way."

Clare paused at the other end. "Well, that's why we want to come out..." Hugo Ménard stood up, kicking his chair back as he did so. "We need to remove the doubt from this, Richard." Antonin Grosmallard took his hands off the bar and stood up to his full height. They were evenly matched, same age, same build. "What do you think?"

"I think blood might be spilt," Richard whispered.

"Oh, Richard, don't say that! I didn't realize you were so miserable!"

"You've destroyed my family!" Ménard shouted, and Richard couldn't help feeling that the young man had peaked too soon. He'd have expected a low, menacing threat as the opening gambit.

"I'll be out there tomorrow. Alicia and Sly can follow at the weekend," Clare continued, clearly concerned.

"*Your* stupid father got what he deserved!" Antonin threw his whisky glass on the floor and let his arms fall loose by his side. It suggested aggression, but wasn't wholly convincing, whereas Ménard looked like he knew what he was doing.

"What is going on there? Are you watching one of your films?" Distracted as he was, the "your" in "your films" still struck home. "Don't tell me. Macho men in hats argue over not much at all, usually a woman. And it's called *They Had It Coming* or some such." She was trying to sound lighthearted but her acerbity was never far from the surface.

"No, this is real, Clare." He tried to sound tough but world-weary at the same time. Suddenly he was in film noir territory, a place he found himself in quite often, if he was honest.

"Hey!" René roared from the front door, brought in by the sound of smashing glass. But the young bucks didn't hear him, lost as they were in their own battle. Even Olivia could feel the tension and started clucking madly as though about to lay.

"Richard, is it a cock fight?"

"In a way," he answered, bending down to soothe Olivia through the air holes but getting a cramp in his leg as he did so.

"Argh!" he cried, unable to control the pain.

"Richard, are you OK?" Clare screamed.

His leg involuntarily shot out in front of him, kicking over the chair opposite. Fortunately, or unfortunately depending on your point of view, this coincided with Hugo Ménard in mid-spring at Antonin Grosmallard, knocking him off balance and giving René enough time to grab them both by the scruff of the neck, making them look very sheepish indeed.

"Richard, are you OK? Will you answer me, for God's sake?"

Richard paused. "I'm fine," he said, sounding absurdly composed. "We've got the situation under control." Olivia *bwokk*ed loudly in confirmation. "I'll see you tomorrow," he added, narrowly avoiding adding "kid" at the end of the sentence, Bogart-style.

"Right, you two," René said with menace. By now both young men were in his clutches and were pulled up to their tiptoes by the smaller, far more dangerous man. "I don't mind a ruck," he continued, "it's good for the soul sometimes, so what do you say? I'll let you two carry on, but I get to fight the winner? Fair?"

Within seconds both Ménard and Grosmallard had fled, leaving a laughing René to search for a dustpan and brush.

"That was nice work, Richard. I'm not as quick as I used to be— you slowed them down for me."

"Oh, you know..." He waved his hand airily like he was James Bond, while at the same time afraid to move in case the cramp returned.

René swept up the broken glass and righted the chair. "Well, it should make tonight's meeting a fiery one if those two are going to carry on like that!"

"What meeting?"

"The big council meeting, plus all the traders, shops, and so on. I'm surprised you're not going. I got the message at lunchtime. Everyone's going to be there. Apparently, the council want a plan of action to rescue the good name of Saint-Sauver." He laughed.

Maybe that's what Madame Tablier had been trying to tell him from inside her helmet. Anyway, it would be a good opportunity to "meet everyone," as Valérie had said she wanted to do. "What time does it start, René?"

"Half six, and I hope it doesn't drag on—I've got bookings tonight."

"We'll be there," he said decisively, and then he thought of Valérie, the full bed and breakfast, the impending arrival of Clare, and the nightmare sleeping-arrangements scenario that had just opened up in front of him. He sighed like a man facing up to the reality of execution.

"I've got stuff to do this afternoon, but one more?" asked René.

"Better had," Richard said. "I think I need it."

11

The early evening sun was hitting the glass doors of the *salle polyvalente*, causing some people to shield their eyes as they mounted the few steps to the entrance. In truth it was one of those buildings that stood out in old French towns, a large square box that, as the name suggests, was multipurpose and usually named after some long-forgotten local councilor or a person of artistic standing who was unlikely ever to have even been to the town. In this case it was the Salle Polyvalente Victor Hugo, and like all these buildings it was a theatre, a dance hall, a wedding reception venue, a polling station, the school concert space, and—by far its most popular manifestation—the location for the fortnightly Sunday afternoon bingo. Victor Hugo's views on bingo go unrecorded.

Richard and Valérie were among the last to arrive, Valérie tugging on his jacket sleeve as they climbed the steps like a mother dragging her reluctant child to a dental appointment. Richard, his shoulders slumped in acknowledgement of yet another of life's defeats, was suddenly caught by the reflective sunlight on the doors. It hit him like a train and he nearly fell backward and into the arms of the buxom *boulangère,* Jeanine, who giggled and managed a loaded, "Good evening, Lord Grantham."

Richard groaned. He'd avoided any major physical pain in his life, no long hospital stays or serious injury, but he could imagine none of it being quite as bad as the early evening hangover. The secret to lunchtime drinking—and he'd worked this out over much scientific research—was to keep going. Don't stop, just plough on through the hard yards until bedtime. Hangovers can be dealt with in the morning; in the evening they offer the potential ruination of two days.

Valérie held the door open for him. She'd been called to pick him up from René's place and was therefore fully aware that he'd overindulged, but she didn't seem to connect that with his current state. She put it down to the doldrums he was feeling at the news that Clare was to visit. To her, he seemed broken by the news, indicating just how bad their marriage had become. She could easily find somewhere else to stay, though, bless him; he really was quite upset about the inconvenience. In the meantime, she was trying to cheer him up with talk of murder, suspects, motives, and the promise of a post-meeting *verre de l'amitié,* the traditional glass of rosé without which no French public meeting could possibly end.

Richard groaned again and he slumped into a plastic chair at the back of the hall, before Valérie quickly grabbed his arm and, showing unsurprising strength, hauled him to his feet. "Come on, Richard, we need to be a little nearer the front," she hissed through a false smile. "We want to be in the action."

They walked up the central aisle, and even through his fug Richard could feel all eyes turn to Valérie, and then, as if registering disbelief, to him. He stood up straighter, determined to acknowledge as many people as possible, to, despite his fragile state, bask in the shocked attention of Saint-Sauver's great and good. He was the benevolent Earl of Grantham, after all.

"I didn't realize you were so important, Richard," Valérie whispered, apparently unaware of her own effect on the throng.

"It's not a very important town." He smiled back, giving it his best Clark Gable.

They were all there. René DuPont, sitting on his own and near the back of the room, winked at them both. Elisabeth Ménard sat on the aisle in the middle; Hugo slouched a seat apart with his leg across the chair next to him, a picture of unnecessary rebellion. All three Grosmallards were across the other side of the hall, as though they had deliberately picked the seats furthest away. Sébastien sat between Antonin and his nervous, red-headed daughter, Karine. Guy Garçon sat a few rows in front, leaning back against a wall so he could take in the rest of the room. Jeanine was offering her condolences to Madame Ménard, who looked exhausted. A few other town dignitaries were about, councilors, the town doctor. Even Madame Tablier stood at the steps leading up to the stage, leaning on a broom, her passport through every door.

Richard and Valérie sat nearer the front than they actually would have liked, but had gotten caught up in the attention that carried them there. Without fanfare and with some awkwardness, Noel Mabit appeared from behind the curtain in the stage wings and walked to a table in the center. Being as thick-skinned as he was, he wouldn't have noticed the collective eye-rolling and barely suppressed groans that greeted his entrance, like a performer who'd come back on for an encore that nobody had asked for. He sat down at the table and tapped the microphone.

"*Bonsoir*, ladies and gentlemen," he began, "thank you all…"

The large doors creaked open at the back of the room and Auguste Tatillon, toupee in place, sneaked in and sat at the nearest chair.

Valérie leaned in to Richard and whispered in his ear, "What's he doing here?"

"Maybe René wants a review as well?" he quipped, before furrowing his brow and adding, "I really don't know. That's very odd, isn't it?" He unfurrowed his brow quickly, wincing at the clanking pain the hangover caused as he did so.

"*Bonsoir*, ladies and gentlemen," Noel Mabit restarted, a tinge of annoyance in his voice. "Thank you all for coming this…"

The doors creaked open again and this time commissaire Henri LaPierre sauntered in and sat a few chairs from Tatillon, who, regardless, felt it was too close for a provincial policeman and moved a couple of seats further away.

Mabit sighed. "*Bonsoir*, ladies and gentlemen…" The doors opened with more force this time and it was old man Clavet, with his enormous set of keys jangling on his shaking arm.

"Have you not started yet?" he demanded of Mabit, feeling no compulsion, like caretakers the world over, to acknowledge anyone other than their direct contact. He looked at his watch. "I've got to get this room ready for a bal musette that starts in thirty minutes."

"We are trying to start now, Monsieur Clavet!" Mabit was rarely flustered, but he was now. Clavet tapped his watch and loudly maneuvered his false teeth back into position. "*Bonsoir*, ladies and gentlemen." Mabit paused, expecting further interruption, which thankfully didn't come. "Thank you all for coming this evening. The mayor, Monsieur Planchet, has asked me to pass on his apologies and beg your forgiveness for his absence as he is incapacitated with gout."

Nobody had seen Monsieur Planchet since the last municipal election, and it was suspected that Noel Mabit actually had him locked in a cellar somewhere while he wielded the power. Not that anybody cared. Anyone who seeks election wasn't to be trusted or liked in the first place anyway; they were all the same, as far as the rural population were concerned.

"I—" He stopped to cough, then began again. "*We* have called this extraordinary meeting today to hit back..." He slammed an ineffectual fist on the table, almost knocking his microphone over. "To hit back," he repeated, "before our enemies go any further in taking advantage of this, er, unfortunate situation."

The room, it has to be said, looked a bit nonplussed by this. To describe the murder of Fabrice Ménard, king of cheese, as an "unfortunate situation" was one thing and could be put down to tact and euphemism, but the big question was: What enemies? Saint-Sauver, represented here by everyone who counted, wasn't aware of any enemies. This was news indeed.

"What enemies, monsieur?" It was the commissaire, who quite rightly assumed this was a new avenue of inquiry about to open up.

Mabit looked blank. He'd clearly written what he thought was a rabble-rousing opener, a prelude to fiery torches and pitchforks, but was short on detail. "Well, there's La Chapelle-sur-Follet." He stopped there, hoping that would suffice.

"La Chapelle-sur-Follet?" It was Clavet at the back, laughing at the suggestion in a way that nearly brought his teeth out.

"Yes! La Chapelle-sur-Follet!" Mabit stood up to underline his point.

"Population 542, La Chapelle-sur-Follet?"

"The numbers do not matter, Monsieur Clavet. What matters is the act of aggression. Have you seen their town sign as you drive in?" Nobody had. "It reads, *La Chapelle-sur-Follet, No vegan cheese allowed*!" He sat down again, waiting for this earth-shattering news to hit home.

"What does it matter?" René asked from the back. "People only ever drive *out* of La Chapelle!"

There was muted laughter from the room, which Mabit responded to by producing a gavel and banging it on the table.

"Who is this little man?" Valérie asked, no longer bothering to whisper.

"Noel Mabit," Richard sighed, "the town woodworm. He creates a hole for himself and burrows in."

"He is very silly."

René stood up, immediately controlling the room. "Look, Mabit, I have to open for the evening shift. What are you proposing—that we invade La Chapelle-sur-Follet?"

All eyes turned back to Noel. "Of course not," Mabit said, in a way that didn't entirely rule out the possibility. He stood again and tried to assume a more dignified air. "I think our town needs to heal. I want to offer all our condolences to Madame Ménard and to Hugo"—there was murmured approval—"and to offer our support to Sébastien Grosmallard, the victim, it seems, of foul play on the cheese front."

"As bad as any murder!" Grosmallard shouted, springing to his feet before Karine pulled him back down to his seat. Richard couldn't help thinking that Grosmallard was taking things a bit far by equating the swapping of real goat's cheese with a vegan substitute to actual, physical murder, but then this was France. He kept it to himself.

Karine stood after settling her father down. She was tall like him and looked drained by the whole thing, her red hair making her skin look pale to the point of being see-through, and she fiddled nervously with her necklace as she spoke. "Monsieur, we accept your kindness. We have had setbacks before; we shall be fine. Our sympathy lies with Madame Ménard. I apologize for my father, but he is hurting over the death of an old friend. It has been a shock to us all." She sat back down and looked to the floor.

"I offer my condolences as well." This time it was Garçon, though he didn't bother standing. "I never met Fabrice Ménard, but his reputation was huge. I have an idea!" Suddenly the youthful exuberance that had the young chef plastered all over every magazine and TV station went off like a bottle of champagne. "Let's have a food festival, here in Saint-Sauver! We have two of France's most famous chefs, the soul of the goat's cheese industry..."

"My café!" René shouted, not entirely without a snarl.

"Why not?" Garçon stood now. "Monsieur Tatillon, what do you say?"

Tatillon pursed his lips in non-committal fashion.

"I want no reviews or reviewers." Grosmallard growled this in a way that suggested rolling thunder and the promise of heaven-sent carpet bombing.

"Why, afraid of the competition?" It was intended as a joke by Garçon but, thanks to youthful exuberance, it lacked judgment.

"You are not, nor have you ever been, nor will you ever be, competition." This time Grosmallard sounded like a bear prematurely roused from hibernation. "Your food is magpie food, shiny, anonymous, and lifted."

Garçon wasn't one to back down. "It's not all about the name, though, is it, chef? I mean, what's in a name?"

There was a pause while the whole room held its breath.

Grosmallard stood slowly. "If you are referring to my son, he will learn from his mistakes." Antonin looked vacant rather than hurt. "I cannot control 100 percent of his genes." With that he walked out, followed by Antonin. Karine was left to shake her head sadly, then she stood as well.

"Monsieur," she addressed Mabit, "I think a food festival could be a good idea. I have spent too long trying to re-establish my father's reputation to have it ruined again by one incident." She turned to the rest of the room. "Good evening," she said quietly, and left.

Again, silence fell after the large door clanked shut.

"Is that it, now?" Clavet asked.

This had the effect of snapping Mabit back into the present. "No, Monsieur Clavet, one more thing." The room groaned again. "I'm sure you've all met Commissaire LaPierre." LaPierre stood and nodded. "The commissaire has asked that we appoint an intermediary to act as a guide to the town and his investigations, someone local, obviously, who knows the place well."

"Why haven't we had a new *police municipale* appointed yet?" Jeanine asked. She liked a man in a uniform.

"The wheels of the state turn slowly," Mabit replied, as if it were the most profound thing ever said in the French language.

92

"A police liaison? Lord," whispered Richard, "what a poisoned chalice that would be!"

Valérie didn't say anything, but kept looking forward to the stage.

"I propose Monsieur Ainsworth," Mabit said with a delicious, malevolent edge.

"Oh no!" cried Richard.

"Oh yes!" cried Jeanine, the *boulangère*.

"Motion carried!" Mabit said swiftly, banging his gavel.

"What?! But I'm a busy man!" Richard jumped to his feet. The rest of the room felt some level of sympathy, but it was outweighed by their relief at dodging the responsibility themselves.

"Too busy to help our town?" Mabit asked unfairly.

"Too busy to help the state investigate a murder, monsieur?" LaPierre joined in.

Richard sat down again, defeated, and felt a tap on his shoulder.

"Bad luck, old man. Tough assignment, that."

"Yes, bad luck, Richard."

He turned round to see Martin and Gennie Thompson grinning at him.

"Hello, Martin. Hello, Gennie." He tried not to show any enthusiasm in his greeting, which didn't take much effort. "You know Valérie."

"We most certainly do!"

"Oh, Martin, put your tongue back in! He's terrible, he really is."

"How's business?" Richard asked, his mild disgust mixed with a salacious curiosity.

"Booming, isn't it, Gennie?"

"Yes, booming."

"These swinging holidays are the way forward, old man. If that's your thing, obviously."

"Have you…" Gennie started.

"No."

"Do you have a room free?" Valérie asked the question but still didn't turn round.

"Why yes!" Gennie clapped. "We do!"

"Just a room, though." Valérie stressed the point. "And I shall insist that everyone wears clothes. All the time." She was referring to the time she'd popped round for tea and got far more than she'd bargained for.

"Of course," Martin and Gennie said in unison.

Richard couldn't help feeling that this was turning into a really rotten day. He breathed out heavily, like the last whiff of air leaving a burst tire. At least it was nearly over, he thought.

"Monsieur Ainsworth." Commissaire LaPierre stood over him, a vicious look in his eye.

"Can it wait until tomorrow, commissaire?" he asked without looking up. "I'm feeling a little fragile." "Fragile" was putting it mildly. He had a vague sense of Martin and Gennie sneaking off, and then of Valérie standing up slowly. *Et tu, Brute?* he thought sourly.

"Good evening, Henri." Valérie's tone wasn't cold as such, but neither was it warm. Richard looked up to see the commissaire's face hit the floor.

"Valérie!"

"It has been some time," she said smoothly. "You've put on weight."

"That's what happens to men after we divorce. We let ourselves go."

"Are you lot still here?" It was Monsieur Clavet, and he wasn't pleased. "You're the only ones left."

"Is there no *verre de l'amitié*?" Richard asked weakly. "I could really do with a drink." Then he turned to the commissaire. "Did you know Olivia de Havilland as well?"

12

The garden bench creaked as Richard sat down on it heavily. He watched the hens closely as he did so, checking to see how the pecking order was taking shape, but they looked calm enough. Lana Turner was eating heartily, nipping deliberately at the ground, Joan Crawford was kicking up the dust behind her, and Olivia de Havilland was keeping a wary distance and watching the others, a regal look in her eye. There was no visible sign of attacks by the other two, but it was best to keep an eye on things anyway. Breakfast for the guests was finished and he could clear up later; for now, he needed time and space to think.

He had intended to sort his head out the previous evening but it was banging and clanging like a busy shipyard, so he'd allowed himself the indulgence of watching a couple of Olivia de Havilland films instead. He'd started with *To Each His Own*, a tearjerker about an unwed mother, and then moved on to *Airport '77*, a disaster movie in every sense but to which she had lent much-needed dignity. He had thought about watching *Gone with the Wind*, but he didn't have the stamina, so he'd gone to bed instead, still sad at the missed opportunity of meeting the great woman. An opportunity he had taken for granted but had never had the nerve to take advantage of, something he realized was perhaps the recurring theme of his adult life.

It's at times like these when the tropes are trotted out. *"Je ne regrette rien,"* people will say or, "Regrets? Too few to mention." This wasn't Richard's way, and he had his many, many regrets, filed away on his own internal hard drive, to be viewed morosely when the chips were down or as a stark reminder when things were going well. Then there were the regrets that he didn't have but which others, namely Clare, carried for him to use like a Taser whenever the need might arise. There was the one about the marriage proposal she had turned down from Stephen Roachford—that was a hardy annual, often given an airing whenever talk of money came up. She had turned down Stephen Roachford because he was a plumber, and she didn't want to be married to a plumber. She would, however, have been delighted to be married to the multi-millionaire Sir Stephen Roachford, owner and founder of Roachford's Domestic Services, and to hobnob with the high and mighty. Instead, she married an unambitious film student who, rather than use his PhD and move into the upper echelons of academia, spent most of his life in a darkened room, his emotions played out for him on a flickering screen.

It was an understatement to say he wasn't looking forward to her coming over. He knew why she was coming and knew it was probably time to make things official, but divorce should be a fight, a to-ing and fro-ing of beleaguered emotions, a tug of war, and a war of words. This was all going to be very amicable. The marriage would end with a whimper, not wholly unlike how it started. He was grateful at least that she couldn't get a plane immediately and was now coming the next day instead. He needed time to take stock.

Valérie had gone to bed early. She had said she was tired but Richard also suspected that she didn't want to talk about her exhusband, commissaire Henri LaPierre. How many ex-husbands was that now? Richard couldn't be sure; he wasn't convinced that even Valérie could be that sure. There was the tall Texan, Tex, who was also a bounty hunter and who, he assumed, had returned to the United States; there was the one who had died last year, though he may have been invented in order to persuade Richard that getting involved with mafia hitmen was the gallant thing to do. She had mentioned, he thought anyway, at least two others. It dawned on him, and not for the first time, that he knew almost nothing about her. Even her surname, d'Orçay, was an anagram of Corday, an eighteenth-century assassin. Was that even her name?

Richard watched the hens still grazing. Did he need to know more? Was it really necessary? On the one hand, he'd lived a careful, discreet, and—if he was honest—a rather dull existence. He was the living embodiment of caution and stability, a byword for staunch. On the other hand there was Valérie, a beautiful, dangerous intruder into his staid world, kicking up dust just like a hen and offering an excitement he'd only ever had vicariously through the movies. If this was a movie, he suddenly realized, there would be no choice. Rightly or wrongly, our hero would choose the path—reluctantly, for sure—of peril and exhilaration. He leaped to his feet, the decision made. He would do the same. He would show Clare. He may not be a millionaire or mix with politicians and business brains, but he could offer brighter lights than Sir Stephen bloody Roachford and his domestic services empire.

He would also show Valérie. She'd seemed embarrassed by the fact that the commissaire was her ex-husband, not because of his dowdy appearance—though it proved she didn't have a "type," as such—but because she hadn't told Richard. He sensed that it was something she regretted, and Valérie was not the sort of woman to entertain regrets.

So, where were they? How did things stand? He sat down again and returned his attention to the hens. Then he stood up again and said out loud, "No, it's no good. I need movement to think. No more being passive, Richard old son.

"So, Olivia," he began, "what have we got? Think of it like *The Dark Mirror*, when you had to investigate a murder by your own twin sister." Olivia made a low clucking noise as if paying attention. "We have a murdered cheesemaker, hit on the head then dumped in a fermentation tank. Not subtle, so whoever it was didn't mind the body being found. The victim supplied said cheese to a world-famous chef whose big comeback is ruined because someone switched the cheese to a vegan substitute. My question there, old girl, is why didn't he notice? Does that mean he wasn't there when it was prepared? Where was he, then? Ménard's place? It's only two hundred meters away. OK, that's one." He held up his thumb, then flicked open his forefinger. "Two. Local gossip says that the cheesemaker victim was putting it about, apparently. We need to know who with. That shouldn't be too difficult to find out in a place like this. Three." He flicked out his middle finger. "Three," he repeated. "There's no love lost between either the son of the cheesemaker victim, Hugo, or the son of the world-famous chef, Antonin. Is that just over this

business or is there a history there? Four." With slightly more difficulty he opened his ring finger. "Guy Garçon, who, whisper it, is
more style than substance, produces a perfect dessert that is basically
Grosmallard's recipe. He calls it an homage. I call it bad taste. Even
though it tasted very nice indeed. And five." He held up an open
hand. "Garçon gets a glowing review for a largely ordinary meal from
a feared critic, and the feared critic, who may or may not have been
the first to spot the vegan faux pas, turns up at a civic meeting for no
good reason whatsoever!"

He sat down again, before immediately shooting back up. "Six! I
am a murder suspect, according to the officer in charge of the murder
investigation. Six B, the officer in charge of the murder investigation is Valérie d'Orçay's ex-husband. Six C, my soon-to-be ex-wife
arrives tomorrow and I've nowhere for her to sleep because the man
accusing me of murder's ex-wife is there at present, and no matter
what's happened I can't stand the idea of her staying with expat per-
verts Martin and Gennie." This time he did sit down and stay there.
"Well?" he asked Olivia, who remained tight-beaked.

"Where else can I stay, Richard?" Valérie stood a few yards away,
her case at her feet and Passepartout inevitably in her arms. She
looked a little lost, like an orphan girl.

"How long have you been there?"

"Since number two. I presume number one was the murder."

"Yes, it was."

"You are right, Richard, there are a lot of questions to be
answered."

"More than I listed there too," he mumbled sullenly.

"Yes."

"Why didn't you tell me?"

"About Henri? I don't know." She sat next to him. "I think I thought he would delegate to someone else and so I wouldn't have to meet him. I don't remember him being a hard worker like this."

"You don't have to tell me any more." His tone was aimed at the right side of martyred stoicism but it had a large sprinkling of I'm-desperate-to-know about it too.

"We met at a police training college," she said quietly. "We were very young. And it didn't last the course."

"I can see that."

"No, it didn't last the police training course. He was an ideal-ist who believed in fighting crime, and I was a young woman con-stantly told that this wasn't my world and I should be doing the filing instead. He got a big breakthrough in a case, which I gave him. I got no credit for it and it broke our marriage."

"That's awful." Richard's indignation was palpable. "And, erm, was he...was he the first?"

"Policeman, yes." She seemed lost in thought. Richard nearly fell off the bench. "As for staying at Martin and Gennie's, there doesn't appear to be much choice. Your wife arrives, then your daughter. The *chambre d'hôte* is full..."

He nodded. "I had hoped that having Madame Tablier serve them breakfast might make them check out early, but no such luck."

"It may not be for very long, just..."

"Just until the end of my marriage? How long will that take? I'm so sorry," he added quickly. "I—I didn't mean..."

"That I've had more practice?" She had a twinkle in her eye as she smiled at him. "Each time is different, but if your minds are made up, then I suggest a quick kill." She sensed Richard stiffen. "I didn't mean like that, Richard. Ha! You couldn't afford me!"

They both laughed this time, though it was a sentence that Richard knew he'd not easily forget.

"So, what now?" he asked.

Valérie produced a business card from her pocket. It was one of Martin and Gennie's more salacious ones, not, he felt, leaving a great deal to the imagination of even your average swinger. "I'll give them a call," she said, though obviously putting it off.

Suddenly, Richard got to his feet again. "Can I borrow that?" He took the card from her. "I'll be back in a tick."

Five minutes later he was sitting next to Valérie again, unable to hide a big grin. "We have a room free now." There was a hint of smug triumph in his voice too.

"Richard!" She paused. "What did you do?"

"I just happened to mention to that new couple that if they were stuck for something to do this evening... Then I gave them Martin and Gennie's card."

"But don't they have children?" She looked aghast.

"I said we could offer crèche services."

"Oh, Richard, brilliant!" She kissed him on the cheek. *That's six C dealt with*, he thought. *Just numbers one to six B to sort out now.*

13

"Oh yeah! What's going on here, then?" Madame Tablier was brandishing her broom as though it were a spear and Richard and Valérie were morally bankrupt intruders.

"Absolutely nothing, madame." Valérie saved Richard from answering with something borderline incriminating. "Your boss has been very clever this morning, that is all."

"Filth, more like!"

"It's nothing of the sort, is it, Richard?"

"Heaven forbid," was the weak, unconvincing response.

"Well, something's going on. That new family have started packing up already. I've cooked eggs for longer than they stayed."

"Yes, well, they decided it wasn't for them. Madame d'Orçay will be taking the room, if you could get it ready."

"I see." Madame Tablier leaned on her broom. "You know in Paris you can rent a room by the hour. Is that what this place is becoming?"

"No."

"A knocking shop?"

"No, Madame Tablier. It is not." This time, and possibly for the first time, Richard tried to be firm with the woman. The look on her face, however, suggested that it hadn't been worth the effort, so he decided to change the subject. "Yesterday you said that Ménard had been having affairs..."

"No, I said other people had said that. I keep my ear to the ground, that's all."

"Rather a vulnerable position, wouldn't you say?"

Madame Tablier glared at Valérie while Richard's brain did a somersault at Valérie's words. Had she been revising on his account or did she completely by accident quote Celeste Holm from *High Society*, the musical adaptation of *The Philadelphia Story*? They were both films very dear to his heart... *Concentrate*, he told himself, as he realized he may be missing some potentially important parts of the conversation.

"...That's what they say, anyway." The older woman had a look of distaste on her face that suggested she'd just swallowed a lemon studded with cloves.

"I don't believe it!" Richard said. "Say that again?"

She tutted in annoyance. "I said that the Ménards and the Grosmallards were all very close. Very close."

"You mean they were all lovers?" Valérie didn't so much need confirmation as she wanted to see how Madame Tablier dealt with the subject non-euphemistically.

"That's what they say."

Richard and Valérie looked at each other. "I mean really, does anyone stay faithful anymore?"

"You did, Richard, so you say."

"Yes." He nodded sadly. "But that wasn't my fault."

"Anyway, I can't stand here gossiping all day. I'll have to go and get your room ready."

"I should clear up after breakfast." Richard stood up. "Every piece of new information just opens the thing up wider. It's very messy," he added inadequately.

"Murder is messy, Richard, come on." Valérie stalked past a surprised Madame Tablier.

"Where are we going?"

"The Ménard cheese factory," she said, as if it were the most obvious thing of all.

"Right-o." He looked at Madame Tablier. "Would you mind, erm...?"

She tutted again.

A few moments later they were in Valérie's car, and once they had got it started, they were speeding along the narrow country lane up to the goat farm. It all felt impossibly exotic to Richard. He was well aware, from previous experience, that things just happened to Valérie d'Orçay, and that he was, by and large, clinging on to her hem and being dragged into the whirlwind. Yes, he had a cautious nature, and yes, this wasn't usually his kind of thing, but it was all such bloody good fun. At least it would be if she didn't drive like a lunatic.

"I could book an appointment with my mechanic if you like?" He tried to sound as nonchalant as possible, as though, excitement or no excitement, Valérie's death-wish driving style wasn't scaring the very life out of him.

"You didn't believe me about my car, did you?"

He gripped the door handle as they went careering around a sharp bend. Even Passepartout—an expert at riding through Valérie's driving idiosyncrasies and with a low center of gravity—nearly rolled out of his bed. She took her eyes off the road, demanding an answer, and he decided to say something quickly before she drove them all into the River Follet.

"I don't know what to believe half of the time." Funny, he thought, that backed into a corner it was honesty that came to mind first. "This all seems so..." He struggled to finish the sentence. "Fictional," he said finally. "It all seems so fictional."

"Like a film?" She smiled at him.

"Please watch the road, Valérie." She had said "like a film" though, not "like *one of your* films, Richard," as Clare would have done. The difference was enormous.

"You are thinking about your wife, aren't you?" Once again, she had an unnerving ability to be in Richard's head, like a squatter.

"How could you tell?"

"There is a vein on your forehead that becomes more pronounced whenever she is mentioned or you think of her. It's a sign of stress, unresolved stress."

Richard stayed silent for a moment. "You shouldn't be looking at my forehead, you should be watching the road." He ran a finger over his forehead nonetheless, feeling for the giveaway vein.

"I thought... Clare, is it?" She knew very well it was. "I thought she was coming out today?"

He looked out of the window. "She's coming tomorrow now, couldn't get a flight, then my daughter and her husband are coming at the weekend. Happy families!" he said, trying and failing to sound chirpy.

"Why not just ask Clare not to come?"

It was a solution offered in the same tone of voice that a computer engineer says something like, "Turn it off, turn it back on again," a mix of ennui and emotionless matter-of-factism. But then, he had to acknowledge, she was the expert in these situations, or, at the very least, was vastly more experienced when it came to marriage breakups.

"I can't." He tried not to sound pathetic. "For one thing, she owns half of the house and business, so I can't just shut her out, even if I wanted to."

"And you don't want to?"

"Not really. I know it's the end and so does Clare, so we have to get things sorted, I suppose, financially and so on."

"And are you sad it is the end, Richard? You sound sad." Valérie slowed the car down a touch.

"Yes, yes of course I am. We had thirty years together, most of them very good." He paused, trying to think of some specific latter-day examples, which he couldn't. "Didn't you ever feel sad when your, er, marriages ended?" He tried to swallow the plural.

"Not really," she replied, as if considering it for the first time. "I never regret a decision once it is made. It is the way I am, you know?" Richard knew.

"And was it always your decision?" He was trying to build up to the question of just how many times this had actually occurred.

"Oh yes. But I could always persuade my husbands that it was in their interests!" She smiled widely, showing her perfect teeth. Richard thought, for the millionth time, that he'd never met anyone quite like Valérie d'Orçay.

"So, what will you do with your newfound freedom, Richard?"

He took a deep breath. He had thought about it, obviously, but always in heroic, man-alone, stoicism terms, taking his leave of the cruel world. A lighthouse keeper was one such option, a remote Amazonian missionary another. Though, in truth, he knew less about religion than he did about lighthouses.

"I don't really know," he sighed, as Valérie turned in to the car park at the Ménard *fromagerie*. "I want, I don't know? Excitement? I think I want excitement. After thirty years of marriage, you get used to most days being the same, one year running into another. Easter here, Christmas there, birthdays at the same restaurant. The same people, the same conversations, the same worries. I like the idea of being free of that, and that's not Clare's fault at all, it's just that's what marriage is or became for us, anyway." Valérie turned the engine off. "So, maybe I quite like the idea of not knowing what's coming next." He was in full James Stewart mode now. "It's daunting, really daunting, but the freedom of it all, the lack of responsibility... It's exciting all the same. I'll have no ties; I could do anything! I could make last-minute decisions for once, go anywhere on a whim. Make things up as I go along. Improvise! That's it, I can improvise now!" He took a deep breath and looked out of the window at a largely empty car park. "So," he said, "what's the plan?"

Valérie smiled. "Why don't we improvise?" she said softly.

"Oh God, really?" Richard looked terrified.

14

They both sat looking out of the windshield for a few minutes. Valérie was trying to formulate a plan based on what was in front of her while Richard, despite his wild talk, wished they had arrived with a plan in the first place, discussed it, printed out a few copies, and maybe even had a dry run. As they sat there, a luxury coach arrived and parked between them and the office reception area. The coach doors hissed open and the coach itself lowered slightly. Its windows were tinted and the bodywork gleaming; it looked more like the tour vehicle for a rock band than a glorified holiday bus.

After a few seconds, an old man stuck his head out of the door. He had a bushy mustache and wore a white, fishing-style hat. The rest of his outfit, a slightly too small shirt and what used to be called slacks, was light blue. On his feet were an enormous pair of white trainers; he looked like he had his feet stuck in polystyrene breeze blocks. He sniffed the air, used the camera slung around his neck to take a picture of what he'd just sniffed, and stepped gingerly off the bottom step onto terra firma. Happy that the ground was solid enough, he turned to help an elderly woman down the steps. She had lilac-colored hair, visible through the top of a sun visor, but apart from that she was exactly the same shape, wore exactly the same colors, and looked equally distrustful of French soil.

"Americans," Richard said definitely as the couple were joined by at least a dozen others, all the same shape, age, and presumably disposition, and each pair representing a different pastel shade as though they were a human swatch booklet for the colors of a tastefully decorated downstairs toilet.

"Also an opportunity," Valérie said, opening her window slightly for Passepartout before stepping out.

Richard did the same and then repeated his question. "So, what's the plan?"

Valérie at first looked slightly annoyed, then smiled warmly and walked off toward the group without saying anything. Richard took a deep breath and followed. As the group of tourists filed in through the double doors, Richard and Valérie sneaked in with them at the back, hiding behind three very tall, elderly gentlemen in garish Hawaiian shirts who were complaining that the leg room on the coach was inadequate. Another felt the same about the air-conditioning, while the third said they'd arrived in the area in "better shape than my old man did in the war," which put a stop to the complaints of the others.

"Welcome, ladies and gentlemen," came a voice at the front, speaking English with a very heavy French accent. "It his a pleasure has always to welcome hour friends from they United States." Richard peered through the foliage of the Hawaiian shirts to see that it was Hugo Ménard himself giving the welcome, and though he was trying his best to be warm, circumstances and his naturally chilly personality weren't making his job any easier. Also, Richard had the sense that the American tour party were having difficulty understanding him and would have preferred someone nearer their own age. They began shuffling and muttering. Poor Hugo, as if he didn't have enough on his plate, was losing the room. After a few minutes, in which the muttering and the agitation grew loud, Hugo paused.

"I ham very sorry, ladies hand gentlemen," he said slowly, trying to enunciate every word, "our usual geede is unwell. He cannot be 'ere today. My *accent anglais*, my Hinglish haccent, is not very good."

"If he talks that slow, I'll be dead before we get out of here," one of the Hawaiian shirts said.

"Ah, give the kid a break, Morty," replied another.

"Yeah, the more time we don't have to be in that goddamn bus, the better for me," the third concluded.

It was then Richard noticed Valérie gently pushing through the crowd and making her way toward the front. Once there, she got Hugo's attention, which wasn't something she found difficult, and spoke quietly in his ear. After a few words, Hugo got as close to a smile as his demeanor would allow and re-addressed the crowd. "Ladies hand gentlemen, we har in luck. Monsieur Ainsworth, my friend, will translate for hus. Richard, are you there? *Vous êtes là?*" The group started to look around for whoever this mysterious Richard Ainsworth was.

"Oh, bloody hellfire!" Richard cursed at the back, attracting the attention of the Hawaiian shirts, who all turned to look down at him.

"You Ainsworth?" one of them snapped.

"Yes," he replied reluctantly.

"Well get up there, will ya? The kid needs a hand here."

A path opened up for Richard as he made his way to the front. He tried not to catch anyone's eye, except Valérie, to make sure that she knew he wasn't best pleased.

"Is that the Earl of Grantham?" he heard an old woman ask, which was something at least.

Shaking Hugo Ménard's hand, and hopefully forgiven for knocking him over with a chair the day before, he said, "Happy to help," with as little enthusiasm as possible, shot Valérie another angry look, and turned to face the throng. There were so many pastel hues and so much bright, impossibly colored hair, it reminded him of his daughter's childhood obsession with My Little Pony sets.

A woman with pink hair and a matching velour tracksuit pointed a sturdy metal walking stick in his direction. "What do you know from cheese?" she said, her heavy Brooklyn accent making it sound like a threat. Still, Richard thought, it was a valid question.

"This his Monsieur Richard Ainsworth," Hugo talked quickly, more comfortable back in his native tongue, "an old friend of the family." Richard translated to little enthusiasm. "And this is..."

"Madame Valérie d'Orçay." She smiled and most of the room melted. "I've come to buy your house." Richard decided that some judicious editing in the translation might be called for.

"It's no longer on the market," Hugo whispered from the side of his mouth in French.

"That is a pity. I was very interested."

"I was going to put it back on tomorrow, though. I have an appointment at the estate agent's in town."

"That's wonderful, I was..."

Richard noticed that they were losing the room and coughed loudly, rolling his eyes as he did so. "Shall we get on?"

They paused to register his obvious complaint and then ignored him. "We can go to my office and discuss the house, madame."

"If you don't mind."

"Not at all." Hugo handed Richard the clipboard he'd been carrying, which had his script and spiel typed out for him. "I am very grateful, Richard."

"Well, of all the bloody nerve!"

"Richard." Valérie winked at him. "Improvise." They disappeared into the back office and Richard turned back to the rapt tourists who, while not understanding much of what had been said, felt like they'd just witnessed the most French scene ever. Age, youth, beauty, and the whiff of infidelity and cheese.

"Goats were first brought to the Loire Valley by the Moors in the eighth century..." he began.

"Are you sure you're not the Earl of Grantham?" someone whose hair resembled cotton candy asked. Richard had the distinct impression it was going to be a long thirty minutes or so, as he led them through the factory doors and past the point of no return.

He would never have admitted it to Valérie—he couldn't let go of the feeling that he'd been royally dumped in it—but it didn't take him long to start enjoying himself. The American tourists, despite the obviously shaky start, proved to be attentive and well mannered, were politely if not remotely interested in goat's cheese production, and to his great relief, didn't ask any awkward questions. He had to confess that he liked being the center of attention for once and wondered idly if it wasn't time for a career change, or at least to dip his toe into amateur dramatics. He scooted past some of the more controversial aspects of the tour—the fermentation tank, for instance, which he couldn't easily see without imagining Fabrice Ménard's legs sticking out of the top. Also the vast, gleaming, obviously expensive annex that had been built solely for the production of the new vegan range and which his script covered in far too much technical detail.

The tour was to finish with old Giscard. Giscard was reputed to be the oldest billy goat, not just in the Follet Valley, but in the Loire Valley as well. At twenty-three years old he had lived twice as long as any other billy goat in the area and was the original Ménard billy, literally where it all began. Richard gave out this information as the group crowded around him at Giscard's perimeter fence and began to take photos of the old fella. He was chewing lazily on some hay and regarded the throng with a bored look in his eye. He'd seen it all before, and now had the air of a contentedly retired stud.

"The old guy looks beat!" It was one of the Hawaiian shirts.

"You would too if you'd seen that much action," said another.

"He does and he didn't see that much action!"

Richard joined in the laughter.

"Hey, Dick?" It took a few seconds to realize that he was being addressed.

"Yes?" He suppressed the urge to say, *It's Richard, actually*.

"That French guy, May-narde. He steal your girl?"

Richard shook his head. "Oh no! No." He decided to play to the crowd. "Well, I hope not!"

The three older men didn't join in the laughter this time. The tallest one leaned in close, as the other two leaned in closer with him. "We'll be in the area a few days..."

"We're following our old man's trail," added the smallest one, getting a look from the other two.

"Like I say, a few days. If you need anything taking care of... You get me?"

"Oh yes, yes. Thank you. That's very kind, thank you." He wondered if there'd always been this much untapped violence in the world or whether it was a more recent phenomenon.

"I'm Morty," said the tall man. "These are my brothers, Abe and Hymie."

"Here's our card." Abe offered the card. "*The Liebowitz Brothers*," it said, "*New Jersey's Finest Moving Company*."

"Well, that's, erm, well, very kind, thank you." Richard had no idea how to take the offer.

"Great tour, Dick!" Hymie clapped him on the back and the three of them made their way into the cheese shop.

Richard waited for them by the bus door, ready to see the whole thing through and to say goodbye. They slowly drifted out of the shop, each one of them carrying some paper-wrapped cheese, which nearly caused the bus driver to hyperventilate at the prospect of his bus ambience being infected with goat's cheese forever. The Liebowitz brothers were among the last to get on the bus.

"Take care, Dick," Morty said as he climbed the steps. "You know where we are if you need something."

"Yes. Thank you again."

"Hey, Dook!" It was the lady with the walking stick and cotton candy hair.

"Really, madam." Richard couldn't help but make himself sound even more English. "I am not a duke."

"Well, whatever. Anyways, we all enjoyed that and we had a little collection for ya." She handed him fifty dollars. "Take care, Dook, and if you're ever over in Pennsylvania..." She blew him a kiss as she was helped up the steps and the door hissed shut behind her. Richard waved them off and turned back to the factory. Set about fifty meters to the side of the factory was the family home, an old *longère*-style farmhouse with a neat garden in front and gabled windows in the roof. To the side of the house was Elisabeth Ménard, wearing a pink dressing gown and peering into the woods behind the old building. She was waving at someone or something, but Richard couldn't see what. Without noticing him, she went back indoors.

"Well, Richard, that was very interesting!" Valérie was at his shoulder. "I have learned a lot from Hugo Ménard..."

They got back in the car and Valérie started the engine. After making sure Passepartout was OK, she roared the car out of the car park, concentrating on the road. She couldn't contain herself for long, though.

"So, Richard, the whole vegan cheese idea...it was Hugo's idea, not his father's, not the idea of Fabrice Ménard."

"But was it him who swapped the cheese at the restaurant?"

"No, he says that was nothing to do with him. He doesn't know how that happened." Richard didn't understand why she was so excited then. "Fabrice was a gambler and had run up some big debts, and with the wrong people." Richard pretended this was news and didn't admit that he knew this already and had forgotten to mention it. "That is why the house is on the market. They're hoping that his life assurance policy will cover the debts, but in the meantime, the demand for this vegan cheese, this now very controversial vegan cheese, is enormous, and the orders are flooding in!"

"And he told you all this?"

"I can be very persuasive, Richard."

He thought about this for a moment while images of Valérie having Hugo Ménard in a half-Nelson flashed through his brain. "Are you saying that what's behind all this is an aggressive vegan cheese marketing campaign?" He couldn't hide his skepticism.

She seemed a little hurt by his lack of enthusiasm for her ideas. "Well, it is a start, Richard." She took her eyes off the road, trying to read his face.

"Look out!" Richard cried just in time so that Valérie could swerve round an oncoming jogger.

"Silly man!" she shouted.

Richard looked through the back window. "That was Antonin Grosmallard," he said slowly.

"He doesn't seem the exercising kind to me," she harrumphed.

"He's not," he replied slowly. "He was wearing Wellington boots." And he told her about Elisabeth Ménard waving at someone in the woods.

15

The center of Tours was heaving with summer tourists. The main shopping drag, the rue Nationale, was a sea of people swaying from one boutique to the next, while all the cafés and restaurants boasted of air-conditioning to tempt people indoors, their terrace tables already full. There was almost a party atmosphere as the old city, with its timbered walls and crooked buildings, looked down benevolently on the carefree holidaymakers and costumed street performers. Richard had had the foresight to book ahead: a favored restaurant in the shade, just off the place Plumereau. It was just what he liked, a set menu at a good price and simple fare that arrived on a white plate and didn't have to be analyzed as though it were a Rorschach test.

"But he's half her age!" was just about all Valérie had had to offer since the events of the day before. A very un-French, bordering on prudish reaction that had come completely out of the blue. For some reason Richard had assumed that Valérie had a somewhat more laissez-faire attitude to matters of the heart. Potentially half a dozen marriages were evidence enough of that to his mind, but her reaction to the Elisabeth Ménard–Antonin Grosmallard liaison was nothing short of matronly, a pearl-clutching response that seemed out of character. Not that he could claim to be in any way an expert on her character, he admitted to himself. In fact, he still knew virtually nothing about her and yet... Yet what? Did he sense there was something there? He had a history of completely misreading the signs since a very early age—it was almost a talent with him—but he had sensed something. And if that something was ever going to be given enough oxygen to turn into an actual thing, he really should get to know a little more about her. Did she really kill people for a living, for instance? He'd been out of the game, as it were, for some considerable time, but knowing things like that really did seem the bare minimum in even the most modern relationships. She had left him in the afternoon to work on "her accounts," she said, which had left him even more confused. Do bounty hunters keep receipts? It seemed unlikely. *Wanted: dead or alive—depending on your mileage and sustenance charges.* He literally had nothing to go on. She did seem quite put out, though.

"But he's half her age!" she kept repeating, with the occasional variation of the theme, "But she's twice his age!" thrown in for good measure. It did seem an unlikely pairing all the same. Technically, Valérie was spot on: he was half her age, and she was twice his, but they were also both adults, so where was the harm? Well, the harm was obvious—a couple, regardless of age, were having an affair, and the husband of the female party had been found murdered and dunked in goat's cheese. Richard picked up his crouton of baguette and spread some murderous goat's cheese on it. *What a way to go, though*, he thought again. Also, if he was to take his role as civic police liaison officer seriously, he really should be reporting this affair to the commissaire, but he couldn't see that happening in a hurry.

His phone beeped to signal a text; it was from Valérie:

Why was Tatillon at the meeting?

He stared at it for a minute or two. The simple answer was that he had no idea; Richard wasn't even sure why *he* had been at the meeting. He suspected that Auguste Tatillon's presence was intended to intimidate someone. But who, and why? He thought again about the various critics he had known over the years, a few of whom had used their make-or-break reputations as a way of terrorizing people. But there was always something behind it, at the very least influence. So, who did Tatillon have that power over? Certainly Grosmallard, possibly Garçon. The bad critics he'd known, the vicious ones, always came with the baggage of failure. They'd tried to be actors or filmmakers and for whatever reason, too much bad luck or too little talent, had failed. He remembered having a lunchtime pint in Soho with an old colleague who that morning had had a run in with a well-known critic for a London evening newspaper. The colleague had had one lunchtime pint too many, but it had made his anger more lucid. "Those who can, do. Those who can't, teach," he'd said, then added, "and those who can't teach, become film critics!" It was harsh on the best critics, but a fair point about the vipers. It was a resentment that they used like a weapon, figuring that their failure gave them greater insight and license. Had Tatillon trained as a chef, maybe? Under whom?

He texted this question to Valérie, but got no immediate response and decided to try to put the culinary events of Saint-Sauver to one side for a bit. He had to pick Clare up in an hour, and he needed to get his head straight.

It was unfair on her to have money tied up in the property and business in France. The question was, would he be able to buy her out? He didn't have the money for that, though he could get a bank loan, he supposed, if he put down the rest of his redundancy payout down as a deposit. It was quite a depressing thought. He was in his early fifties, about to be single, and might need a loan to keep the roof over his head. This was not how he had imagined things would turn out. In fact, he'd given no time at all to imagining how things might turn out—they would just turn out. That's how things happened. Still, he would be free. He gulped nervously at the thought. Free to do what, though? Just keep plodding along? He needed to give his future some clear thought. Yes, he decided definitely, folding up his napkin. He would spend time this evening doing exactly that, just as soon as he'd chosen an appropriate film to watch as "man faces life-changing decision" inspiration: *Sullivan's Travels*, maybe, *It's a Wonderful Life*, or perhaps...

The chair opposite him scraped back and Clare sat down with a superior grin on her face. Inside his head, he screamed like Janet Leigh in *Psycho*.

"I knew I'd find you here." Her smile became warmer and she poured herself some water from the carafe. Richard said nothing. Even if he could have found the words, he wasn't sure his vocal cords had recovered from the shock. She looked well, and was getting admiring glances from men as they walked by, her striking, carefully grayed hair catching them first before they were brought to a halt by her tanned cleavage, given full rein by a low-cut, leopard-print top.

"Bu..." was about all he managed.

"My flight was earlier than I told you. I knew you wouldn't check. And so, I wanted to see if you were the same old Richard, still sitting in the shade away from the action." She looked about her. "I never really liked this place."

"Tours?" Richard found his voice.

"No, not Tours. Just this restaurant. I know you think you've found a gem because you can always get a table, but there's a reason for that. Anyway"—she suddenly smiled at him—"you're here, and I was right. And in a way, it's quite comforting. How are you, and what on earth was going on when I phoned the other day?"

"Well, it's a long story," Richard said in such a way as to avoid telling it.

"And?" Clare was eager to know. "I'm going to be here for a while, hopefully. I've got time."

This didn't seem to fit with why Richard thought Clare was here at all—here for a while? And since when was his to-the-minute-predictability so comforting? As far as he recalled, it was the main reason she'd upped and left, that and the City accountant from Petersfield. He filled her in on the facts, leaving out only a small detail.

Clare shook her head. "I don't know which I find most shocking." Her eyebrows were right at the top of her forehead, signaling that she was about to try humor. "That there's been a murder about cheese, that Madame Ménard has a toy boy—and by the way, *good on her*—or that a backwater like Saint-Sauver has two Michelin-starred restaurants!"

"The place is going up in the world." He couldn't help being slightly put out by her dismissiveness; after all, he was the civic police liaison officer. "It's why we're so busy," he added defensively.

"We? Oh, Richard, that's definitely your business. And I'm pleased it's going so well."

Dammit, he thought, *that's just cost me a few grand.*

"Surely, you've left something out, though, from all this excitement?"

"Oh? No, I don't think so." He drank some water.

"Really? So that Valérie woman isn't here, then?"

Janet Leigh screamed again. "Here? No."

"There?"

"Ah. Yes."

"I thought so." Her eyes narrowed slightly. In that top, she now looked like a female leopard who'd sensed a rival in her territory.

"She's house-hunting," he squeaked.

"Manhunting, more like."

He blushed. He was being made to feel guilty and yet had absolutely nothing to feel guilty about. *More's the pity*, he thought sourly. It was the story of his bloody life.

"Well, she's not hunting me."

Clare looked at him for a few seconds, then laughed. "No," she said, "you're probably right."

That hurt.

"Why the charade with the plane times anyway?" He called for the bill, trying not to look insulted.

"I wanted to see if you would still do the same routine. The restaurant, the same table—did you have the *entrecôte*?" He nodded and she shook her head, but not in pity. "A small *pichet* of rosé?" He nodded again. "I knew you would, but I wanted to see it. I've been watching you for a while. You are still a good-looking man, Richard, but you shouldn't slouch so much."

This was not going the way he had been expecting. Clare seemed different and yet not different at the same time, as though she was making her mind up about something. Him, for instance. As though she were making her mind up about him. He paid the bill.

"Did you bring that awful 2CV?"

"Yes, well, it's all I have."

"Then I'm glad I hired a car, dreadful thing. I'll meet you back at home, then." She stood up, moving her figure like a film star sliding out of a limousine, and making sure she was watched in the same way. She looked down at him across the table, a position every other man looking at them would have loved to be in. "Race you!" she said, in a way verging on saucy-postcard eroticism, and walked off down the road.

That's it, he thought, *no* Sullivan's Travels *for me tonight, no* It's a Wonderful Life. *It's* The Birdman of Alcatraz *instead*. He left a small tip and walked quietly away. There was no point in racing; he knew he'd lose.

16

It usually took about thirty-five minutes to get back to Saint-Sauver from the center of Tours. That was if he took the A85 and was keen on getting back to Saint-Sauver in the first place. Today, Richard meandered along the much more picturesque country route instead. He couldn't have beaten Clare back to the house even if he'd wanted to, and also—he had to reluctantly admit this—he had no reason to do so. There was no reason to keep Clare and Valérie separated, nothing suggestive that Valérie might let slip. He was a romantic hero, without romance, so best to just leave the two of them to it. He knew damn well that there was a large element of cowardice to his decision and he didn't care one jot. Sometimes it was the wiser course of action to sit back and let things play out.

He slowed the car down to a crawl, annoying the other drivers behind him. Still, he thought, he would love to be a fly on the wall when, or even if, they confronted each other. Cinema history was littered with such big beast showdowns. Literally, in some cases— Godzilla versus Cosmic Monster, for instance, though he wouldn't want to ascribe those parts to Clare and Valérie. There was the much heralded De Niro–Pacino confrontation in *Heat*, which was some way after Richard's preferred era so left him a bit cold. There was Bette Davis and almost every other actress she appeared with, but mainly Joan Crawford. There was Joan Crawford and every other actress *she* appeared with, but most notably Bette Davis. His own favorite was Dame Margaret Rutherford and Irene Handl going at it like heavyweights in *I'm All Right Jack*. Of course, there was Olivia de Havilland and her own sister, Joan Fontaine, but...

The growing row of cars behind him all started angrily beeping their horns at the same time and he realized he was practically stationary. He sped up, for what it was worth, and shrugged his shoulders in the rearview mirror as an apology. He really should stop dawdling and just face whatever was going on at home. He sped up some more and then decided to stop by a favored vineyard and pick up some white wine. It was an hour later when he carefully parked the 2CV at Les Vignes *chambre d'hôte*. Valérie's car was parked sensibly under the shade of a willow tree while Clare's rental car, a behemoth of an SUV, dominated the small parking area like a tank on a putting green.

He opened the gate cautiously, though he didn't know why, and stepped through into the large garden area. Beyond the rhododendron hedge that separated the bed and breakfast from his own house, he heard laughter. Female laughter. Confident female laughter. He didn't know whether to feel relief or panic.

"Richard, is that you? We could hear your battered little car a mile away. Do join us."

Richard did as he was told and walked into the walled garden area. Valérie and Clare were sitting at the white painted iron table, a jug of Pimm's between them. Valérie was wearing her enormous sunhat, while Clare had her feet on the chair opposite, her skirt rolled up to her midthigh, trying to catch the sun, and most improbably of all, Passepartout was asleep on her lap.

"Richard, you've taken ages—did you get lost?" She laughed and rolled her eyes at Valérie, who smiled warmly, conspiratorially even, back.

"I needed to pick up some necessary supplies," was his subdued response.

"Well, I'm just introducing your friend Valérie here to Pimm's. Would you believe she's never had a Pimm's before?" Clare was at her ebullient best, never happier than when directing society.

"Well, we can't get it around here."

"Lucky I brought a few bottles with me, then!"

Valérie smiled again. Or was it the same smile, fixed in place for the duration? Richard couldn't tell under her huge floppy hat and behind large cat-eye sunglasses.

"Is there one for me?" he asked, sitting down.

"Oh yes, could you pour your own? I don't want to disturb the little doggy. He's very comfortable in my lap." Richard had rarely seen Clare like this; she was trying too hard and quite possibly looking for evidence of infidelity on his part. More divorce leverage, perhaps? "Valérie has been telling me about 'your case'—do you call it a case? You should, you know. Anyway, you didn't mention that the famous Auguste Tatillon was also staying nearby. Saint-Sauver is really going places. It's a pity you're full, Richard, he could have stayed here rather than at Martin and Gennie's bordello." She laughed again. "Poor man. That will prick his pomp! Or," she snorted, "the other way around!"

"I didn't know he was staying there." Richard turned to Valérie for a reaction, which wasn't forthcoming. For one brief moment Richard even thought Clare might have poisoned her, which would explain why she hadn't moved or spoken.

"I spoke to Martin and Gennie this afternoon," she eventually said.

"And how long is he staying for?" he asked, without trying to sound too interested.

"Indefinitely, they said. Apparently, he finds the area 'charming and inspirational.' He wants to finish his *memoirs* here."

She turned her head toward him for the first time, making it clear, imperceptibly, that this was important information. Memoirs, thought Richard, that certainly was important. In his experience, and he had read a lot, they could be either dull, boring affairs or absolutely explosive, bridge-burning efforts. There was no doubt that Tatillon would have a lot of secrets to share if he was willing to do so, and that he was doing so on the doorstep of Grosmallard looked very deliberate indeed.

"Valérie also tells me that you are the civic police liaison officer for Saint-Sauver, Richard. I always knew you had it in you to be important. Well done you." She raised her glass and he raised his back. Once he would have suspected that to be a back-handed compliment, but it felt genuine. She smiled at him, and he smiled back. Valérie stood up to go just as Madame Tablier came out through the double doors to the walled garden.

"Oh, hello!" Madame Tablier sniggered, her eyes bulging with excitement at the potential for gossip and confrontation in front of her. "All three of you, eh?" She leaned on her mop as if it were the best seat in the house, making them feel altogether more uncomfortable than they had been, which in Richard's case was quite some achievement.

"Madame Tablier, it's so nice to see you again," Clare gushed in English.

"Yep, keeping something warm in your lap as usual," the old woman replied in French, knowing that Clare wasn't fluent. Valérie coughed out her Pimm's and Richard stood up, as if that would make a difference.

"You can nip off early if you like, madame. I think we're done for the day."

"Nip off early? I've already done eight minutes overtime. Nip off early! Want to be alone, the three of you, no doubt." She threw her bucket of dirty water across the terrace, making as much noise as she could. "There's too much of it about, if you ask me. Bed-hopping!" she shouted.

"What did she say?" Clare asked.

"Too much bed-hopping, apparently," Richard translated morosely.

"Oh really? And does she have anyone in mind?"

"Poor Monsieur Ménard," she wailed, as she brushed the water into the flower beds, "hardly cold as yet and she's already running around."

"Elisabeth Ménard?" It was Valérie this time.

"Yes! Madame Ménard. Well, what do you expect from a foreigner? No offense."

"I thought she was from Lyon." Richard was confused.

"It's practically foreign," snapped Madame Tablier. "They're all the same."

Valérie lowered her glasses. "And who is she having an affair with, madame, do you know?" She winked at Richard, who hoped Clare hadn't seen it.

"I don't know! None of my business, is it?" She did some more brushing. "But the gossips in town, they're full of it, aren't they? Her and that Grosmallard. Disgusting. At her age."

Richard translated for Clare. "I thought you knew all that?" she whispered needlessly.

"It's good to have confirmation, though." Valérie nodded. "I mean"— Madame Tablier leaned on her mop once more—"I know they're both widowed but some decency wouldn't go a miss, a bit of discretion." She slammed the mop into the floor like she was slaying a dragon.

"What do you mean they're both widowed?" Richard was confused.

"Her, Elisabeth Ménard"—she talked to him like he was an idiot—"and that chef fella, Sébastien Grosmallard! Honestly, I'd have thought you'd have found that out by now. She's been seen coming out of his kitchen late the last two nights now. Shameless hussy."

"Who has seen them?" Valérie asked indignantly. And it was a fair question given that you'd have to be making a special effort to be in the restaurant car park late at night to see any goings-on, therefore it could be argued that they were being discreet.

"Practically the horse itself!" She picked up her bucket. "Grosmallard's daughter was seen at the station, waiting for a train to Paris. In tears she was, with her brother. 'I can't stand that woman!' she says to him. 'She'll ruin everything!' And her brother says, 'I'll talk to her, she's just lost her husband.' Well…"

"This is fantastic, Madame Tablier. Where do you get all this stuff?"

"Never you mind, Mr. Civic Police Liaison Officer. I'm no grass. Well, I'll be off now." And off she clanked without an au revoir.

"She really is the most extraordinary woman." Clare looked stunned by the performance. "I've no idea why you keep her on, Richard. I really haven't."

"I like her." Valérie smiled as the old lady waddled into the distance.

"Me too." Richard shook his head, dazed.

"Well, no doubt you two know what you're doing. You're old hands at this sort of thing now, aren't you?" Clare picked up Passepartout and put him gently on the floor, obviously feeling left out of things and not just because of the language barrier. "Well, I'm going to unpack. Richard, I'll take our room if that's OK with you; you can sleep in your cinema room. No doubt you have something to watch that you've only seen a few hundred times before." It was all very pointed but it was lost entirely on Richard and Valérie, whose minds were elsewhere. "It was charming to see you again, Valérie. We must go shopping while I'm here. Richard has such appalling taste. It'll be fun, a girls' day out."

"Yes, that would be nice," Valérie said, as light as a breeze.

"And, Richard?"

He looked up. "Yes?"

"I'm going for an aperitif this evening with Andrew and Tanya over in Clocheville—do you remember them?" Richard couldn't remember them. "Nice couple, he's an architect. I don't suppose you'll join me?"

He didn't feel like he had a choice. "Yes." He tried to sound as unenthusiastic as possible. "If I must."

"Good, we'll leave in an hour." She walked off toward the main house.

"Blast it," he said under his breath, "I don't even know who these bloody people are!"

"Well"—Valérie looked at him with a compassion that comes from expertise—"sometimes we have to do things in a marriage that we do not want to do. Meet other people, especially."

He sighed a tired, "Yes, you're right."

"But, Richard"—her tone changed slightly—"you must do me two favors: don't be too late and don't drink too much."

His imagination went into stratospheric overdrive.

"Why not?" he babbled.

"Because tonight we keep watch on the Grosmallard restaurant for ourselves. We'll see just who is having the affair!" And with that she took off her glasses and showed eyes wide with excitement.

17

"Well, how was your aperitif?"

On the face of it, it was a strange time for Valérie to start making small talk, but as they were effectively on an old-fashioned cop-style stakeout, it also made sense. That Richard had completely misunderstood the evening thus far was evident by his attire. He was head to toe in black and had even used some of the dark mudpack that Valérie had lent him on a previous night mission. Valérie was in a light, flowery summer dress and wedge sandals, and even though it was nighttime, had the ubiquitous sunglasses on her head, holding her hair back.

"Oh, OK," was his slightly petulant reply. He'd just been admonished for his costume in no uncertain terms, and felt not just unwise but worse, unworldly. He had assumed that "stakeout" meant undercover and had prepared accordingly. Valérie had taken a different course. They would be in the car and hiding in the corner of the darkened car park because, if they were seen, they didn't want to be seen. They would be playing the part of illicit lovers. That was her plan; that was the story. Richard's take on the cover story made it look more like she was the victim of a kidnapping. She'd given him some face wipes and told him to remove his gloves and black bobble hat.

"Just OK?" The car was parked facing away from the restaurant, in the furthest corner, but her eyes were constantly looking into the rearview mirror.

Richard felt, probably wrongly, that Valérie was probing for something, some information on the Richard–Clare marriage. An optimist might look on it as a form of jealousy, but Richard had given up optimism sometime around puberty as a trap to catch the unwary traveler in life. The truth was that if she was looking for some insight into the current Ainsworth marital status, she was looking in the wrong direction. He was as much in the dark as anyone, probably more so. Clare's behavior since she had arrived had veered between the acidly dismissive, verbally beating him about the head with a sledgehammer, which he was accustomed to, and the territorial, which he most certainly was not accustomed to. It was like she herself was undecided about him. He puffed out his smeared cheeks. He knew one thing: once Clare had made up her mind there would be very little he could do about it either way.

"A good OK or a bad OK?" Valérie persisted, still acting as if it were small talk and that she had nothing really invested in the answer.

"I don't honestly know. I can't work Clare out at the moment, if I'm honest. And my mind is elsewhere," he added suggestively.

"Yes, I know what you mean, Richard." Did she? The excitement was almost screeching in his head. "This case is very complicated." The excitement came to an immediate and crushing halt, like an insect hitting a windshield. "There is something we are not seeing here. Everybody involved knows each other and has done for years, yet now it comes to a murderous conclusion." For something so complicated and lethal, which he conceded it was, she spoke with an almost indecent fervor for the thrill of the thing.

They sat quietly again for a few minutes. "There was one thing about this evening that I found interesting," he said, hoping it was relevant. "This architect fellow, Andrew Shipman—we were talking about the two restaurants, and he was saying just how expensive it is to set up a place like this, at least half a million euros just to get the thing off the ground. Even around here. René said much the same thing."

"So what are you saying?" She took her eyes off the mirror, interested in his train of thought.

"It's just an idle thought really, but where has the money come from?" He could see her nodding in the dark, thinking it over.

"Surely his reputation would guarantee investment?"

"Well, that's what I said, but this architect was saying that as far as he knew, Grosmallard's reputation for culinary genius is dwarfed by a much greater reputation for being an unreliable has-been. He's been on a downward spiral since his wife died, which is pretty much what Tatillon told us too. So the question is, who has invested the money and to what lengths would they go to protect that investment?"

The moonlight caught her eye as she looked at him. "Richard, that is brilliant."

"Thank you. Follow the money, as they say." He felt very pleased with himself.

"This evening hasn't been a waste of time after all." She indicated the dark of the restaurant behind them and the singular lack of activity.

"Ah." There was an air of confession in his voice. "What day is it?"

"It's Sunday."

He sighed, the martyr about to take the blame. "Of course it is. They're shut on a Sunday evening. Sorry, I should have remembered that." He could sense her thinking this through.

"So they will have chosen a less obvious meeting place, you mean?"

"Something like that, yes. Sorry, I forgot."

Valérie drummed her elegant fingers on the steering wheel, which to Richard was historically suggestive of annoyance. She turned to face him suddenly and he suspected all his good work on the investment angle might be lost in the aftermath.

"It's perfect!" she hissed, again the gleam in her eye.

"What is?"

"There's no one here, Richard. The place is deserted."

"Ye-es."

"So we should take the opportunity to have a look in the office, don't you think?"

"No," he said.

"Yes," she countered, "there might be some clue as to where the money has come from!"

He thought about it. He could sit there and argue all he liked but he knew it would make no difference, plus he was dressed for the role.

"Come on, then!" he said, making it sound like a child's cry of "Geronimo!" as they jump off a bridge.

Valérie got some tools from the boot of her car, a large flashlight, and a bag, presumably containing her lock-picking equipment. They made their way cautiously across the car park, sticking to the shadows and Valérie leading the way despite her implausible outfit, Richard hovering behind almost like he was her shadow. If they were expecting security lights then none came on, even as they reached the doors at the back of the kitchen.

"That's good," Richard whispered. "They must have spent so much money on cell phone jammers they had none left for adequate security." He could tell that Valérie wasn't convinced, though.

She shone the flashlight upward above the door, revealing an expensive-looking alarm system, its box immaculate, showing how new it was. "That's odd," she muttered as she unzipped her tool kit.

"What are you doing?" Richard panicked. "Shouldn't you disable the alarm first?"

"There is no need, Richard. I know these systems—they are very expensive, possibly the most expensive." She gave him a pair of medical gloves from the bag, putting her own on as well.

"So you know how to work it then?"

"Richard." He was trying her patience. "It is not on." She shone the flashlight upward again. "There is a blue light if it is programmed, and there isn't. It has been disabled already, or Grosmallard forgot to activate it, which is probable." She worked briefly on the door lock with something from what Richard called her "breaking-and-entering purse." It opened easily, a smile of triumph on her face and the almost feverish excitement that he was becoming accustomed to. This time she didn't bother to whisper. "Follow me!" she said, and stepped inside. More cautiously, Richard followed her.

It was a sinister-looking place in the half gloom. The narrow windows above the sinks against the wall allowed a sliver of moonlight, which caught the shadow of state-of-the-art kitchen equipment, making it all look like aggressive machinery rather than the tools of culinary invention. Richard felt like he was in a laboratory. The surfaces gleamed even in the shadow, the chrome racks contained pans of every size and shape, and the heat lamps above the range of hobs and ovens in the center of the kitchen looked like rocket boosters. There was a hum of fridges and freezers and the smell of cleaning product everywhere. It was cleaner than a hospital.

Valérie shone the flashlight around, taking it all in. Richard did the same with the surprisingly bright flashlight on his cell phone. "Let's start with the office." Valérie was quieter this time and shone the flashlight toward an open door at the far end of the room, next to a window, which showed a desk and chair in the harsh light. She moved off quietly but at speed, showing the professional she was, leaving Richard to make his own mind up where to take himself. He decided to follow her to the office and took the same route, but more cautiously. Valérie was sitting at the desk when he got to the partitioned office, taking in the view and deciding where best to start. Quietly she opened a drawer, which was the same as everyone's utility top drawer the world over. It contained stationery, batteries, elastic bands, and a cell phone charger. She closed it quietly and got to work on the drawer below.

Richard shone his flashlight on the walls. There were certificates of health and safety, licensing, and so on by the door, but on the other wall there were the trophies, as it were. There was a framed certificate for the two Michelin stars Grosmallard had been awarded in his first solo adventure, newspaper cuttings of the presentation and of his famous dessert, which Richard was surprised about, knowing that Grosmallard was apparently paranoid about sharing images of his creations. There were other photos on the wall too. The great and the good of French life shaking the hand of the famous chef. Politicians mainly, writers, television personalities, sports stars, all not quite what they were, all from a few years ago, except the politicians, who never seemed to fade. There were no recent photos. It was quite a sad collection, really, and he couldn't imagine Grosmallard putting it together himself. It was probably the work of his daughter, Karine, who was so desperate to put her beloved father back where he belonged, though even she had now left in tears.

Valérie made a sound that meant she'd had some success in the search. "Bank statements," she whispered, "dating back a few years. There was a large deposit a few years ago but it dwindled, and there's not much left. At the time they would have started building and planning this place, there was no increase in their funds at all, and this is a business account."

"They might have paid everything in cash?"

"Or someone else did? Or these aren't the official accounts. There must be another account somewhere, but it's probably not here." She was thinking aloud and then looked at the computer screen. "I might be able to find it on here."

"How long will that take?" Richard didn't want to be here any longer than was absolutely necessary, and even if they found the account, it was unlikely to show clearly where the money was coming from. He shone his flashlight back on the wall. "Oh, look," he said enthusiastically, and Valérie responded to his tone, thinking he'd found something. She looked at the photograph he was highlighting: it was a thinner, smilier Grosmallard standing next to an old woman. She turned back to the computer.

"It's probably his mother; a lot of these chefs dote on their mothers."

Richard said nothing. The old woman in the picture was Olivia de Havilland, and Valérie hadn't recognized her neighbor and apparent *millefeuille* companion. He didn't know what to think, so he left her to it in the office and went back out to the kitchen, telling himself that the light and the angle from which she was looking may have caused the error. In the kitchen he picked up an old recipe book that stood on a shelf, almost like a trophy itself. It was more a notebook in size, with papers and Post-it notes stuffed in it as new recipes were tried or old ones adjusted. He shone his flashlight on it and began to walk around the central cooking island.

Suddenly his foot hit something and he went rolling over onto the floor, knocking some silver presentation platters over in the process and making one hell of a racket as he did so. He didn't dare move initially and lay there until Valérie came rushing over and hissed in his face, "What on earth are you doing?" which wasn't an unreasonable question under the circumstances.

"I tripped over something. It wasn't bloody deliberate." He sat up, picking up his phone and the notebook.

Valérie shone her flashlight haphazardly on the floor to find the culprit that had tripped Richard, and as she did so they both jumped back in shock. Two feet, presumably attached to two legs and therefore the rest of a body, were sticking out from under the shelves. They both got on the floor and followed the flashlight as she moved it up the body. The light ended finally on the agonized face of Antonin Grosmallard, his lifeless eyes bulging, his neck covered in blood, and a large knife sticking rather awkwardly out of his throat.

18

So many situations in life demand established protocol, thought Richard as he served breakfast even more distractedly than usual. He'd already spilt some coffee while serving his gay couple, who were up and out early as usual. He'd managed to blame it on them rather than face the ire of Madame Tablier, though, who, while in his shocked state, represented a bridge too far. Protocol was a tricky one. There's the rather old-fashioned protocol of asking a prospective father-in-law's permission to marry his daughter, something which he remembered with fondness; there's the complicated French protocols of greeting, how many kisses, which cheek, and so on, and which was a political and social minefield; and then there was the rather thornier, much less explored protocol of what to do when stumbling across a dead body in a place you have just illegally broken into.

It was a tricky one and it had left them both largely speechless on the short trip back. Antonin Grosmallard, stabbed in the throat, clearly dead, but left in a place that was surely meant to be discovered, though not by amateur sleuths looking for explanatory bank details. Valérie had driven back with caution for once, her jaw tight, and had asked the same question more than once: "Why?"

Richard had replied as best he could with the evidence that they so far had at hand. That Antonin Grosmallard, like Fabrice Ménard, was paying the price for involvement in his father's disastrous opening evening, particularly with the dessert: that was the first potential motive. That other people knew of his affair with Elisabeth Ménard was another. It left the list of suspects exactly the same as for the murder of Fabrice Ménard; the only one that could with certainty be crossed off the list was poor Antonin Grosmallard himself.

He refilled the coffee machine. His Parisian family were silently, stiffly almost, going through their breakfast, perhaps sensing the tension in the air. Valérie descended with Passepartout, and she showed no signs of the shock she had shown the night before. And it had been obvious that she was shocked. Richard imagined her as a hardened professional, perhaps even a killer herself, though that was something of a gray area, but neither of them had been prepared for that. This morning she looked refreshed, however, inevitably glamorous, but with a steely determination to get things sorted out. She smiled at Richard, giving nothing away, and sat at her usual table in the corner.

Richard took over the pot of coffee and poured some out. "How are you this morning, Madame d'Orçay, did you sleep well?" It was one thing to keep up appearances; it was quite another to take this route, and it felt like even Passepartout rolled his eyes.

"Morning everyone, bonjour!" Clare entered through the double doors, looking as glamorous as Valérie but in a more—for want of a better word—British way; it was the classic "Frenchness" of Jean

Seberg versus Shirley Eaton, to Richard's mind, *À bout de souffle* versus *Goldfinger*. She looked fantastic; she swept in, kissed Richard on the cheek, and sat confidently at Valérie's table. Some men might have reacted to this with a sense of flattery, that he was the center of attention between two beautiful women, Chihuahuas notwithstanding. Richard wasn't one of those men, and if a CT scan of his brain had been available at that moment it may have resembled Edvard Munch's *The Scream*.

The father of the Parisian family looked at Richard with new respect, while his patently nonplussed wife obviously couldn't see what attraction he had. The children ignored the whole thing, and were putting mini pains au chocolat in their pockets while their parents were momentarily distracted.

"Oh, Richard, don't stand there with your mouth open like that, it looks most unhygienic."

He snapped his mouth shut and returned to their table with the coffee pot.

"So," Clare breathed in gossipy fashion, leaning in conspiratorially, "where did you two head off to last night?"

So that was it, he thought, partly in relief. Clare wasn't glammed up necessarily for his benefit; it was just her natural competitive instinct shining through. She was determined to win Richard over Valérie, whether she actually wanted him or not, and without knowing that Valérie probably wasn't even in the fight. He relaxed; his ego wouldn't have been able to cope with the thought that he was a prize to be a fought over, but he was perfectly comfortable with the idea that, in essence, it had absolutely nothing to do with him.

"I cannot lie, madame," Valérie answered smoothly, feeding

Passepartout a morsel of croissant as she did so. "I borrowed your husband last night."

"Lucky Richard," Clare said icily. Richard laughed nervously.

"Yes, I admit I was bored and I was looking at properties for sale on the internet. I asked Richard if he wouldn't mind showing me where they were. He did say that you were already in bed." Passepartout grinned on her behalf.

"And was it a success? Did you find what you were looking for?"

"Much more than I bargained for, actually, yes."

"Are you sure you wouldn't be bored living out here in the country?" Clare stirred her coffee. "I always felt I was cut off from the world."

"Oh no!" Valérie laughed and repositioned the inevitable sunglasses on top of her head. "I have already seen the world!"

Richard, with his rictus smile losing its sheen, didn't notice his other guests get up and leave. He was disturbed, however, by Madame Tablier grumbling to herself as she came down the stairs. He went back to the relative safety of his breakfast bar, as though seeking shelter from a bombardment, and poured himself a strong coffee. Madame Tablier nodded a wordless good morning to the two ladies and sat down at a vacant chair, removing her slip-on shoes and rubbing her feet. "I have to leave a bit earlier this morning," she said, without looking up. "Maître Renaud wants me to give the office a quick clean before the will-reading this morning."

Richard caught Valérie's eye.

"What did she say?" asked Clare, not wishing to be left out of anything.

"Madame Tablier is to clean the *notaire's* office this morning before the reading of the Ménard will," Valérie translated.

Clare snorted. "I really think she is the only cleaner in the whole of the Follet Valley!"

"Of course, Madame Tablier," Richard interjected, the older woman having heard her name and looked up at Clare with something approaching contempt.

Clare was oblivious, however, and buttered a piece of baguette. "Richard"—there was a pretend innocence in her voice—"I wonder if *I* could borrow you today?" It was a pointed question, which Valérie ignored and which Madame Tablier, while not understanding the English, certainly caught the tone of.

"Well, yes, I, er...of course!"

"Good!" Clare beamed. "I'd like to go for a picnic by the river. Do you remember that spot we used to go to? It was so romantic, so... private." She made it sound like a secret trysting place, though he was sure he'd have remembered if anything like that had gone on.

"Yes," he replied cautiously, "why not?"

"Oh, Richard, you could show more enthusiasm than that!" She laughed at him and stood up to leave. "I'll take care of the picnic; I'm very good at that kind of thing. Au revoir, Valérie, I do hope you won't mind house-hunting alone today." She left without saying a word to Madame Tablier, who muttered something about just being staff before going back upstairs.

Richard breathed out heavily. "I didn't realize she had seen us going out."

"I'm not sure that she did." Valérie smiled. "She may just have been playing a game. She is a very beautiful woman, and she doesn't want to lose you. She seems also to think that I am a rival."

Richard would later tell himself that he was on the cusp of asking if she actually was a rival, but he never got the chance. There was a knock at the door and commissaire Henri LaPierre walked in, a look of concern on his face. Valérie nodded to Richard, a silent signal that he understood as "leave the talking to me."

"Monsieur Ainsworth, your wife said that you were in here." He stressed the word "wife," and clearly Clare had wanted to stress it too. "Valérie," he said, "you look delightful as always."

"Henri, how nice to see you. Or shall I call you commissaire? Is this official business?"

"Henri, commissaire, it makes no difference." He was definitely on a charm offensive.

"Morning, Henri." Richard smiled.

The charm vanished quickly. "I think commissaire works better for you, monsieur, in your capacity as my envoy, that is."

"Ah, right-o." He saw Valérie roll her eyes behind her ex-husband's back. They really must have made a most odd couple.

"Anyway." He looked slightly apologetic. "I have a confession to make. It was I, monsieur, who requested that you be made my go-between, shall we say. I was convinced you know more than you actually do." He looked at Valérie. "Valérie managed to convince me yesterday that maybe I was being premature with that."

"Oh well, really..." Richard felt slightly embarrassed and was also assuming, by the lack of urgency that LaPierre was showing, that he had no idea as yet of the murder of Antonin Grosmallard.

"But I have decided to keep you in that role and, to that end, I want you to come with me this morning."

"To the reading of the will?" Valérie asked.

"You know about that?" LaPierre's eyes narrowed.

"Madame Tablier told us."

"And who is this Madame Tablier?"

"I am." Madame Tablier came heavily down the stairs, holding her back this time. "Who wants to know?"

"I am commissaire Henri LaPierre!"

"Bully for you."

"Look," Valérie interrupted, "this is getting us nowhere. Why do you want someone else there, Henri? It's not like you."

"Because *everyone* will be there," he replied with a whine. "Maître le Notaire called me this morning, and by the terms of the will there is something for almost everyone in Saint-Sauver!"

"Really? But Grosmallard and Garçon haven't been here long enough, have they?"

"Ah, monsieur, that is the point. This will was drawn up two days before the murder of Fabrice Ménard!"

"Blimey!" Richard said. "And everyone's in it?"

"Yes."

"Even the Grosmallards?"

"Yes, even the Grosmallards! I went to see them this morning, but I only saw the father. The daughter is in Paris, and Sébastien Grosmallard hadn't seen his son. He had assumed the boy had gone running. He usually does. He was preparing the kitchen himself, which annoyed him greatly."

"You saw him at the restaurant?" Valérie asked nonchalantly.

"Yes."

"In the kitchen?"

"Yes. Why?"

"Oh, nothing."

"So everybody is in the will?" Richard tried to change the subject slightly. "That doesn't help you, I suppose? No one to scrub off the suspects list."

"Henri, I must come also." The commissaire went to raise an objection but Valérie was insistent. "Some of the language used at the reading of a will is quite archaic. I wouldn't want Richard to be out of his depth with that, in his role as..."

"Yes, yes, yes. OK then." He knew he couldn't win. "I shall see you both at eleven at the *notaire's* office." He sighed and turned to go, then leaned in to Richard closely. "Watch that one," he whispered, and then more loudly, "And, monsieur, I have not scrubbed you off my list of suspects. Not yet."

Richard and Valérie just looked at each other. Where on earth had the corpse of Antonin Grosmallard disappeared to, then?

19

I n every small French town there is one building, a large house, almost Gothic in architecture, that dominates the very center of the place, usually looming ominously, overlooking the central square. It casts its shadow both literally and figuratively, the very embodiment of small-town power, success, and wealth. For whatever reason, and regardless for whom these houses were built for, they are now almost always owned by the town *notaire*, that peculiarity of French life, the "amicable judge" who processes all legal work and requests in the civic arena, much like a powerful local solicitor in England, for example, but appointed by and backed by the state and therefore a dispenser of local justice.

That said, Maître François Renaud did not look like an all-powerful dispenser of local justice. Instead he looked like a portly vicar, the staple of black-and-white British comedy films of the 1950s, absentminded and kindly. He was slightly balding with clouds of white hair protruding at odd angles, and though his role demanded regular conferences with clients, he wasn't a fan of people in general, preferring the company of enormous, old-fashioned ledgers and dusty files. It was reported that the *notaire* in La Chapelle-sur-Follet had entirely digitized his arcane filing system and could now carry his office around on a key ring. Monsieur Renard had posted him a letter expressing his disapproval and had cut off all ties. The letter had been digitized, archived, and re-sent to the *notaire's* computer by email, where it lay in a spam file before no doubt disappearing forever.

Richard and Valérie climbed the ornate wooden stairs to the public meeting room on the first floor, where they were the last to arrive. The meeting room was an extension of the stairs, the same solid oak paneling giving the place an austere, Victorian atmosphere. The chairs were the same, though there weren't enough of them; in fact, there were only three arranged around the public side of a leather-topped desk and a plush, leather chair facing them, presumably for the *notaire* himself. There was an excited buzz in the air. Elisabeth and Hugo Ménard sat at two of the chairs, with an empty one between them as if the spirit of the deceased Fabrice might need a sit-down at some point in proceedings, while everyone else stood toward the back of the room. They all tried to look somber as the occasion demanded, but curiosity was also getting the better of them. Nobody, apart from the Ménards, knew why they were there. Sébastien Grosmallard stood with his back to the room, staring out of the window. His daughter had not yet returned from Paris and as far as he knew Antonin was otherwise disposed, though God knew where. Guy Garçon was there too, talking to René DuPont. Madame Tablier was pretending to dust some of the paneling, while Jeanine had cornered Commissaire LaPierre and was animatedly explaining something that looked like kneading, but which could have easily been misconstrued. There were various other traders and personages dotted about too; in fact, the only person missing, as far as Richard could tell, was Noel Mabit.

A door hidden in the paneling behind the desk creaked open and Noel Mabit tiptoed in. Richard felt almost comforted by his presence. He didn't like the man at all, but if he hadn't been present, serious questions would have needed to be raised. Mabit looked about the room, waiting for everyone to shush. He coughed and indicated for everyone to stand up. "*Mesdames et messieurs*, Maître Renaud!"

Renaud shuffled in and had the good grace to look baffled not just by Mabit's role in the whole procedure but by who the infernal man might be. He gestured for the Ménards to sit down and briefly welcomed everyone else without looking up at them.

"Ladies and gentlemen, we are here on the, er, today, for the reading of the last will and testament of Monsieur Fabrice Christophe Ménard. This document, the last will of the above named, is what we call a *testament mystique* and replaces the previous *testament authentique*." There was a murmur in the room. "It was lodged with me and sealed in the presence of two employees just two days before his death. It has been registered with the Fichier Central des Dispositions de Dernières Volontés and therefore, as a legal document, it is"—he looked up to make his point clear—"it is beyond reproach."

Valérie had been inadvertently correct when she'd said Richard might not understand everything; he was lost. He understood the words but not their meaning and turned to Valérie for an explanation as a worried Hugo comforted his mother. "As Henri said,

Fabrice Ménard changed his will just a few days ago and had told no one about it. And as this will is what they call a *testament mystique*, a mythical will, no one knows what the envelope contains."

Richard looked confused. "So how did the *notaire* know to ask everyone to attend?"

"That's a very good question, Richard."

The noise grew with the speculation in the room and Mabit stepped forward from the shadows, produced his gavel, and banged on the desk. Maître Renaud again looked cross and bewildered. "Ladies and gentlemen, please. Monsieur Ménard told me privately, without revealing any of the details, that he wished all of you to be present. I appreciate this will cause some speculation, but I am as much in the dark as you are." He paused, allowing his irritability to rise to the surface. "So can we get on with it, please?"

The room quieted down to a more respectful silence. The *notaire* opened a drawer and produced a slim white envelope, which he placed on the desk. He rummaged further in the drawer, looking for something, and was further irritated by not finding whatever it was. Inevitably, at this point, Noel Mabit coughed gently and stepped forward to produce a letter opener. The *notaire* took it as though he was considering using it for other purposes but instead took his frustration out on the envelope.

He read a few lines to himself without giving anything away, then turned the single piece of A4 paper over to see if there was anything else. He looked surprised to see that there wasn't much more to it than he had in his hand.

"Oh well. Ladies and gentlemen," he began, "*testament en forme mystique de Monsieur Fabrice Christophe Ménard*." A hush descended.

"'First of all, I leave a goat's cheese to every man and woman in Saint-Sauver.'" The crowd didn't know whether to laugh or not.

"He wanted a crowd," Richard whispered to Valérie.

Renaud continued, "'I leave all my worldly possessions, my house, and business to be divided equally among my surviving family members: my dear wife, Elisabeth, who has been my strength and has supported me since we were young; to my son Hugo, who I know will make me proud.'" The noise from the crowded room was one of relief and everyone, except the solitary figure of Grosmallard, turned to one another to express what they thought was a job well done.

Noel Mabit banged his gavel. "Maître Renaud has not finished yet, ladies and gentlemen."

"Yes, yes, thank you, monsieur, erm...well, anyway. He's right, there is more. 'I leave all my worldly possessions, my house and business'...oh I've done that bit, haven't I? Never mind." He sped up considerably. "Er, surviving family members, dear Elisabeth and so on, my son Hugo, proud etcetera. 'And to our other son, who goes by the name of Antonin Grosmallard.'" He looked up, satisfied that that was a job well done, a look which he quickly dropped when he noticed the reaction in the room.

Elisabeth Ménard cried loudly and began to sob. Hugo Ménard stood up, looking for someone to lash out at. Sébastien Grosmallard stormed out of the room without saying a word to anyone, while everyone else looked at each other in shock, even the commissaire. Noel Mabit started banging his gavel and Maître Renaud, happy to be nearly finished, read out the closing formalities as if pandemonium hadn't kicked off around him. Richard and Valérie left, quietly followed by Commissaire LaPierre.

The three of them crossed the square, walking toward Valérie's car, the policeman a few yards behind.

"Valérie," he called out, not raising his voice exactly but making it clear that she should wait. "And Monsieur Ainsworth." He had now caught up with them. "May I have a word?"

Richard and Valérie looked at each other.

"Here?" Valérie asked innocently.

"Here will do," he said with a touch of menace. "So, as far as I understand all of this," he began, circling them as he did so, "there is a scandal involving a famous chef, his son, and some cheese. The same night, the supplier of said cheese is murdered. In his will, the dead man names the son of the famous chef as his own son, and leaves him partly in charge of the cheese business." He stopped.

"Yes, that seems about it." Richard tried to sound encouraging.

"I have a feeling, monsieur, that you know more about this than you say. And you, madame, for you that goes without saying!"

"Now, Henri..."

"This is no time for a 'now, Henri.' This is official, this is serious. You must stop playing games."

Here we go, thought Richard, just as he'd suspected. The man was dogged and incorruptible. There would be no leeway or favors just because Valérie was his ex-wife; he would not only put a stop to all this, he would drag everything, everything they knew, out of them. It was time to come clean, he concluded, and opened his mouth to speak.

"Wait one moment, Monsieur Ainsworth, I am still speaking. I do not know what is going on with this investigation. I also do not know what is going on with you two, whether you are together or not." Richard and Valérie both went to interrupt, whereupon LaPierre held up his hand to signal he wanted immediate silence. "And let me be clear," he continued slowly, "I care nothing for either. I was posted here at my own request. I was owed a favor. I regard it, I regarded it, as being as close to retirement as one can get and still draw full pay. This is the Follet Valley. Nothing is supposed to happen here. You know what I thought? *I will spend my days fishing,* that is what I thought. But then I arrive and a body turns up, previously happy, successful families are ripped apart, secrets emerge, and everywhere I turn there is my ex-wife, bounty hunter, *possible* assassin, and her lapdog."

"And me!" Richard didn't know if he was being chivalrous or was just put out at the omission; either way, he couldn't help himself.

"Yes, monsieur, her lapdog."

"Ah." *Bloody cheek*, he thought.

"Now, both of you, listen to me and listen carefully." He had them now lined up like they were children about to be punished by a headmaster. "All I want is a quiet life, you understand? A quiet life. I suspect that you both know more than I do about what is going on, and I am trying not to take offense at that but then I see a possibility. If we can work together, and I mean together, I may get some fishing done. Do I make myself clear? We. Work. Together."

"*Bonjour*, Richard! *Bonjour*, Valérie!" It occurred to Richard that he and Valérie weren't the only ones who turned up everywhere—Martin and Gennie had exactly the same habit and were at it again now, hailing the two of them as they rounded Valérie's car. They looked like they were going to stop and chat, which would have been poor timing, but then they got a proper view of the commissaire head on and Gennie said, somewhat demurely and with practiced innocence, "Oh, and *bonjour* to you also, Monsieur Vigoureux."

The commissaire blushed and said a brusque "Madame," making it clear he wasn't at home, so to speak, and Martin and Gennie hurried on.

The commissaire knew he was defeated, the wind gone completely from his sails. He tried to look sanguine, which for a man who looks like he's spent his whole life looking sanguine should be easy, but he actually looked seasick.

Richard and Valérie shared a brief look of triumph and he saw Valérie cross her fingers and put her hands behind her back. "You are right, Henri, we have been snooping about. It was me more than Richard, who is certainly not my lapdog, and I think you should apologize." He mumbled something inaudible, so she continued anyway. "From our investigations we thought that Elisabeth Ménard and Antonin Grosmallard were lovers, certainly not mother and son. We are as surprised as you are. It seems we have been mistaken all along." She looked apologetic, which Richard didn't believe for one minute, and he was surprised that the commissaire seemed to be falling for it. *Maybe that's how you become an ex of Valérie*, he was thinking. *She loses respect for your judgment.*

"I am not surprised," was the haughtier reply as LaPierre tried to regain the upper hand.

"Don't take that tone with me, Henri. Or is it Monsieur Vigoureux?"

He nodded, a broken man, and looked like he'd had enough of amateurs, ex-wives, and life in general. "And so you two snoopers are now in full possession of the facts; what was going to be your next move?"

Richard began to feel a bit sorry for him. "Well, I don't know that we had a plan yet," Valérie said innocently, "but I would certainly like to talk to Antonin Grosmallard to find out exactly what he knew."

"I see. Please leave that to me for now," begged the commissaire.

"But you will let us know what you discover from the young man?" Valérie spoke with the certainty of a hypnotist dishing out instructions.

"Yes, Valérie, I will let you know what I discover." He walked off sadly to find his own car.

Valérie undid her crossed fingers and looked at Richard. "What?" she asked, the very picture of virtue. "Somebody has to find that body; it may as well be the police." She smiled up at Richard. "Martin and Gennie are really wonderful at times, aren't they?" She beamed.

20

Clare smoothed the picnic rug on the riverbank with a care and attention to detail that suggested this was going to be no informal, light lunch. The riverbank sloped gently down to the water's edge in a secluded spot where dragonflies hovered majestically and the river drifted by silently. On the opposite bank stood a heron, biding his time for any passing fish, and further upstream stood a wooden cabin, the office of the local river paddle-boat hire, which was shut for lunch. The large wicker picnic hamper was set between them as they sat and took in the serenity of the scene.

"It's at moments like this I remember why we moved here," Clare said wistfully. "It really is so peaceful."

Although he could see exactly what she meant and that her thoughts were backed up by the vista in front of them, Richard was also currently struggling with a double murder and historical infidelity. It's the kind of thing that puts dragonflies, majestic or otherwise, into perspective, so he stayed silent.

"Are you hungry?" she asked, undoing the leather straps on the basket. "I've brought some of your favorites."

"How did you get this hamper on your flight? Didn't they kick up a fuss?"

"It was here, silly. Have you not used it since I left?"

Richard shook his head. "No," he said. "I haven't had much call to."

"Do you remember the last time we used it?" It was the kind of question that sends a shockwave through any male. Any inquiry regarding relationship dates or specific memories should be tabled well in advance, in his opinion, and not just sprung on you out of the blue. He thought about it and decided to be brave.

"No, not really."

She nodded as if in confirmation of her thoughts and then said quietly, "No. Me neither."

"It would probably be doing something like this, I suppose." He was trying to cheer them both up. "Probably before we even moved here."

She opened the basket. "Yes, that would make sense. That's the problem with moving somewhere you enjoy as a holiday. It stops being a holiday."

"Oh, I don't know."

"It did for us, Richard. Scotch egg?"

He wanted to argue the point that although Clare had never gotten used to the slow pace of the Follet Valley, it suited him very much indeed. But he also really wanted a Scotch egg, so decided not to argue the point at all.

"Did you smuggle them into France?" he asked, his tone very much like that of a gold prospector who spies a potential seam.

"I did!" She laughed. "And not only Scotch eggs, either." She unpacked the basket, proudly reeling off the very British picnic goods that Richard hadn't had for years and up until that point didn't know he'd missed. "We have the aforementioned Scotch eggs; Melton Mowbray pork pies; I've made my own coronation chicken; there is potato salad; Red Leicester cheese; Jacob's cream crackers; Marks & Spencer's cloudy lemonade; I have those dreadful mango chutney popadams that you love. And..." She paused for effect. "Ta-da!" She pulled out a family size bar of Cadbury's Fruit and Nut. The woman was a temptress and she had gone to an enormous effort.

"Wow, that's...wow. Thank you," he said quietly.

"I was right." There was a note of I-told-you-so triumph in her voice. "There are things you miss and maybe it's time you admitted that to yourself." She looked out at the river, dramatically waiting for Richard's response.

He picked up the packet of Red Leicester cheese, holding it like a curator holds a precious artifact. "I have missed you so much," he said with almost breaking emotion.

She turned toward him and said urgently, "I knew it, Richard. I've known it all along." She put her hand on his. "Now, leave every-thing to me."

He looked at her, confusion etched on his face, his giveaway forehead vein working overtime. He was just about to address the mistake when in the background, and moving along the river with some determination, was Elisabeth Ménard in an orange pedal boat. Some twenty meters behind her and pedaling furiously was Sébastien Grosmallard, his yellow pedal boat leaving behind it a substantial wake. Richard stood up suddenly, taking a substantial bite out of a Scotch egg as he did so. It was then he noticed, a fur-ther twenty meters behind Grosmallard and just appearing around a bend in the river, a heavier-laden red pedal boat containing the

Liebowitz brothers. Ménard and Grosmallard he could just about understand, and clearly they had mutual points of interest and probably quite a lot to discuss. But a family moving firm from New Jersey? Something was up.

"Let's take a pedal boat!" he said suddenly.

"What?"

"Let's take a pedal boat. It'll be like old times!"

"Richard, we've never taken a pedal boat."

"Then it's high time we did!" He started packing up the food, throwing it into the hamper.

"Richard?" She didn't sound angry, more confused, as if she didn't really know this man like she thought she did. Richard picked up a corner of the blanket, practically rolling Clare off it.

"Come on! It'll be so romantic!" He knew he would regret that as an attempt at persuasion, but this was an emergency.

"But what about lunch?"

"We can eat it on the pedal boat! Come on!" He picked up the hamper, hurriedly helped Clare to her feet, and marched her off to the boat rental office.

The office was still shut when they got there, which Clare looked relieved about. "Let's have lunch, and then go on a pedal boat after," she reasoned, but Richard was having none of it.

"No, we can pay the man when we come back!" He chose a blue pedal boat at the end of the short wooden jetty and clambered in clumsily, almost losing his balance.

Clare held back. "I've never seen you like this," she said, though smiling as she did so.

"Come on, then!" He was determined to play up to it if it helped her get a move on. "The game's afoot, Watson!" he added, overdoing it somewhat, and helped her onto the wobbling craft.

If Clare had imagined Richard's apparent impetuosity was the prelude to a potentially tranquil interlude drifting along the River Follet, she quickly became aware that it wasn't. In their student days they had spent dreamy afternoons together doing exactly that, rowing around the lakes at Keele University and planning a successful future together. Now, though, Richard was most certainly distracted and pedaling like a professional cyclist trying to break free of the peloton. For his part, Richard had a pretty good idea of where the others were heading. This section of the River Follet also connected to a largish lake, the Lac des Petites Îles, which in turn was linked to the old canal system that had once served the valley so well. The lake was dotted with small islands, as the name suggests, well-known trysting places for couples. It was a matter, considering the others had such a head start, of finding the right one.

"Do you need to pedal quite so quickly, Richard?"

He was already out of breath but trying to hide the fact. "If I can build up enough momentum, the thing will just power itself."

"If you say so," she replied with a wistful sigh. To Richard's great annoyance she then put her hand in the water, in his eyes slowing their progress. "Do you remember our afternoons on the lake, Richard? We had the whole world before us..."

"Yes," he said, through gasps of air.

"I was going to be a PR guru and you were going to be an academic, with a doctorate in film studies... We were so young, so hopeful."

"Yes," he gasped again. "I don't suppose you fancy taking over for a stint, do you?"

She ignored him.

He circled around the lake once, but couldn't see either Ménard, Grosmallard, or the Liebowitz brothers. He couldn't for the life of him work out why the three Americans would be there anyway. It may be pure coincidence, the three of them trying to relive their old man's D-Day landings—he didn't know. What he did know for sure was that he had overdone it and had so little oxygen left in his brain he might conceivably pass out.

Clare was still in rose-tinted mode behind him, sucking on cloudy lemonade through a straw and sunning herself. "Why do you never use your doctor title, Richard? It's very distinguished."

They had had this conversation so many times over the years, and Richard wasn't going to use possibly his last few remaining breaths going over old ground again. She knew very well why. They were on a flight to Copenhagen once, a business jaunt of Clare's, and a passenger had become ill. Inevitably the pilot had called over the intercom asking if there was a doctor on board and Clare, a few gin and tonics into a full head of steam, had offered Richard up. The passenger survived thanks to the ministrations of the aircrew, whereas Richard was shunned as a phoney and a dangerous prankster who, when asked for his medical expertise, Clare had scornfully offered up, "Nothing strictly medicinal as it were, but he's seen *Carry On Nurse* a few times!"

He stopped pedaling, letting the craft drift as he got some breath back, and then he spotted them. On one of the larger islands there were two pedal boats pulled up onto the sand, one orange and one yellow. A few yards up the beach stood Elisabeth Ménard, who looked almost like a child beside the bulk of Grosmallard. It didn't take much for a doctor in film studies and a man possibly on the cusp of reconciliation or divorce to work out the dynamics of the conversation, if not the specifics. They both looked guilty. She had her arms folded, though she was still able to nervously bite her nails, while he hung back a few yards, his hands deep in his pockets, kicking at the sand. What was the guilt for, though? Post-coital? Surely post-coital guilt was just an English thing? Were they in it together? And what was "it," exactly? Her husband had been murdered and, unless he was the killer, he might not even know that the same fate had befallen his son. Her son, actually. Their son? But Fabrice's will had specifically said "our" son. Maybe Grosmallard didn't even know which, though Richard couldn't see how that was possible, and he wished Valérie were here to spark off, which was very unfair on Clare, who had gone to such trouble. He felt like guiltily thrusting his own hands in his pockets.

"Hey, Dick!"

The Liebowitz brothers pedaled slowly by in the opposite direction, and it was obvious now that they were also keeping an eye on proceedings.

"Good afternoon—not touring today?"

"Nah, you seen one goddamn chateau, you seen 'em all," Morty said as they passed. Behind him, Abe had a small pair of binoculars trained on the beach. "Bird-watching." Morty's tone changed.

Elisabeth Ménard got back into her pedal boat and was pushed off, surprisingly gently, by Sébastien, who then did the same to his craft; they were heading back to the jetty. The Liebowitz brothers cleverly decided to go in front of them rather than follow this time and left with a cheery, "So long, Dick!"

Clare had sat through all of this looking lost. It was obvious that she had a lot of questions to ask, maybe even more than Richard, but she gave the impression that she didn't want to know the answers. Answers would get in the way. "Who are those people?" she asked eventually.

"Oh, you know, a moving company from New Jersey."

"If you say so." He was relieved to see that she wasn't that interested after all. "You really shouldn't let them call you Dick, you know. It's not becoming for a man with a PhD."

Eventually they reached the shore, where the old man started to give Richard a fearful telling off, threatening police action for theft. Then Richard collapsed in cramp on the jetty, his face purple with exhaustion and possible sunstroke. Together the old man and Clare revived him; she gave him some of the lemonade and then produced the Fruit and Nut for a sugar boost, but it had melted to liquid. Richard was vaguely aware that whatever plans anyone seemed to have these days, none of them were working.

21

Now you must rest, Richard. I don't know what that show of romantic bravado was all about but gadding about like that at your age, and in the full heat of the sun, just isn't wise."

From his prone position on the lounge sofa, he was vaguely aware of Clare pacing back and forth with a mixture of annoyance and concern, though the tone of her voice suggested that annoyance was streets ahead. She was an opaque shadow from where he lay, and he was grateful for that; he didn't fancy direct eye contact. She had nursed him as well as she could, part practical management, part infuriated maternalism. She never did like him being unwell; she liked her men strong. As such, she had admonished him for his ill-advised youthful exuberance, while at the same time preparing cold towels, ice packs under each armpit, a moisturizing face mask, and a slice of cucumber over each eye. He looked like a salad buffet. She wasn't letting up, either.

"I had supposed you'd have plans with that woman for this evening?"

Dangerous territory, this, he thought, and whined a pathetic "No" in reply.

She ignored him. "Well, I'll tell her that whatever you were planning, it's canceled. You need rest. No more of this Cagney and Lacey act. You're both in your fifties, Richard, though I'd say she's slightly older than us."

Meow! thought Richard.

"Enjoying life is one thing, but you're not the Avengers!"

"Chapeau Melon," he said instinctively, though he didn't know why.

"What was that?"

"Chapeau Melon. It's what the French call the Avengers."

There was a steamy silence and Richard cowered behind his cucumber.

"I honestly don't know if the sun has got to you and you are delirious or you're completely back to normal. It's very difficult to tell!" she said, her frustration evident.

Richard heard a polite knock on the lounge door. "I am so sorry to disturb you." It was Valérie, and he sensed the pause as she took in the view. "Are you OK, Richard?"

"Oh, fine," he replied, trying to sound cheerful.

"He has sunstroke." Clare made it sound terminal, before changing her tone. "He overdid the romance this afternoon, didn't you, darling?" Richard whined again. "I'm afraid he can't come out to play this evening, Valérie."

"That is a shame," she replied. "The commissaire of the police specifically requested his assistance." Valérie and Clare hadn't known each other very long at all, but it was clear that the former already had the measure of the latter, and the latter loved a title and the reflected glow of prominence.

"You still have cucumber on your collar, Richard," Valérie said, handing him some makeup wipes from her bag and struggling to start her car. "Really, what have you two been up to?" She clearly found the whole thing rather amusing. "And at your age!" she mocked. He really wished everyone would stop saying that.

"If you must know, I was trying to follow our suspects." He was being a trifle petulant but he also knew that it would get her attention. "I spotted Elisabeth Ménard on a pedal boat on the river, then I saw Sébastien Grosmallard following her!"

"So you followed them?"

"Yes."

"Well done, Richard."

"And not only those two, but the Liebowitz brothers as well." He watched her reaction carefully for any hint of recognition at the name. He hadn't the faintest idea how the Liebowitz brothers fitted into all this, but the most obvious way would be if they were colleagues of Valérie's in some way, either bounty hunters or assassins or bodyguards.

"Who are the Liebowitz brothers?" she asked without the slightest hint of recognition, as she took her eyes off the road and addressed him directly. He told her what he knew of the Jewish moving experts from New Jersey. "That is odd," she mused. "I've not heard of them, but I'll make some enquiries."

She sped the car up impatiently, causing Passepartout to bury his head in his bed.

"So why does the commissaire want my assistance, then?" He couldn't hide the note of self-importance in his voice.

"It was both of us, really, Richard. Anyway, they have found the body of Antonin Grosmallard!"

"So they gave the kitchen a proper clean this time, did they?"

"He is not at the restaurant."

"Oh. Where is he?"

"At the goat farm." They both sat silently for a few moments.

"That doesn't look good for Grosmallard, does it? His son is killed in his kitchen, then he finds out he's not his son and his body turns up at his real parents' place."

"The police do not know that he was killed in Sébastien's kitchen; only we know that. I think that whoever killed him knew about the will."

"Which suggests Hugo, as he loses control of the business."

"Or Sébastien Grosmallard because of the humiliation?"

"Or Karine—presumably without Antonin she would inherit the Grosmallard restaurant and name."

"Or Elisabeth? But then why would Elisabeth kill her own son?"

"Because she had an affair with him and it unhinged her?"

"But how could she not know he was her own son?"

They thought about it for a while, then Richard said, "If it is any of these people, and for those reasons, where do Garçon and Tatillon come into it?"

She thought about this as she parked the car. "Maybe they don't?" she said. "Maybe it is just bad luck. They might not be connected at all." Which was perfectly viable, but were they really innocents caught up in something that didn't directly concern them?

Somehow, they are involved, Richard thought. It was too much of a coincidence otherwise.

Giscard the goat eyed them lazily. He stood there chewing silently, completely unimpressed with all the attention he was suddenly getting. Behind him was a large pile of hay, out of which the legs of young Antonin Grosmallard were sticking up directly, reminding Richard nauseatingly of Guy Garçon's frog-legs dish.

"You're sure it's him?" he asked.

The commissaire looked weary. "I have been closer than this, monsieur," he sighed. "It is Antonin Grosmallard. His throat has been cut."

"But why here?" Richard and Valérie said simultaneously.

LaPierre looked from one to another. "He wasn't killed here; there is not the blood. He was killed elsewhere and placed here for our benefit."

"Why?" Valérie asked, the picture of innocence.

The commissaire balanced on the balls of his feet, swaying back and forth slightly. "I was hoping you might tell me that, the pair of you." He was standing right in front of the two of them.

Richard and Valérie protested their innocence and ignorance, causing the commissaire to raise his hand, demanding they stop.

"As I told you, I will work together because I want to go fishing; I really like fishing. It is so peaceful." He leaned in closer. "But you must tell me what you know! There are two murders now, and I will get pressure from above because these are famous names. I demand—"

He was interrupted by a cry from the door as Elisabeth Ménard saw poor Antonin's legs aloft. The commissaire motioned to a colleague to take her away and for forensics to continue their investigations. Sébastien Grosmallard appeared behind Elisabeth, as usual the fiery maniacal look in his eye and the hair like Medusa's. He looked like he might howl in paternal pain, but this was a different Grosmallard; he put his head to one side and said quietly, "My child." He put his arms around Elisabeth's shoulders and guided her out.

"Had they not seen the body?" Richard asked incredulously.

"No, I wanted them kept out at this point. I wanted forensics and your...knowledge." He scowled at them again.

"So who found him?" Valérie asked.

"That we do not know, madame. We received an anonymous call this evening. This is where you'll find the body of Antonin Grosmallard, it said."

"A man or a woman?"

"A man, monsieur, with a bad French accent." He turned to Richard and looked him in the eye. "That is why I wanted you here."

Richard went as white as his sun-pinked face would allow him. "I didn't call you!" he stammered.

"No. Having seen your reaction, I think not." Richard wobbled and Valérie grabbed his arm. "But you do know more about this than you are telling me." LaPierre's cell phone rang, which he cursed, and he wandered off, seeking privacy.

"Come on," whispered Valérie, and she made her way over to Elisabeth and Sébastien. They were both smoking, neither saying a word.

"This must be an awful shock for you both," Valérie offered quietly.

"Yes, if there's anything we..." Richard tailed off.

"Shall we call your daughter? I believe she is in Paris," Valérie probed.

"She was due back today anyway, madame. After Antonin

disappeared, I asked her to return." They stood in silence. "He was my son!" Grosmallard suddenly announced, though it was difficult to tell whether he was upset or if his pride was battered. "Fabrice was playing games from the grave."

"Fabrice did not play games," Elisabeth answered quietly.

"He knew about the affair. It is his revenge."

Richard thought that this didn't really add up, unless Fabrice had threatened to reveal the truth and was killed for that.

"He wouldn't do that to our son." Again, Elisabeth spoke so quietly it was difficult to make out her words, almost like she was talking to herself. Richard wanted to ask if she meant Antonin or Hugo but couldn't think of a delicate way to do so.

"Monsieur Sébastien Grosmallard." The commissaire looked less weary than he had done, and more like he had a solemn duty to perform which demanded more authority. "I am arresting you for the murder of Antonin Grosmallard and Fabrice Ménard. You will please accompany me to the station..."

Elisabeth let out a cry of anguish, while Grosmallard looked wearily at LaPierre. He said nothing.

"That was a colleague of mine," the commissaire explained as officers put handcuffs on the great chef. "There is a knife missing from Monsieur Grosmallard's kitchen, and there is blood under the units. The blood will be tested but I am certain it is that of his son, her son, er, Antonin Grosmallard."

Grosmallard towered above the officers either side of him. "I was broken into the other night." His tone was matter-of-fact, neither pleading nor confrontational.

"And yet you did not report it, monsieur?"

He shrugged. "I noticed a knife was missing, my office drawers had been opened, and a notebook, my recipe notebook, had been taken."

The commissaire snorted. "Are you suggesting someone is framing you because they want your recipe for onion soup?"

Grosmallard stiffened. "No, Monsieur le Commissaire, I am not. But somebody broke into my office and stole my notebook. That book is a bible of modern cookery. It is not a recipe book. It is an autobiography of French cuisine, describing how the recipes were born, why, and the emotional state behind them. That book would prove my innocence. Tell that to your colleagues!" It was a powerful speech, though Richard couldn't help thinking that a missing notebook was nothing compared to the murder of two people. He knew great chefs could be a bit single-minded, but he rather seemed to have his priorities all wrong. *Show a bit of contrition, man, sorrow at least.*

They led him off to a waiting car and a policewoman comforted Elisabeth.

"He is making it up, of course," the commissaire said to Richard and Valérie as the car pulled off. "Why not say all of this before?"

"I suppose he's had a lot on his mind."

"Yes, Monsieur Ainsworth, murder!"

Valérie stared after the car, deep in thought. "Richard," she said without looking round, "can you drop me at the station later? I need to go to Paris this evening."

He was taken aback by this, and just uttered a surprised, "Yes, OK," in response while she walked back to the car. He turned to say goodbye to the commissaire, who had one eyebrow raised in a suspicious fashion.

"Be careful, monsieur, be very careful. Ask yourself a question: How well do you really know Valérie d'Orçay? What might she be keeping from you?" He turned and walked slowly back to the crime scene.

It was a warning, that was for sure. He was implying that he himself didn't know her at all; the man had been married to her and he didn't seem to have a handle on the woman either. Yes, she might be keeping something from him, but she didn't know that he had Sébastien Grosmallard's apparently explosive notebook. At least, he thought he did—he just didn't know where.

22

Richard parked Valérie's sports car outside the train station, the lowered roof giving off a more carefree image than either were feeling, and they sat without moving, knowing that they were a good fifteen minutes early for Valérie's Paris train.

"I shouldn't be gone more than a couple of days," she said. "Could you get the car looked at for me? Do you know anyone?"

"Yes," was the stoic reply, "I'll get it booked in tomorrow for you." They resumed their silence, which in the end Richard broke. "I don't get it," he said. "Why Paris and why now? Just when things are getting really interesting." He didn't want to sound desperate, like some lovelorn teenager, and that wasn't his overriding feeling anyway. In truth he wasn't sure how to cope with the fallout of Grosmallard's arrest, the increasing insinuation from Commissaire LaPierre that Richard knew far more than he was letting on, and the very uncomfortable feeling that he was very capable of knowing far, far more than he was letting on—but the key to that, Grosmallard's notebook, was nowhere to be found.

Valérie pushed her sunglasses up onto her head and turned to him. "Richard, we have been through this. Whatever is behind all this goes a long way back, to when they were young, I believe. And almost everyone has come here, then, to Saint-Sauver, either looking to wipe away the past or to deliberately, I think, rake it up again."

"But can't you just google what you need to know?"

She gave him a withering look. "No. I want the truth, not official news or Wikipedia references."

"Fair enough."

"I know people in Paris who could help with that, and while everyone is here in the Follet Valley, I can do it discreetly, in person." She started buffing her nails before adding enigmatically, "I also have some appointments there."

"Work appointments?"

"Work appointments," she confirmed, though in a tone of voice that put an end to that line of inquiry.

"Dangerous work appointments?" he ventured, ignoring her tone.

"Oh no!" was her over-enthusiastic reply, and they fell back into silence. "Richard, would you do me a favor?"

"Of course."

"Could I leave Passepartout with you until I return?"

Blimey, he thought. It must be a very dangerous mission indeed if she was leaving her beloved Passepartout behind. He was also aware that it was a huge honor to be asked to dog-sit the pampered Chihuahua, and an even greater responsibility.

"Yes, of course," he said, trying to hide the panic in his voice. He turned to look at the small dog on the back seat, who seemed keenly aware of the conversation in front of him and was not full of confidence about its outcome. "I'll stay in your room until you return, so that he's not too upset at the upheaval."

"You are not staying in your own bed?"

"Er, no. No. That's er...no."

She turned to look at Passepartout as if she was having second thoughts already, wondering if Richard was indeed mature enough for the task.

He tried to laugh it off. "Well, Clare will be happy to not have you around for a while. I think she sees you as competition." He knew it was a rather obvious attempt at fishing, but he also knew that Valérie's almost Olympian ability to take things literally meant that, obvious or not, it would probably go unnoticed.

She put her sunglasses back over her eyes. "Then it is a good thing that I am out of your way, don't you think?" He felt like shouting, *No, it bloody isn't!* but managed to control himself. "I am not—what do you call it in English?—'the other woman.'"

That was a far more unequivocal response than he had been expecting from his fishing expedition, and he continued to laugh off the idea. "I should think not!" was all he said.

Valérie's phone started to vibrate in her handbag and she reached in to get it. "Hello, ah, commissaire." She made sure that she had Richard's attention and pushed her glasses back up on her head again; she used them like a shop used an open/closed door sign. It was also odd that she could be so formal with an ex-husband. There was no "Henri," just "commissaire." The past was the past to Valérie; she lived entirely in the present. "Yes, I am waiting at the train station now. I shall be away for a couple of days." She paused and Richard could hear the muffled voice on the other end. "He has been released already?" She moved the phone away from her mouth. "They've released Sébastien Grosmallard," she whispered. The voice on the other end continued for a couple of minutes, with Valérie offering the occasional "I see" or nodding as if everything she heard had been predicted. "Thank you, commissaire," she said eventually and ended the call.

"I don't get it." Richard shook his head. "Why have they released him already?"

"No evidence," was her muted response.

"But the blood in the kitchen? You mean it wasn't Antonin's blood?"

"The blood sample, shall we say, *disappeared* on the way to the laboratory." She gave him a look that signaled very clearly that she was having none of it.

"Disappeared? That sounds very unlikely," Richard agreed. "And they don't have the knife either, so yes, I suppose they had no choice. What do you think happened?"

She pursed her lips in thought. "I think we are dealing with something much bigger than a murky family history here, Richard, much bigger. I wondered why he was so calm when he was arrested." She turned to face him urgently. "That notebook, Richard, it is the key, I think. I wonder who has it, though?" It was a good question. What on earth had Richard done with the thing was also a good question. He wasn't even sure now that he had pocketed it. Either way he decided to stay quiet on the subject for the foreseeable future. If Valérie became aware that he had found and quickly lost the damn notebook, the key to the whole case, she'd said, he stood little chance of ever clawing his way back into her good books at all from that position.

"He did seem very nonchalant when they cuffed him," he agreed. "I just put that down to his cheffy arrogance. Looking back, I suppose..."

She ignored him. "Richard, while I'm gone, I want you to go back to the Ménard place..."

"I'm not breaking in!"

"No, nothing like that. You couldn't do that without me. No, say that you want to look at the house that's for sale. Try to get Hugo chatting. He must have something to say about Antonin, about being his brother. And about his mother. Is there something going on between this Elisabeth and Sébastien? Could you do that?"

He answered in the affirmative and with what he hoped had a whiff of the aforementioned cheffy arrogance, but for someone who generally regards small talk as a rickety bridge on the way to conversational depth and substance, he was appalled at the prospect. Subterfuge wasn't his forté.

"You can rely on me." He didn't sound entirely convinced or convincing.

"I know that," was her warm reply, though, which did wonders for his confidence.

Down the line they heard the bells of a train-crossing barrier as it closed, signaling her train was close. Valérie slid elegantly out of the car and took her small case off the back seat. She bent down and gave Passepartout a quick kiss and a warning to be on his best behavior for "Uncle Richard." Uncle Richard got awkwardly out of the car and stood to one side like a nervous boy at a school dance.

"Please take care," he mumbled, though it was clear to Valérie that he meant it.

"I will." She smiled at him and kissed him on the cheek. "Now, I must go!" And she skipped off with the energy of a woman half her age, the train already at the station.

"Daddy!" came the cry of a woman exactly half Valérie's age. "Who was that woman?"

His daughter, Alicia, had inherited all of her mother's good looks, but whereas Clare was worldly and calm, poor Alicia still carried an air of immaturity and had a whine in her voice that could smash terracotta.

"Alicia! Perfect timing! And Sly! You're here too."

Sly was just emerging up the stairs from the underpass, lugging the most enormous suitcase. It may once have been called a trunk, it was that big, but it was also pink and had "Sandy Toes, Sun-kissed Nose" written on the side in a nauseating font. Phileas Fogg would not have approved, nor did Richard, and to his credit, Sly looked none too pleased to be heaving the thing about either. Richard had some sympathy for the man.

"*Bonjour*, Dick!" he said breathlessly, coming up the last few steps. Richard's sympathy vanished, though it was strange how he could accept being called Dick by a dubious family of New Jersey moving men but not by his son-in-law, a London-based estate agent. Sly reached the top with one last heave and offered his hand to Richard, leaving the case to wobble dangerously on the top step before the younger man grabbed it quickly, arresting its fall. He did have that going for him, Richard conceded; he was as awkward and clumsy as Richard was.

"Mummy!" Richard felt his eardrums buckle and he turned to see Clare, her arms folded, leaning against her enormous SUV.

"I didn't know you were coming, Richard?" Her tone lacked warmth.

"Oh, you know... Been here long?"

"Long enough."

"Right-o." *Awkward*, he thought.

"Will she be gone long, your Valérie?" He wasn't thrilled by the "your" in that sentence.

"A couple of days."

"Good. That will give us some space, Richard."

"That's what she said, actually."

Clare didn't reply, though he saw her smile, a slight note of triumph, perhaps.

"Alicia, Sly, how lovely to see you. Sly, you'd better put that case in my car. I doubt it will fit in Richard's."

"Hello, Mother," Sly said enthusiastically, and Richard saw Clare wince. "Nice wheels, Dick—is it yours?"

"I'm looking after it for a friend. Do you want a hand lifting that case?"

Between them they struggled to put the case in the hire car thanks to a combination of its weight and the fact that the car was so big that the boot was about four feet off the ground, giving the lie to the practicality of the urban SUV. Clare and Alicia were already in place and ready to drive off.

"Can I ride with you, Dick? I've never been in one of these Renaults."

"Of course," he replied coolly. He'd never felt more midlife crisis-y. An attractive woman's sports car, an estranged wife: he had become a classic stereotype. But then Sly was a modern stereotype himself. In Richard's day, estate agents wore suits as shiny as their slicked-back hair and had either a "hurry-up, this thing will sell in five minutes" aggression about them or an obsequious stoop, like they needed a favor. Sly was too stocky for suits, and his combat shorts nearly reached his walking boots but left enough bare skin to reveal some circular, Celtic tattoos on each calf. His curly hair was shaved at the back and sides but left unruly at the top and disconnected from the kind of beard that forgotten prisoners had in films about medieval dungeons, only it was groomed to shaped perfection. He also had a hole in his left earlobe with what looked like a large boot eyelet keeping it there. Richard could see right through it, which made him feel uncomfortable. All in all, Sly looked like a Viking, but one kitted out by one of those pricey, outdoor lifestyle accessory shops.

But, Viking or hipster, he was an estate agent and therefore the perfect cover to visit the Ménard place as per Valérie's instructions. Sly wandered around the car and whistled. "She's lovely," he said, going for the old-fashioned "cars are female" angle. He reached in to stroke Passepartout, who let him do so without complaint, something Valérie would say was very much in the young man's favor. "So the trunk space is at the front?" He leaned in to pull the opening lever.

"Yes, it is." Richard was trying to give the impression that he was an expert, but then panicked as Sly opened the trunk. *Christ*, he thought. He hoped Valérie had tidied away her firearms.

"Er, Dick," asked Sly from behind the bonnet cover, "is this yours?" Richard began to sweat, dreading what was coming next. "My old man had one just like it; they're worth quite a lot these days." He came back into view holding up Richard's leather jacket. And out of the side pocket Richard could see the brown leather corner of a notebook.

"I'm glad you're here Sly." He beamed. "Shall we go?"

23

If Richard had been expecting an awkward family evening, he was wrong. Clare was charming throughout, wanting to put on a united front, no doubt. Almost as soon as they all arrived, she had been very keen to give Alicia and Sly a guided tour of any changes that had been made since their last visit a few years earlier. The young couple showed a more willing interest than he would have expected, and also, he was pleasantly surprised to realize, they were very much in love. He didn't know why that should be such a surprise, but then he realized he had become a cynic, jaded at the idea of romance, and that was something he didn't ever want to be. Though things had turned sour for Clare and him, they were hopefully the exception to the rule, not the norm. He decided that his pre-bedtime film that evening would be something uplifting and romantic, *The Shop Around the Corner*, perhaps, or *Roman Holiday*.

They all mooched about as though it were a sales visit, asking questions about electrical consumption, seasonal yield, and so on, which he put down to Sly's vocational habits. Richard followed behind, there when needed, which wasn't often, until he realized that it was something of a procession and he was no longer at the back of it. They were being shadowed by Madame Tablier with a suspicious look in her eye.

"All new bookings get a tour now, do they?" she asked as Richard waited for her to catch up.

"No, madame, that's my daughter and her husband. You remember my daughter, Alicia?"

Madame Tablier peered round Richard and squinted into the near distance. "I see it now, yes." She didn't seem at all pleased. "She looks like her mother, which is just as well, I suppose."

Richard tried hard not to see it as an insult, more just a physiological preference. "Let me introduce you, or reintroduce you, anyway. Alicia, Sly? I'd like to introduce you to Madame Tablier, who basically keeps the whole thing running for me. Without her..." He translated for the old woman, to let her know the esteem in which he held her. Clare didn't look like she was at all keen on the billing she'd been given, but then facts were facts.

"Ha! Tablier! Apron! That's brilliant. *Tablier*, apron, geddit? Apron is *tablier* in French."

"It's good, isn't it?" Richard encouraged until he saw that Madame Tablier actually thought she was the butt of whatever the joke was and he swallowed his smile quickly. "I didn't know you had any French, Sly—not many people get that."

"Oh well, I've been brushing up since I knew we were coming out."

Good on him, Richard thought, feeling a little guilty that he had done the lad a disservice these last few years. "Well, look," he said, anxious to get on and look at Grosmallard's notebook in peace, "I'm going to go and feed my hens, see how they're doing."

"Dick, can I ask a favor?" No, it was no good, sooner or later he was going to have to correct him on that.

"Yes, what is it?"

"We're going to get an early night tonight. I'm bushed from all the travel. But can I help you with the guests' breakfasts tomorrow? I'd like to see how it's done."

To be frank, and all things considered, being called Dick was a small price to pay to have someone around the place who didn't just boss him about and seemed genuinely interested in what went on.

"Yes, of course I'd be delighted to show you the ropes. Ha! I might even get a lie-in while you're here!"

Clare smiled, pleased at how everyone was getting on. "Well, Alicia and I are going to have cocktails at that bar in town," she said, "if they do cocktails. Can you look after yourself tonight, Richard?"

It was an odd question considering he'd been looking after himself for at least eighteen months now, but he went along with it. "I'll try," he said, and went off to his hens while the other three made for the main house, leaving just Madame Tablier tutting and shaking her head. She didn't like it, whatever it was, she didn't like it.

Richard pulled a small beer out of the travel fridge he'd installed in the hen food trunk and sat down on the bench in their run. He produced the notebook from his back pocket and held it carefully. It was about the size of a reporter's notebook, but rather than ring-bound with a cardboard cover it had a soft tan leather cover, and the leaves of paper, some lined, some not, were bound in by what looked like a shoelace. It gave the whole thing an antiquarian feel, and rather than a collection of notes and recipes, it could double as an explorer's journal. It was stuffed with sketches, equations, questions, like Grosmallard was hunting for the Holy Grail itself rather than the perfect pavlova.

It seemed to have no order to it, no organization, which was not only confusing but, to someone who alphabetized his DVD collection according to at least three different cross-sectioned criteria, quite upsetting. But Valérie was convinced it was important. Grosmallard had said it was important and two people had been murdered, potentially because of its contents. He must remember to hide it somewhere safe when he'd finished deciphering it this evening. That's if he even started deciphering it this evening, and the omens didn't look good on that score. He needed a plan of attack with the thing.

He had found himself another beer and was now sitting on the edge of the bed in Valérie's room. Pleasingly, Passepartout lay asleep in his own bed, obviously comfortable with the sudden change in domestic arrangements and not pining for his mistress. He toyed with the journal, as he was now calling it. Grosmallard had called it an "autobiography of modern French cuisine," which was obviously giving himself a lot of credit. He'd also suggested that it had been stolen from an office drawer though, whereas Richard had picked it up in the kitchen itself. The thought struck him that whoever had killed Antonin, then, had meant the book to be found; they may even have been there when he and Valérie... He shivered at the thought and texted Valérie to make sure she was OK.

His phone pinged back almost immediately, but it wasn't from Valérie—it was from Sly.

Hey Dick! Can't sleep now. Mind if I watch a DVD in your cinema space? Not seen *Psycho* in years

He replied that it was fine and got back to work on the journal. Whenever he'd read books or seen films about code-breaking—and he assumed that this book was some kind of code, as the thought that a double murder hung on the precise ingredients of bouillabaisse was too ridiculous to contemplate—they all searched for a common thread. In *Sherlock Holmes and the Secret Weapon*, Basil Rathbone had decoded a cipher consisting of dancing men, taken from the original short story, by working out which figure appeared most often and ascribing that figure the letter "E." From there he managed to build up almost the entire alphabet; the code was broken, the baddie jailed, Holmes delivers a rousing patriotic speech, fade to black. Well, Richard had been through the book front to back, back to front, upside down, and even tried to take it by surprise. Apart from food, obviously, there was little else as to what you might call a natural thread.

Purely as a Grosmallard cookery book, as it were, it was a very interesting document. It was twenty-three years old (page one was dated), and therefore started a couple of years after Antonin would have been born. Some pages had been stuck together, splashed by long-dried ingredients, but carefully prised apart so that their detail wouldn't be lost. The diagrams were fascinating, showing how a plate would be built up. It was almost a work of art in itself. There was more than one hand at work, too. Some notes were in a scratchy, difficult-to-read, masculine scrawl, while others, certainly in the first half of the book, were complemented with notes in what Richard thought, while acknowledging he was no expert, were larger, feminine loops. Presumably, assuming he had this right, that was the famed Angélique, Grosmallard's dead wife. Her writing disappeared altogether just before halfway through, and from there it was just the Grosmallard scribble, almost more manic than before and with certainly far more crossings out, as if he had lost his muse.

A fascinating document, no doubt. He yawned and finished his beer. But he really couldn't see its significance. If the killer had meant it to be found, why? And apart from easy access to his creations, why had Grosmallard made such a song and dance about it? He determined to give it one more shot before bed, and decided that the best thing to do was to start with the infamous dessert, the *parfait de fromage de chèvre de Grosmallard*. At first it wasn't easy to find, so he decided to try looking for a design of the final plate, in particular the handprint made from coulis. He was surprised to see that it was nearer the end than he had thought it would be, but once there he could see how the masterpiece had grown. As with many dishes in the journal, it began with a name. It was surprising how many plates of food Grosmallard had created that were named after people. Beef Wellington having started the trend generally, he supposed. Many of them were long-forgotten names, the bright star of celebrity fizzling out almost before dessert could be served. But some he still vaguely recognized, politicians, talking heads on the news, and so on—all very Parisian, in his opinion.

Grosmallard's dessert had begun with a simple title, *dessert pour Angélique*, and was probably the most splashed set of pages in the book. Again, it looked like a complicated math equation rather than the topper to a full meal, but it told its story nonetheless, and Richard had an image of the young couple working furiously in a kitchen somewhere perfecting his, their, creation. Bickering, excited—Tracy and Hepburn, Powell and Loy, Hudson and Day. He lay back and closed his eyes. This was all very well, but he still didn't have a thread or a motive or a reply from Valérie. Passepartout jumped onto the bed as if sensing Richard's concern. They had both expected to hear something by now.

24

It was half past eleven and by any standards, the day was not going well thus far. He was half tempted to go back to bed and try to reset, but the fact that he had woken up late in the first instance was a major contributory factor to the day's woes and his own mood. The current reading on the mood barometer registered hacked-off with more to come.

That he'd woken up with a face full of Passepartout wasn't the best of starts. And that Valérie had not only not responded to his late-night text but, according to WhatsApp, hadn't even seen it was a cause of genuine concern. Maybe that was why Passepartout was sticking close? Dogs have a sixth sense for these things, apparently. And if those two things weren't enough, he had woken up late. A good hour late too, which, while being a good advertisement for his expensive beds and mattresses, would mean nothing if his guests were starving in the breakfast room. Cursing, he'd shot out of bed, almost sending the tiny Passepartout flying off the duvet, dressed hurriedly, and rushed downstairs, hoping he wasn't too late and that all the guests had slept in too.

They hadn't. It was worse than that. He had been invaded; his citadel had fallen, his private empire usurped. The Hiking Viking had taken over.

"Hey, Dick! I thought I'd let you lie in; you can't have had many of them in the last few years, eh?" Sly was serving coffee to the Fontaines, a tea towel slung over his shoulder.

"I'm usually an early riser," he'd replied, a bit baffled by the whole thing and still groggy.

"*Bonjour*, monsieur!" the two young children sang simultaneously, though without real enthusiasm, with their parents conducting them, and he tried smiling in response but he was feeling weak. It all felt like a dream. The place was laid out immaculately, not the way he would do it himself, possibly better organized, if he was of a mind to admit such things, and everything seemed to be going very well indeed. The only thing missing was him and it made him feel like the Ghost of Christmas Future. If it felt like a dream, however, then the scowling presence of Madame Tablier leaning on her mop by the double doors gave it a darker edge, a much darker edge.

"Morning, Madame Tablier, how are you today?" He'd decided to go for the jovial, "Everything is under control, sorry, did I forget to mention it?" approach. It was worth a go but the look on the old woman's face suggested menacingly that it would yield nothing.

"Madame Tablier," Sly had interrupted, "if I can help you in any way this morning, please just ask." He'd clearly been working on his little speech, and though not perfect French, it was obviously heartfelt. She didn't appreciate it, though, quite the opposite. In fact, she seemed to be emitting a low growl instead, and Sly had wisely retreated to the safety of the breakfast bar. Richard's breakfast bar.

He felt like a deposed mountain gorilla, a wounded silverback no longer needed by the troop. He went out to feed his hens and gather his thoughts, but not before quietly taking an old decorative biscuit tin down from the large dresser. He had some wits about him.

Standing by the chicken coop, he wrapped Grosmallard's notebook in a plastic bag and shut it in the tin. The fact that at first glance he hadn't been able to glean much relevant information from it didn't take away from the fact that it was hot property for someone. Two people had died, and he didn't much fancy being the third. He put the tin in the far corner of the coop and covered it with straw, getting a telling off from Joan Crawford in the process, always the angriest of layers. Emerging from the coop, he'd brushed himself down and was immediately confronted by the ominous figure of Madame Tablier, who still had a face like a cliff in winter.

"What's going on?" She never had been one for preliminaries.

He plucked some straw from his hair. "On?" he said innocently. "Nothing, just feeding the hens."

Her eyes narrowed. "I don't mean with the bloody hens. He wants my job, doesn't he?"

"My son-in-law?" He tried to laugh it off.

"Yes."

"No!"

"He wants your job, then?"

"Eh? No!" He tried laughing again, but he wasn't convincing himself, let alone the formidable Madame Tablier. "He just offered to help, that's all. He's an estate agent; he probably wants to do some good for a change, put something back into the world."

If she got the joke, she ignored it. All she heard were the words "estate agent," and that was the clincher as far as she was concerned, estate agents coming some way below politicians and people who didn't like her favorite singer, Johnny Hallyday, as those who can't be trusted. She took a step closer to Richard, and in a low voice said slowly, "I have my duties here. If he crosses a line, I strike!" She stepped back and put her mop up to her shoulder like a soldier on parade, at the same time giving the impression that strike could mean either industrial action or a swift blow to the back of the head.

He remembered sighing heavily at that point, gamely thinking that things could really only get better from then on. He was wrong. His phone rang and he scrambled to get it out of his pocket, hoping it was Valérie ringing to say she was safe.

"Richard?" It was Clare. "How are you this morning?" She sounded very bright.

"Oh, you know..."

"Oh, has your friend not come back?" He didn't like her tone at all. Jealousy he could have handled, anger even. But not mockery.

"No," he replied tartly, though it was probably lost on the line.

"Poor Richard." She sounded genuine now, which made him even more worried. "We've all been there, I'm afraid. Now look, what are your plans this evening?" He went to answer but was overridden. "Because I've booked a table at that new restaurant, you know, the one where there was all that goat's cheese fuss. Just the four of us. We have to face up to this, darling—there a lot of details to be ironed out here."

She was right, of course. "Yes, yes, that makes sense. What time?"

They'd made arrangements for later that evening and Richard made a decision to just let Sly get on with breakfast himself. He obviously didn't need his help in any way, though he also arranged with him to go and visit the Ménard house late morning. He'd then gone for a shower, picked up Passepartout, and taken Valérie's car to the mechanic, a visit that did nothing whatsoever to lift his spirits.

"Nice," the *garagiste* had said smoothly. "You don't see many of them around here." Richard didn't at all like the way he'd then caressed the bonnet; it was almost sexual and felt somehow invasive despite it not being his car. He'd never been comfortable around mechanics anyway; they always seemed to sense immediately that his knowledge of cars and how they worked was minuscule, and therefore that he should be treated like a rube. This one was worse than usual. He had his overalls turned down to the waist, revealing a white T-shirt and the muscles beneath. He looked like he'd stepped out of a mechanics calendar. "What's the trouble?" he'd sneered, probably wanting to add, *As if you'd know*.

"It's having trouble starting. Sometimes it's fine and sometimes... well, it isn't."

"Had her long?"

"I'm looking after it for a friend."

"I see. Well, open her up."

Richard pulled the lever, hoping that the front bonnet wouldn't lift up instead. He had it right and the mechanic opened up the engine hood at the back. "She's very clean." He was impressed. "I'd say it's been steam-cleaned recently, probably serviced too." He bent down further into the engine and began the predictable speech of mechanic's smokescreen, wittering on about an incorrectly adjusted floating needle or some such. Richard had no idea but he recognized the tactic of mechanics the world over. It was like snake-oil salesmen or religious shamans: throw in a lot of complicated, jargon-heavy rhetoric and just wait for your victim to buckle under the weight of your expertise. Like the way a cobra hypnotizes a mongoose. Richard was happy to let him gabble on but he also wanted information, and if anyone was going to be able to help him with this rather specialized data, it was likely to be this smug, car-caressing auto-pervert.

"If, erm..." He wasn't sure how to broach the subject, though. "Say I wanted the car not to start, not that I am here, but you know. It's difficult to think of a reason why, of course, but just suppose that, oh, for whatever reason I wanted the car temporarily disabled. How would, erm..."

The mechanic stood up slowly, wiping his hands on a rag. "What have you heard?"

"Heard? Nothing. Nothing at all." Blimey, talk about going straight to the horse's mouth.

The *garagiste* went back under the bonnet again. "You'd need to remove the distributor cap and disconnect the VT cable," he said, without looking up.

"Just like *The Sound of Music*, then!" Richard thumped a fist into the palm of his other hand.

"Eh?"

"Nothing. Has that been done recently, can you tell?"

"Yes, no problem," he said, this time standing up again. "I'll just get my fingerprint kit from the office. What are you after?" He sounded threatening.

"I'm not after anything. I just want to know if the car has been tampered with, that's all."

The mechanic wiped his hands again and nodded. "OK. Well

look, if it has, it's either been done by an expert or your mate who owns this has a really bad mechanic. Look." Richard leaned under the bonnet with him and was given a lecture about petrol filters and a *"papillon de starter,"* none of which he understood, and none of which brought him closer to confirming whether Valérie had sabotaged her own vehicle or not, or explained why he was still contemplating that possibility when he was also worried sick about her.

Now, here he was in the passenger seat of the Renault Alpine, about whose internal workings he knew more than he wanted, and with Sly having asked to drive. He also had a needy Chihuahua on his lap, one that wouldn't leave his side, possibly because he knew something Richard didn't.

"So where are we going then?" Sly said, enjoying easing through the gears.

"A friend of mine is interested in buying a house. I said you were an expert and that we'd look it over for her." He had to admit, despite everything, he was beginning to secretly enjoy all the subterfuge.

"Right." Sly was nodding along to some imaginary tune in his head. "You know I'm not an estate agent anymore, yeah?"

Richard did not know that. "You still know what a house is, though, right? Sorry, you know what to look for?"

"I'm not sure I ever did! That's why they got rid of me." He seemed proud of the fact. Richard had known that Sly was a useless estate agent; he was famous for it. It was one of his few endearing qualities that he could work in the very heart of one of the world's busiest real estate markets in Central London and as a "property sales executive" still sell virtually nothing. It was to his credit.

"So what will you do now, any plans?"

"Oh, a few irons in the fire, Dick." He winked at Richard, who had no idea why.

Hugo Ménard was there to greet them when they arrived, looking remarkably breezy for a man who had recently lost a father, gained a brother, and then lost the same brother, and all on his property. Too breezy, was Richard's view, and he had a strong suspicion that he either didn't care what people thought of him or, more likely, was one of those people who had no real idea how to behave around others, had tried to work it out, and just thought, "Sod it," and given up. In a small way, Richard was quite jealous.

"I'm sorry I haven't got much time to show you around," he said after the usual greetings. "To be honest with you"—he affected a guilty smile—"business has gone through the roof."

"Is that a seasonal thing?" Sly asked, giving it the full estate agent.

"No, since my father, erm, well, there's no nice way of putting it, is there? Since my father was killed." He made it sound as though it were a business decision like "re-structuring" or "operational alignment." In a way, for Richard at least, it ruled Hugo out of any involvement. Surely no guilty person would be so blasé about self-incrimination as young Hugo Ménard? Richard decided it would be a smart move to get him on his own while he was in such a talkative mood.

"Hugo, do you mind if I just sit down while my son-in-law has a look around? He's the expert; he knows what to look for."

"No, not at all. Do you want me to show you the place?"

Richard gave Sly a signal to say that he didn't and Sly strode off looking as professional as possible.

"Can I get you a drink?" Hugo asked. It was about the best thing Richard had heard all day. "I've got goat's milk kefir, goat's milk triple smoothie or, if you want something different, I can do you a goat's milk latte."

The man was obsessed. "Could I just have a glass of water, please?" he asked, hoping he hadn't put Hugo out by turning down the goat's milk selection. "I didn't know that you did a drinks range?"

"I've been working on it for some time." The enthusiasm was back. "My father, God rest his soul, didn't like the idea."

"He was more traditional?"

"That's one way of putting it! Old-fashioned would be closer to the mark. Like I said, and I don't mean to be disrespectful, but with the old man gone, we can really start building again."

He was so remarkably unguarded, Richard thought, realizing he had to try to take advantage. What would Valérie ask now? "Would Antonin Grosmallard have got in the way of that?"

Hugo snorted. "You mean the will? I wouldn't set too much store by that if I were you. We'd have contested that."

"Your mother denies that Antonin was her son?"

Hugo looked at him blankly. "Do you know? I didn't actually ask her, but yes, of course she would! Anyway, it's neither here nor there. Poor Antonin..." He tailed off, for the first time showing that he was upset.

"I saw you fighting the other day. You said he'd ruined your family."

"Yes. I was wrong. I was upset about my father." He paused. "But then I realized the potential we had here." A wide smile came across his face again. It was most unnerving.

"I thought you were going to attack Antonin."

"Ha! I probably was, but you put a stop to it quickly. Just as well. But we've often fought. We've known each other since we were babies. We all lived pretty much together when we were born. Our parents were quite hippyish. Then my father found some money for this place and Sébastien and Angélique went back to cookery school."

Richard thought about this for a moment; the two families were so intertwined. He'd read about the hippy communes in the late 1960s. They were almost as fervent as religious sects but with a pure dedication to hedonism and, in his opinion, a quite obvious lack of hygiene. But that would have been long before all this started. "Quite hippyish." A shared family experience, customer/supplier, same town, living two hundred meters apart. Almost like a commune itself, in a way. He paused before asking the next question.

"Hugo, who do you think killed your father and Antonin?"

The reply was immediate. "No idea! I have no idea at all. Really. And you move on." Richard got the uncomfortable feeling that he was speaking to a child, not a grown man in his mid-twenties.

"There's quite a lot of damp upstairs, Dick." Sly strode back into the room, pencil and notepad in hand. "And as for the bathroom... I think they kept goats in there! It stinks!"

Hugo looked at Richard for a translation. "My son-in-law is an estate agent, was an estate agent. He'll try to knock the price down."

"I'm not sure I need to sell anymore. We're going to get investment, I know. We have won the contract to supply the Guy Garçon restaurant. Auguste Tatillon wants to do a piece on us for *Le Figaro*, and lots of vegan restaurants in Paris are in contact." He smiled that wide, innocent, childish smile again, making Richard feel a bit queasy. "Business is booming!"

25

Despite the unnerving aspect of Hugo's display, Richard had rarely felt as electrified or energized in his life and couldn't wait to tell Valérie what he'd been up to. OK, Grosmallard's notebook was still proving a difficult hurdle, but at least he had it. They were making real progress, and though he was increasingly concerned by her phone silence, that he wasn't reliant on her made him feel well disposed even toward a potentially awkward family evening. So having left Passepartout in the hands of the Fontaines, who had worn themselves out with sightseeing, he approached the evening with some confidence, a bit of self-esteem for a change. It was a feeling that didn't last for long. As he arrived at the restaurant with the others, he found that the table was booked under the name of Dr. Richard Ainsworth. He didn't like the sound of that one bit.

He checked his phone for messages one last time and then Dr. Ainsworth and his family were shown to their table by his waiter nemesis, who had clearly recovered his sangfroid from the previous evening. They sat down in silence, the formality of the place adding to the inevitable tension in the group. Only Clare seemed anywhere near relaxed, looking stunning in a V-necked jumper, a discreet hint of cleavage showing above the neckline. She was completely at ease with herself, and completely in control of the evening. Richard was expecting the formal announcement of the divorce, as he assumed everyone was, which was why Alicia looked flustered and Sly looked like he wanted to be somewhere else. Richard would have liked to be somewhere else too, but he realized that this had to be gone through and if Clare wanted to do that in an expensive Michelin-starred restaurant, with a glass of champagne in her hand and surrounded by the family that was about to be broken up, good on her—why not? It was a classy thing to do.

The waiter brought the menus, which, although not as extravagant as the opening night's *menu dégustation*, were still very impressive.

Sly got to work on his French translations. "What's *homard*, again?"

"Lobster," Alicia replied. "Is there a vegetarian option?" A cold chill ran down Richard's spine and he had visions of Grosmallard running amok with the missing kitchen knife.

"Alicia, darling, I..."

"I'm joking, Daddy! I'm having the gin-soaked salmon for starters."

The amuse-bouche arrived with the aperitif, and Richard began to relax. Conversation was naturally stilted. How could it not be? It had a "last supper" air to it, but despite still fretting over Valérie's lack of communication, Richard felt that things might be on the up. Clare was enthusiastically flirting with all the waiters, including Richard's archenemy, and Sly and Alicia looked happy together. There were worse ways for the lights to go out on a marriage, and he felt emboldened enough to propose a toast.

"To the future!" he said, raising his glass of Kir. They all responded likewise and were finished just as the starters arrived, which they ate in a very English way—that is, in silence.

Further into the meal, people were beginning to relax a bit more. Sly's confidence in his French was now such that he could ask the waiters about the food or the presentation, if he could get their attention away from Clare, that is. Alicia was reminiscing about family meals growing up and holidays in France. Even Richard was beginning to properly relax until he felt a presence at his shoulder, and a shadow fell across the table. At first, he thought it was the waiter, who had finally had enough and would tell Richard what he thought of him rather than convey his animosity through sneer and silent judgment.

"*Doctor* Ainsworth, is it?"

He looked up to see the quite terrifying shape of Sébastien Grosmallard standing over him, his chef's whites struggling to contain the bulk, the matted hair on the forehead struggling to contain the sweat, and the man himself struggling to contain his anger.

"Well, I don't use the 'doctor' very often," he stammered.

"Ah, I see." For some reason this punctured his aggression. "I thought that was why you were at the Ménard place when Antonin was found."

Antonin, Richard noted, *not "my son,"* though his grief was clear at the mention of the name.

"Oh no! I'm not official in any way."

"That's to your credit. As you see, monsieur, or *docteur*, they released me almost immediately." The way he said it was like he had triumphed over the Olympian gods. It was a declaration of his own will.

"Yes, erm, congratulations."

"Richard?" Clare wore a coquettish look. "Aren't you going to introduce us?"

"Ah, right, yes. This is Sébastien Grosmallard, chef and proprietor of Les Gens Qui Mangent. Monsieur Grosmallard, this is Clare. Er, well, my wife. That is Alicia and—"

"Madame, are you a doctor too?" he interrupted in perfect English, taking her hand as he did so, kissing the back of it a bit more slowly than would be normally acceptable.

"Oh no!" Clare giggled.

"But your hands are the hands of a surgeon."

"I'd say it was your hands that are clearly the more skilled, monsieur."

"And you smell, I must say, divine."

Even Clare started blushing. "Oh, but I'm not wearing any perfume..."

Inside, Richard found the whole thing highly amusing, like some innuendo-heavy fan dance at the court of Louis XIV, all heaving bosoms and men in bouffant britches. But publicly he made a show of wanting this mutual fawning to stop.

"So why were you released so quickly, monsieur?" Richard asked as nonchalantly as he could, even crumbling a crouton as he did so, though he was still wary of any retaliation. He needn't have been. Grosmallard's natural arrogance meant that he couldn't see the attempted dig.

Still holding Clare's hand, he replied, "Because I am Sébastien Grosmallard, monsieur, that is why!"

Richard was pretty sure that that wouldn't stand up as much of a defense in a court of law, but the response was still a fascinating one. If it was him in that position he would probably have opened with *"Because I'm not guilty."*

"Are you saying that you're untouchable, monsieur?" Clare seemed determined to carry on with her attempt at *Dangerous Liaisons*, and in Grosmallard she had a willing partner.

"No one is untouchable, madam." And he kissed her hand again.

Richard found it hard to suppress a laugh. "You must have friends in high places, then?"

The effect of this innocent question on Grosmallard was instant. He dropped Clare's hand as if it were diseased and, for the first time Richard could remember—and that included the man's arrest—Grosmallard looked worried, wary even.

"I must get back to work, mesdames, messieurs. I hope you enjoy your meal. François!" He called Richard's waiter over. "A bottle of champagne for my guests and, François, a good one, eh?" He flashed a smile at the table. "Bon appétit!" he said, his flourish returning, before striding back to the heat of the kitchen.

"What on earth did you say, Daddy? He went as white as a sheet." Alicia wasn't often impressed with her father, but she seemed to have sided with him over her mother's rather obvious flirting.

"I don't really know," he replied distractedly, watching the chef as he disappeared through the swing doors.

"Friends in high places," said Sly, "that's what."

"What do you mean?" asked Clare, put out that her fun had been stopped.

"*Friends in High Places*. He was on it today. I've been watching French news since I've been here; it helps with my vocabulary."

"Who was on it today? Grosmallard?"

"That's him, yes. There's some slot on the news, like a social diary thing. What's he called? I can't remember his name—what was it? Pierre something, Pierre Pot, Pierre Patreaux...no. Potineaux, that's it. Pierre Potineaux. Anyway, he knows everyone so the program is called *Friends in High Places.*"

They waited as Sly cut into his food. "And?" Richard asked impatiently. "Our chef was on it today?"

"Well, they were talking about some food festival here. It's going to be a big showdown or something."

"Ah." Suddenly it made sense. "No, he wouldn't have liked that."

"Also..." Sly was eager to impress with his knowledge. "Do you remember that African Marxist dictator who disappeared last year? General Winston Cash, I think. All 'No man has a right to own anything that isn't shared by the masses'? South Sudeliland, it was. Anyway, he disappeared with about three billion in a Swiss bank account and today he turned up in a wheelie bin outside the South Sudeliland embassy in Paris. Alive, but naked except for a woman's headscarf over his mouth."

The image of that cut conversation for a moment.

"Well, anyway," Clare said, "you see what using your doctor title does, Richard—it gets you noticed. You'll have to start using it more."

The champagne arrived, allowing Richard not to answer. And the waiter, François, was notably more obsequious than he had been. He poured their glasses, though as he came last to Richard's there was a noticeable verbal eruption from the kitchen. The waiter's hand shook slightly at the noise, and half the restaurant stopped chattering. Grosmallard was giving full vent to some poor soul in the kitchen and Richard couldn't help feeling slightly responsible, his innocuous jibe about friends in high places clearly having rattled the volatile chef. The waiter moved off and Clare picked up her glass to indicate she wanted to make a toast.

"I'd like to repeat Richard's toast of earlier," she said. "To us, to the future."

Richard took a sip, half an ear on Clare's toast and half an ear on the kitchen. Grosmallard was still giving out, but their table was just out of earshot. "Excuse me a second." He stood up, without catching anyone's eye. "I need to break the seal." He wished he'd said something classier than that as he made his way in the direction of the toilets, which were next to the kitchen. A film noir detective, or George Sanders in *The Saint*, would never have said they were going to break the bloody seal!

Luckily, the men's toilet was occupied, allowing Richard to legitimately loiter around the kitchen door area, and he could now hear what was going on. Grosmallard was still talking, more quietly, but still with some anger.

"Why, Karine, why? I trusted you; you are my daughter. All I have left and this is how you treat me! You are a betrayer! A Delilah to my Samson!"

It occurred to Richard, not for the first time, that Sébastien Grosmallard was a right old drama queen.

"I have not betrayed you." Karine spoke softly, controlling her emotions, her voice on the verge of cracking.

"Yet you had dinner with that jackal, that vulture, that *faux frère*!" Richard recognized the French equivalent of a "snake in the grass," or *faux frère* could literally mean "false brother," and there were enough of them knocking about, though admittedly fewer than before. Who was he talking about?

"He could help us, Father; he is well connected. That's why I had dinner with him. We need help to get you back where you belong."

"Can I help you, monsieur?" François the waiter had noticed Richard skulking about.

"No, no thank you. Just, just, erm, I need a wee." He slid into the now vacant toilet, again remonstrating with himself that despite watching all of the man's films, at least once, the effortless class of George Sanders had singularly failed to rub off on him.

"I'm afraid we've rather made a dent in the champagne, Richard, you were gone so long." Clare sounded slightly tipsy, but not annoyed at all at his prolonged absence.

"Congratulations, Daddy!" Alicia raised what was left in her glass and a smiling Sly did the same.

"Erm, thanks," he said, sipping his own. The noise from the kitchen had stopped.

"So when do you start, Dick?"

"Eh? Start what?"

"Your new job?"

"My new job?"

"I've been telling them all about your new job, Richard." Clare smiled, but didn't look him in the eye.

It felt like a trap. "Right. You couldn't throw a few details my way, could you?"

"Professor of Film Aesthetics. At Cambridge University. Mummy's been telling us all about it."

He looked from one to another and back again, and finally Clare broke the silence.

"You remember Stephen Roachford? Well, he's *Sir* Stephen Roachford now." She always said this like it was the first time she'd told him. "Well, he wanted to invest in his son's old college at Cambridge, and I convinced him to create a chair for you. It turns out the college was looking to go that route anyway. And you being a doctor in... Well, it was a perfect fit." She leaned in closer and whispered in his ear while the others averted their eyes. "We can start again, Richard." She gently kissed his earlobe. "It's clearly too dangerous for you around here, and anyway, you could never have afforded to divorce me." She finished her glass of champagne.

Richard looked green around the gills, and Alicia didn't look much brighter either.

"It's perfect!" There was a time and a place for Sly's enthusiasm, and this wasn't it. "It means that we can take over the B&B from you, eh, Al? Congratulations, Dick!"

26

The hens stood there, three abreast, looking at him. They weren't used to an awful lot of energy from the man who regularly fed them, but they were used to more than this. He was just sitting there on his bench, throwing seed erratically, sometimes at them directly, sometimes way over their heads. So they'd banded together and were seeking to make a stand, but the man just stared through them, sometimes shaking his head, sometimes muttering to himself.

Richard felt like a puppet, an amiable piece of entertainment for the audience but one that was completely under the control of whoever held the strings. He realized that it was largely his fault, of course. It usually was anyway, he'd learned, but this time it was true. He'd been happy to be a passenger in his own life for so long that he had gotten out of the habit of making the big decisions for himself and allowed others to do so for him. It was a power that others—well, Clare—were either not willing to relinquish or feared for Richard if they did, his judgment having remained untested for so long. She would say she was doing it for his own benefit; maybe she was. He had his doubts, though, and he wasn't the only one.

Alicia had found her father in the salon, nursing a late whisky before bed, Passepartout asleep on the chair next to him.

"Hello, love!" He'd tried his best to look cheerful and upbeat but he'd soon run out of oomph and sat back down.

"Can I have one of those, Daddy?"

He looked at in her surprise. It felt odd to be serving whisky to someone who called you "Daddy," but it was a rare moment of father–daughter time. And at least she wasn't calling him Dick.

"Are you OK?" she asked in a way that suggested she knew the answer.

He looked at her, and didn't bother to hide the fact that he wasn't at all sure.

She took a sip from her glass and shivered at the taste of it. "I'm not sure I like whisky," she said as if mulling it over.

He took a sip too. "You know what, love? I'm not sure I do either."

"But whisky is what men drink when they need to feel sorry for themselves, is that it?" He looked at her in surprise again. "I'm twenty-six, Dad. I know the tropes."

"I think that's the first time you've ever called me dad."

"Maybe. So where are we? Frank Sinatra in *Pal Joey* or Humphrey Bogart in *Casablanca* again? Oh yes, it rubs off, you know?" She gave him a big smile, put her arm around his shoulder, and kissed him on the temple. Then she looked him in the eye, and her smile faded. "We didn't know about that, you know? The Cambridge post, us taking over here."

He took a long gulp of whisky and winced. "Here's looking at you, kid." He coughed.

She smiled warmly at him. "You used to tuck me in with that every night. You'd kiss me on the forehead and say, 'Here's looking at you, kid.' I felt very safe."

He smiled back at her and kissed her on the forehead. "Feel safe now?"

"Safer than you."

"Well, that's my job, I suppose."

She looked at him, looked hard into his eyes. "Sly and I talked about this with Mummy, a few weeks back. Sly was made redundant and I'm sick of my job, sick of London too. We decided a complete change would do us good."

"A *chambre d'hôte?*"

"No. A B&B. We want to stay in England; all our friends are there. Mummy said she knew someone who could help."

"Stephen Roachford?"

"*Sir* Stephen Roachford." She snorted playfully. "Do get it right, Daddy! One of the ideas was to set Sly up as an estate agent in Cambridge." Richard looked at her, raising his eyebrows. "Yes. He lives there." So, that all fitted and they both knew it.

"But?"

"But Sly said no. He had a meeting with Stephen and told him that he didn't want to be an estate agent, because he was no good at it. 'I like people,' he told him, 'so estate agency is not for me.'"

"He's too nice a bloke, you mean?"

"Exactly."

"Good for him."

"We'll convince Mummy that this"—she waved her arm around the salon—"lovely though it is, isn't for us."

"She'll hit the roof."

"It will also end your marriage."

"There is that."

"Which will do you both a power of good, in my opinion."

He turned to look at her, and then he hugged her. "Where did you get all this common sense from?" he asked genuinely.

"My husband. Also, I learn from other peoples' mistakes," she replied pointedly. She poured her drink into his glass and stood up. "Don't drink too much, will you? We've got a lot to do." He could have sworn that she'd then winked at him. "By the way," she asked, turning for the door, "what are film aesthetics?"

He snorted and swirled his drink around the glass, playing his role to perfection. "Aesthetics are the barriers philosophers put up to stop the appreciation of art," he said bitterly. "Mending things that don't need fixing."

"Daddy! It's almost like you don't want the job! Good night," she said. "And don't get drunk—go and watch a film."

He hadn't been close to Alicia in years, probably more his fault than hers. But right now, he'd never felt closer, and that made a difference. He was still standing on the scaffolding; the noose was being lowered around his neck, but at least he had an ally, and that at least meant something to the condemned man. He finished his whisky and made a decision. He would leave Grosmallard's journal until tomorrow; he probably couldn't concentrate now anyway. Instead, he would sleep in his cinema room and introduce Passepartout to some classic Hollywood entertainment, aesthetically acceptable or not. Something like *North by Northwest*, classic mistaken-identity, man-on-the-run stuff, or *Sunset Boulevard*, life through the cynical eyes of a corpse.

It would also give him a chance to mull over the issues at hand. Did he want to be a professor of film aesthetics at Cambridge University? Did he want to stay married to Clare? Did she really want to stay married to him? Could he afford to buy Clare out? Would Alicia and Sly decide that this wasn't for them? And finally, was it too late to run away, change his name, and go and live on a tiny island somewhere?

None of that having been resolved by morning, he at least decided to be more positive, or proactive, one of the two anyway. Firstly, he set Sly to work on setting up breakfast, which he was more than happy to do until Madame Tablier, still in union mode, felt aggrieved at not being asked herself and grumbled darkly about demarcation lines and liberties. "It's getting like one of them cults around here. All these comings and goings."

"It's not a cult, I promise you, madame."

"Well, all I can say is that it feels like that. You read about these things. Everyone being just a big family, if you know what I mean. Nobody knowing who's who. It's wrong!"

Something struck in Richard's memory. Hugo Ménard, that was it. What did he say? "We all lived pretty much together. Our parents were quite hippyish." He wondered if there was ever some kind of commune around here?

"Don't worry, madame, I'm sure that kind of thing could never happen in the Follet Valley..." He knew it was the best way to get her to open up about anything, by closing it down first.

"Ha! Well, that's what you think! There was a place like that, closed down it was. All sex and drugs." The fierce old lady paused.

"And sex!" she repeated as if her needle had got stuck. "People said it was just kids dancing, but we all know what kids and dancing leads to, don't we?"

"Yes, we do," he said, concern masking his jealousy of youth. "But around here, really? When?"

"Oh, not long. Thirty years, twenty? On one of the islands in the Lac des Petites Îles."

Well now, he thought. *I wonder...*

After this, he texted Valérie again, but this time to tell her that he had the all-important notebook, hoping this would break her silence. He'd decipher the thing properly, uncover the whole hippy commune, and solve the whole case. He would then recline regally like Ronald Colman at the end of *The Prisoner of Zenda* and say, "My work here is done," before being dragged reluctantly into the world of cultural aesthetics.

Well, that was the plan anyway, and all was going well until he tried to recover the notebook from the chicken coop. It wasn't there. The tin was there, but the notebook wasn't in it. It had gone. More specifically, it had been taken, because the hens couldn't open the tin and eat the book. Not even Joan Crawford, who had a reputation for wanton destruction should the mood take her. He turned the thing upside down, was shouted at by the hens, unnerved the guests who had come out to see what all the fuss was about, and caused Madame Tablier to tut with such a crack it sounded like her tongue was a bullwhip. It had gone. Not only had the main piece of evidence vanished, but he sorely regretted telling Valérie that he had ever had it. Assuming she was even still alive.

He sat, stunned, on the bench. It was a crushing blow. You expect bad news every now and then, but things were now piling up, and the notebook being taken was just about the last straw. He had turned into whatever is the opposite of King Midas, and now it appeared that even the hens, his beloved hens, had turned on him, as the three of them lined up, facing him like an avian firing squad. Passepartout began to move away from his side too, as if Richard's bad luck was not only contagious but stank like rotting fish. The small dog jumped off the bench and disappeared around the corner. Richard sighed; he should go after him, he knew that, but as things stood, and with his current run of form, he'd probably round the corner, trip over the animal, and be injured just enough to carry on living. So he stayed where he was and waited for trouble to come to him for once.

He didn't have to wait long.

27

A few moments later, Passepartout returned. His eyes were wild with excitement, a wide doggy grin across his face, and he was pawing at the arms of his mistress. She placed him gently on the bench and sat beside him. Richard, of course, tried to take this sudden reappearance of Valérie in his stride, looking up with a nonchalant air while also trying not to fall off the bench.

"I thought I would find you here." There was a slight note of relief in her voice, which cheered him up enormously. "It has been a hectic two days, Richard. To find you on your bench with your hens is very reassuring."

"I texted you a few times." He tried not to sound petulant, but it was funny how neither of them had felt the need to offer formal French greetings, they'd just settled quickly back into whatever their relationship status was.

"I found them when I returned last night. It was very late. I did not want to disturb you."

"You don't have your phone on, then? Not when you're working, that is." They were both skirting round an issue that neither of them, in all honesty, wanted to talk about anyway.

"I use a different phone," she said flatly, ending that topic of conversation.

They sat in silence for a brief moment. "Well, Passepartout missed you. He's very happy to have you back, obviously."

"And I missed him too." She hugged him tightly. "But he likes it here, and I knew he would be safe. Did he behave?"

"Oh yes, good as gold. He's not much of a film fan, though. He fell asleep during *Sunset Boulevard* last night. I thought about showing him an old *Lassie* film but he didn't seem fussed." She looked at him in confusion. "Never mind. How was Paris?"

"Quite revealing." She had a sly smile on her face, which meant that it had gone very well indeed.

"I only ask because there was quite a hoo-hah there yesterday. The food festival was on TV and an African dictator turned up."

"An ooh-ah?" Again, her pronunciation of English slang-euphemism was enough to make a statue go weak at the knees. "Is that the same as 'kerfuffle'?"

"Yes, though you can say 'hubbub' or 'ballyhoo.'"

"How was the restaurant?"

He laughed. "Grosmallard really is a very difficult man to like. He was all over Clare. He said she smelled divine, even. Clare never wears perfume."

"Were you jealous?" He didn't know the answer to that. "Now, about that notebook. Well done for finding it; you didn't tell me you picked it up."

"No. Well, I couldn't remember where it was and I didn't want to get your hopes up."

"Well, at least we have it now."

"Yes. Erm, about that..." He was about to confess that the thing had been stolen by a person or persons unknown when she pulled the small, leatherbound journal out from under Passepartout, who looked reasonably calm about the thing. "Where did you get that?" Richard couldn't hide his surprise or relief.

"In the hen food tin," she answered as though it were a trick question, "where you left it."

"Yes, but how did you know it was there?"

"Oh, Richard." She half giggled at the naivety he didn't know he had. "But it's very interesting, isn't it? What do you make of it?"

He took a deep breath. "Well, not much, really. I was surprised at how many dishes are named after people in the news, though. Or the news as it was. Celebrities, politicians, and so on. Do you think that's a starting point for most chefs? Think of an actress, say, and develop a dish around her? It's a way of getting the food noticed, I suppose."

"Maybe," she said quietly, "but I think it's more than that."

"A code, you mean?"

"In a way. I think it's an inventory—well, partly it's an inventory and partly it is what it is, a chef's recipe notebook. There are genuine recipes in there, look." She turned to a page and pointed. "The *loup de mer en papillote coco curry*."

"Curried sea bass." He shook his head. "Not my thing."

"No," she said with forced patience, "but it is an established recipe, a little safe for a Michelin-starred chef perhaps, but a proper recipe. Now"—she turned over a few pages—"look at this one."

Richard put his glasses on. "*Gâteau de Gaston Cormier*. Yes, well, I mean it looks a bit rich with all that butter, but..." He tailed off, at a loss and worried he was making a fool of himself.

She smiled at him. "Exactly, Richard! Brilliant."

"Good." He was none the wiser.

She turned a few more pages. "Do you know the phrase '*mettre du beurre dans ses épinards*'?"

He thought about it. "To put butter in one's spinach?"

"That is the literal translation, yes. But it's a French idiom. Butter is a slang word for money; putting it in your spinach makes the spinach richer. It adds to what you have, you see?"

"Like a sideline, extra income?"

"Yes."

"OK," he said slowly, trying to work it out. "So, are you saying that Gaston Cormier, whoever he is, provided a lucrative sideline and that's the code in this recipe?"

"That's exactly what I'm saying!" Her eyes were shining with excitement.

"So who's Gaston Cormier?"

"He was a politician. He died a few years ago."

"So no more butter there, then."

"No, but look at this one. *Pot-au-feu Potineaux.*"

He looked. "What about it? I mean there's a lot of butter, obviously, but..."

"But who puts butter in a pot-au-feu?"

"Ah. Good point. Hang on!" He clapped his hands. "Potineaux. That's the journalist who announced the food festival yesterday, isn't it?" He looked at her for confirmation, guessing that she knew more than she was letting on.

"Yes," was the reply without any addition.

"So, what you're saying is that this book, aside from recipes, is a kind of ledger of people who pay Grosmallard extra butter, or money. But why?" And then he had it and they both said it at exactly the same time: "Blackmail!"

"I am sure of it!"

"So he's blackmailing the rich and famous? That's how he gets funding for a new restaurant despite his Michelin star being on the wane, so to speak. Clever. Do you think Tatillon knows? And that's why he's writing a book?"

"It is possible, yes. Or that he has guessed something doesn't make sense."

"And this Potineaux, shouldn't we tell the police about the blackmail?"

"Eventually," she said after thinking this over. "We don't know yet if Potineaux supplied Grosmallard with his information or if he was being blackmailed himself. The butter in the pot-au-feu might refer to his cut."

"Difficult to cut a pot-au-feu," Richard said, immediately regretting his flippancy.

"Anyway, there is more with the notebook. Look." From her pocket she produced a scrap of paper that he recognized as the other half of Ménard's supposed suicide note. She placed the note on a page chosen at random. The handwriting was close enough to look the same.

"He wrote Ménard's suicide note? The more I find out about this Grosmallard chap, the less I like him. He's up to his eyeballs in this."

"And yet, there's even more."

"You have been busy," he said in awe.

"Did you notice anything else about the book?"

He thought hard about this. He remembered looking for the famous Grosmallard dessert and eventually finding it somewhere near the back, but...

"Wait a minute, yes! The Grosmallard pudding, dessert, whatever. I found it surprising that it wasn't nearer the front of the book. It was nearer the back, but I thought it was one of his earliest creations, the thing that kick-started the career."

"Exactly, Richard." She looked genuinely pleased at his intuition. "Now why do you think that is? What else is different between the beginning of the book and the rest of it?" She gave it to him to look at again and he flicked through. It was as he remembered it: the recipes were a combination of different handwriting. The hardly legible scrawl of Sébastien Grosmallard and the more feminine hand, presumably of his late wife, Angélique. Her additional notes ended when she died. He said this to Valérie, who nodded and pursed her lips.

"Yes," she said, suddenly quite angry. "How I hate the world of the French kitchen. Where men are great chefs and the little women are cooks. Men are the main course; women are the pretty dessert." He nodded in agreement but decided to stay silent on the issue. "So why is the recipe there after she has died? She was very much alive when it was created and he received his star. There is a picture of them both on the wall of his office."

"Maybe he wanted to update it?"

"I don't think so. It is his one true signature dish. His entire reputation is built on that one plate of food. I don't think he would change it."

"*Dessert pour Angélique.*" He read the smudged title out loud. "I see what you mean."

"No, Richard, I don't think you do." He was quite relieved by that. He could now stop treating this conversation like an oral exam. "Turn back to the front, there!" She stopped him as he turned the pages. "Do you see anything?"

He looked more closely. "It looks like there's a page been torn out," he offered cautiously.

"Exactly."

"But everybody tears pages out of notebooks. I don't think I've ever finished a notebook with all the pages intact."

"Yes, but now go back to the recipe."

He shook his head, partly in bewilderment and partly in wonder that she had managed to see so much in the book, and by extension how much he had missed.

"OK, *dessert pour Angélique...*"

"Look more closely, Richard."

"*Dessert. Pour. Angélique.*" He read each word slowly, hoping that some spark would ignite in his brain. "Dessert for Angélique. I don't get it; what am I looking for?"

"That stain on the word '*pour*.' It makes it difficult to read, yes?"

"Yes?"

"Just suppose it is not '*pour*'—or 'for'—but '*par*'—or 'by.'" She looked at him in solid-gold triumph, her eyes burning with intensity. "Not a dessert for Angélique but a dessert *by* Angélique."

He met her eyes with a similar excitement. "So that's why the page is missing. She made the dessert, not her husband. She was the talent, you mean?"

"I think so, yes."

"Right," he said, making an effort to tread carefully with what he was going to say next. "Just playing devil's advocate. What if your conclusion is wrong? You might be blinded by, you know...erm."

She was giving him a withering look. "By being a woman?"

"No. Just, er, preconceptions. Like I say"—he gulped nervously—"just playing devil's advocate."

"Very well." She nodded. "But our great chef hasn't been near the heights of his previous success since Angélique died; Tatillon told us that. 'A return to form,' he said, 'after all these years.' A page is missing from that time of his career. A dessert *by* Angélique."

"I must admit, it seems pretty clear-cut when you put it like that. But why kill Ménard and his own son? If he was his own son. Just because they screwed up the dessert he had finally resurrected? It's a bit much, don't you think?"

"He is a man who considers himself untouchable, I think, for one. But also, imagine the frustration he must have felt. He simply cannot remake the dish that Angélique perfected. It must torment him to extremes, drive him insane."

"Well, he's certainly very unpleasant. When I was at the restaurant last night..." He paused, wondering if he should tell her about his proposed move back to England and academia.

"Yes?"

"Well, I heard him bawling his daughter out, something about how she had betrayed him by trying to get help for their restaurant. Someone with contacts, he said. I don't know who, though. Oh, and another thing. I spoke to Hugo Ménard. The Ménards and the Grosmallards were in some hippy commune type thing, very near here. And I think it was where I and the Liebowitzes followed Elisabeth and Sébastien the other day. The Lac des Petites Îles."

She looked at him, this time returning his admiration. "Richard, that is brilliant! You are so clever!"

"Oh you know..." He stood up to bask.

"For a man," she added, a warm smile on her face.

"Well, I couldn't have done it without you," he said in mock grandeur.

"Now." She stood up next to him and put Passepartout on the bench. "Put this book back in your hiding place."

"Why? It obviously wasn't a good hiding place!"

"I found it, Richard, but I think I know you very well." She didn't make it sound exactly a compliment, but he'd take it anyway, as he took the book and disappeared into the large pen that held the coop. Olivia de Havilland was sitting serenely in her straw nest, calmly keeping an egg warm, so he tried to be as quiet as possible while picking her up and replacing the notebook.

From outside he could hear approaching footsteps. "Ah," a voice said. It was Clare. "I was looking for my husband, but anyway, I'm glad I have you on your own." Valérie did not reply, leaving Richard to sit in the coop in silence with his screen heroine on his lap.

28

I suppose he's told you about last night at the restaurant?"

Richard could just about see through the wooden slats on the coop wall and he didn't know whether to be terrified or pleased at what he saw. Clare stood straight backed with her arms hanging loosely by her side, like a barroom brawler, whereas Valérie was still sitting and looking very relaxed as she stroked Passepartout gently. One way of looking at it was that two women were fighting over him. Obviously, he knew that wasn't the case, but he was never happier than when cocooned in delusion. The truth was that Clare didn't really want *him* at all but fancied the life as the wife of an academic, presumably having read somewhere that Cambridge college society was something like the last days of the British Raj, all aristocratic bed-hopping and terribly refined back-stabbing. Valérie, he could tell, was quietly bemused by it all.

"The restaurant?" she said. "Yes, he did. He was very excited by the news."

Ah, thought Richard. *Maybe I should have told Valérie the whole story and not just the father–daughter Grosmallard argument.*

"Oh. Oh really? Well, that's good." Clare relaxed and sat down on the bench next to what Richard was now calling "her rival." "Obviously, there's a lot to sort out, but I think they will want him to start at the beginning of the academic year."

Valérie didn't skip a beat; in fact, she carried on stroking Passepartout as if this was all information that she already had. "That makes sense," she said quietly.

"It would never have worked out between the two of you, you know?" Clare's accent had become more clipped, sounding like a stopper being put back on a crystal decanter.

"The two of us?"

"Yes. It would never have worked out. You see, I know Richard. I've known him a long time and this isn't him. All this running around and sleuthing. He'll get bored of it sooner or later. When it becomes mundane or commonplace or rare, even. Richard is a watcher, not a doer. He likes to imagine he's a lover or a detective or on the run, but he wouldn't *actually* be any good at any of those things. He's too English for all that."

Richard felt like storming out of the coop at that point and giving a rigorous defense, but Joan Crawford jumped from her nesting shelf onto his shoulder making him look like a low-value pirate. From this position, he could also hear the small bird's stomach gurgling. If he was going to go, he needed to go now. What was stopping him?

"He is very English." There was no edge or judgment in Valérie's tone, just a repetition of Clare's—in his view harsh—judgment.

"Yes. Which is why a well-paid position at a stuffy old university— well, I say that, but it's one of the best Cambridge colleges—is just perfect for him. Watching his films and talking about them to bored students. And they will be bored, bless them!" She laid her hand on Valérie's arm. It was their little joke, the gesture said, though Valérie remained cool, not responding.

Aside from hearing this very definite and very low opinion of him, Richard, now covered in Joan Crawford's processed breakfast, decided he was quite happy to remain where he was. He wasn't surprised at Clare's dim view of his qualities, he didn't even blame her for them, but there was something about watching these two very strong women that frightened the bloody life out of him. They were so different; they represented different worlds, their futures and their pasts defining what they now were, which was much stronger than him. They both knew what they wanted, that was one of the main differences, as he hadn't a clue what he wanted, which is one reason why he never used his doctor title. It forced responsibility on him. Inevitably Richard saw the confrontation, if that's even what it was, in terms of cinematic fiction rather than feminist fact. He had made a decision not to get involved in politics years ago, especially gender politics, which looked like quicksand on a minefield, literally in no-man's land.

No. Richard wasn't capable of seeing this as liberal versus radical versus Marxist versus cultural feminist. To him, it was just two strong women sorting things out. He was, however, more than capable of seeing it, once again, as Bette Davis versus Joan Crawford in *What Ever Happened to Baby Jane?* or as Bette Davis and Olivia de Havilland in *Hush... Hush, Sweet Charlotte*, or even as the real-life rivalry of Olivia de Havilland and her sister, Joan Fontaine. Suddenly a thought struck him: sisters! Supposing Elisabeth and Angélique had been sisters? Maybe not even "real" sisters, but as close as.

Elisabeth had always loved Sébastien. She thought by removing her husband that they could be together. But why kill Antonin? Because he stood in the way? It seemed a bit of a stretch but it was something to do with family feuding, he was convinced of that. He was also convinced that if he stayed in this stooped position much longer he would be permanently disabled, and he tried to right himself, causing Joan Crawford to start clucking, depositing some more anger on his shirt. He kept as still as he could and watched as Clare looked with disgust at the chicken coop.

"I don't like hens," she said. "Never have. Filthy creatures."

He saw Valérie look in his direction, a playful smile on her lips. He calmed Joan Crawford down, but she was a volatile creature, not unlike the real Joan Crawford. What had Bette Davis said about her when she'd heard of her death? *You should never say bad things about the dead, only good. Joan Crawford is dead. Good.*

"Anyway, it's not completely in the bag yet." He heard Clare continue. "I mean, it's as good as. He has an interview this evening. An online interview with the master and a couple of other important people." She looked nervously at Valérie, a rare moment of weakness perhaps caused by Valérie's silence. "It's a formality, really," she added.

Joan Crawford clucked again, the noise echoing off the corrugated roof.

"I will miss staying here, but then I will buy my own house soon, I think." Valérie smiled charmingly at Clare. "I wish you both the very best."

Clare stood, seemingly satisfied with how things had gone. "It will do Richard good, you know. He can go back to fantasizing about being Cary Grant or Humphrey Bogart or Hercule Poirot or whoever, not trying to be them. Midlife crises are supposed to be about younger women and fast cars... Well, he has the use of a fast car, at least."

Ouch, thought Richard. He also thought that it was a bit rich for Clare to start being jealous and territorial when she'd had more flings than a Highland dance festival.

"I really—" Valérie began but was interrupted by her phone ringing. "Do excuse me," she said with apparent warmth, "but I must take this call. Ah, Commissaire..."

Richard's cramp started up again and as the pain shot through his leg he reeled in agony, banging his head on the roof. He saw Clare glance at the coop again, then back at Valérie. She nodded, pursed her lips, and walked away. Richard decided to give it a few minutes, nonetheless.

When he did emerge, he had in his mind Alec Guinness in *The Bridge on the River Kwai*. A heroic dignity in the face of Japanese torture methods, a stoic determination against all the odds. Of course, the Alec Guinness character had been placed in "the oven" for days in searing Burmese heat and with no food or water, so it was hardly comparable to cramps in a chicken coop and bird poop on his shirt. Richard had even emerged with a fresh egg.

"That was the commissaire." If Valérie had wished to talk about her conversation with Clare or Richard's move back to the UK and into high-end academia, then whatever the commissaire had told her had put that definitively on a back burner. She had that look in her eye that Richard recognized now all too well.

"What's happened?" he asked, wiping chicken poo off his shoulder.

"Auguste Tatillon is dead!"

Richard looked stunned.

"He's been found in the freezer..."

"At Grosmallard's?"

"No! At Guy Garçon's restaurant. With a knife in his throat!"

"Grosmallard's knife?"

"Yes!"

"Blimey!"

"And Henri—" Oh, it was Henri now, was it? "He wants us to go there. He knows we know as much as he does and he wants us there."

"But I'm a watcher, not a doer," Richard said, still smarting at some of the things that had been said about him.

"I disagree, Richard. But let's finish this before you have to go back, yes?"

"Yes. Yes," he said again with determination. "Come on, then, let's go to Garçon's place."

Valérie paused. "No," she said, "let's go to Martin and Gennie's?"

"What? This is no time for naked cocktails!"

"No! To search Auguste Tatillon's room before the police do."

"But they might already be there..." She had already marched past him. "OK." He hurried to follow her. "But can I drive your fast car?"

29

ichard." Valérie was talking slowly. The tone of her voice suggested she was well aware that his ego had taken a bit of a pummeling that morning, what with the rather unflattering comments from his wife, and while Valérie had no wish to add further bruising to his fragile male psyche, this was too much. "Richard," she began again, softening her tone even more, "could you please speed up! The police will be there before us at this rate; we must get a move on!"

Later, he would come to regard this as a turning point, the moment he chose a different path, and rather than ponder the consequences or sit by the side of the road and draw up a list of pros and cons, something inside made the decision for him. He didn't blame Clare. In her own way she was looking out for him, looking out for herself too, of course, but why shouldn't she? It was just that he didn't want to be that person that she wanted him to be and, if she were honest, she didn't want him to be that person either. It was a sobering thought, and he didn't know if it was the most lucid thought of his adult life or utter gibberish. Either way, his feelings on the matter aside, Clare usually got what she wanted, so if this was to be his last adventure before the shackles of academia were clasped to his ankles, he may as well get on with it. It was time to be a bit more *The Italian Job* and *The French Connection* than *Genevieve* and *The Titfield Thunderbolt*, which was actually about a train but, annoyingly, he couldn't think of another slow car in a film, so to cover his fit of pique he slammed his foot on the accelerator and was immediately Steve McQueen in *Bullitt*. Valérie's head shot back and her hat blew off behind the car, allowing her hair to flow with the increased speed. Over the sound of the engine, he apologized fulsomely for the hat.

He came to a skidding halt on Martin and Gennie's gravel drive and with some difficulty prised his fingers off the steering wheel. It may have been one of the most freeing moments of his life but it was also one of the most stressful. He had nearly hit at least three tractors and probably screamed on each occasion. Valérie turned to face him, and somehow her hair was already once again immaculate.

"Well, we got here eventually," she said, though with a twinkle of mischief in her eye.

The back door of Martin and Gennie's house opened and Martin strode out. At least, they assumed it was Martin.

"Good God," moaned Richard, at once unable to look upon the man but also finding it difficult to tear his eyes away from the sight.

The portly figure standing on the threshold of the back door, an innuendo Martin would have delighted in, looked like a pony who'd had his saddle put on badly. He was wearing leather studded briefs and a kind of central belt system that seemed like it was designed to help with heavy lifting for those with sciatica issues. His nipples—and this was something Richard knew would haunt him until his dying days—were attached by chains to a dog collar around his neck. The whole ensemble was topped off with a gas mask.

"Hel-lo," Martin said cheerfully, as if he weren't dressed like a belted pork joint. He tried to wave but a chain pulled on another chain somewhere, a complicated mechanism no doubt, and he let out a cry of pain followed swiftly by a satisfied sigh. "Fancy a cup of tea? Gennie's just getting the kettle on." He turned and went back in, and Richard knew he would also never forget the sight of Martin's red-raw bottom wobbling onto the porch.

"I think we'll just leave Passepartout here." Valérie couldn't hide her disgust but knew there was no time to waste. "He prefers the fresh air."

Gennie appeared at the back doorstep, thankfully wearing a pink dressing gown that looked oddly old-maidish, covering her, as it did, from ankle right up to her neck, where she demurely held the collar closed tight. Richard could only imagine what it was concealing and had no wish to concentrate on the issue. "You should have phoned to say you were coming." She had an enormous, friendly, and welcoming smile on her face. "We were just going to sit down and watch an old episode of *Countdown*."

Richard tried to say something but nothing came out and thankfully Valérie took over.

"We have come to ask a favor."

"Ask away old girl." Martin had reappeared at the step, his gas mask now removed.

"We need to look around Monsieur Tatillon's room..."

"Oh, I don't know about that. Invasion of privacy and so on."

It didn't seem right to be lectured on the invasion of anything by a man dressed as a Visigoth warrior who'd forgotten his underwear, but these were strange times.

"Well, he won't mind," Richard said. "He's dead."

Martin and Gennie looked at each other. In the same way that Richard and Valérie had come to accept, if not entirely tolerate, the fact that quite often the couple made an arresting sight, Martin and Gennie had made peace with the knowledge that Richard and Valérie had their own foibles, and as such were pretty open-minded about the pair of them in return.

"Oh well," said Gennie, "in that case, I'll get the key." Valérie followed her inside.

"That's bad luck for the fella." Martin made it sound like Tatillon had just sprained his wrist and was not, as Valérie had explained on the drive over, hanging from a butcher's hook in a catering-sized freezer with an expensive chef's knife sticking out of his gullet. "Still..." Martin seemed to have exhausted the Tatillon issue. "They say it might rain later, be good for the garden."

"Yes," Richard replied. "My lobelias are parched." He could sense Martin struggle to suppress another innuendo.

"I say, old man," Martin said with disdain, "is that chicken mess on your shirt?"

Richard was about to respond with something tart about glass houses, but Gennie and Valérie returned just in time.

"I'm giving Valérie some of that sponge cake I made last night." She handed a plastic bag and a key to Valérie while still holding her dressing gown collar tight. "What are you looking for anyway?"

Richard thought that was a very good question.

"So?" Richard asked from the bedroom doorway. "What *are* we looking for?"

"I don't know yet." Valérie was searching under the bed. "If he's writing a book, then notes, perhaps, a laptop? I don't know."

He moved to the wardrobe and opened the doors. "Do you think they dress like that all the time?"

"Who?"

"Martin and Gennie. Do you think they dress like that all the time?"

She looked at him. "I would rather not think about it, Richard."

"No. Fair enough." He rifled through the coat hangers, but there was nothing of interest there, though he could see that all the clothes were expensive. "Still," he mused, "if you were to dress like that all the time, what constitutes dressing up for a special occasion? Put it this way, they were planning to watch a daytime quiz show just then, and they're done up like the king and queen of suburban fetishism. I mean, what do you think Valentine's Day is like? How much higher, or lower, can you go? It makes me shudder to think about it..."

"Richard, I really think we need to hurry. Why don't you look in the drawers over there?"

"Yes. Right." He moved to the chest of drawers. Again a selection of expensive underwear, some wig glue—there didn't seem to be much else. He even felt a bit sorry for Tatillon. Why kill him? "I suppose he'd made a lot of enemies," he said.

"What?"

"I was just thinking aloud. I suppose Tatillon must have made a lot of enemies over the years. And friends too, of course."

"Sébastien Grosmallard was both. Tatillon made his reputation and was in the process of now destroying it, I think."

"And that's why he was killed?"

"It looks like that way to me."

"I don't see how we nail him, though. If he's protected from on high like he is, how do we break that up? Hang on, what's this?" He was rooting around in the bottom drawer, where there were neatly folded silk pajamas. "It's another notebook!" He plucked it from the drawer and whirled round, where Valérie was already standing up and stretching after crouching on the floor. She lost her balance momentarily and tried to grab Richard's arm before she fell. She missed his arm and poked him hard in the eye instead. "Ow!" he cried, dropping his findings on the bed and covering his eye in pain; it was already starting to weep.

"Oh Richard, I am so sorry!" Her contrition was diluted somewhat by the fact that she immediately sat down and started picking through the notebook. Richard bumped into the furniture while trying to get his vision straight.

"I think I'm blind," he whined, trying to focus.

"Richard! This isn't a notebook as such—it is a scrapbook. A lot of the names from the recipe book are here, but with photographs and diary entries. Look!"

"I can't bloody look!" His frustration was evident. "Look at what?"

"Here. Gaston Cormier, the politician."

With his one good eye, Richard could make out the figures of a man and a woman, the picture having been taken from above. "He liked to stay close to his constituents, didn't he?" he said, turning the photo the other way up. "Too close, you might say."

"And here." She handed him another photo.

"Who is that?"

"Potineaux."

"And the other man?"

"I don't know for sure. A sportsman, I think."

"Blimey!"

"And here. The one in the middle. Tatillon."

Richard turned the photograph around again. "Having his cake *and* eating it." It wasn't his cup of tea.

"There are older photos too. Look at this one; it looks like a campsite. Maybe even that commune thing you mentioned." She looked more closely, trying to make out the faces in the picture. "And who is that lurking in the background there?"

"I don't know, but he looks very out of place."

"Sénateur Royer. The longest-serving senator in the French parliament. And..."

"And Angélique Royer's dad? Uncle?"

"So this is how Grosmallard was protected. I should have thought about this. But it's as we thought: blackmail."

He mulled this over. "But why is it here, though? I don't get it. Unless Tatillon stole it and that's why he was killed."

"However it got here, Richard, a lot of people want this book. A lot of very important people."

He stood up. "Right, then. Let's get out of here sharpish."

They rushed down the stairs and Richard got into the driver's seat. "No," he cried, "it's no good. You'll have to drive."

"Yes, that makes sense. I drive faster than you."

"No, Valérie," he said, looking in from over the hood as she slid from one seat to the other. "It's because you've bloody blinded me!"

30

They drove at some speed the fifteen minutes or so from Martin and Gennie's place to Guy Garçon's restaurant. Even Richard wasn't so unnerved by Valérie's driving on this occasion, as his bad eye—now weeping like a hungry baby—couldn't see much of the road anyway. He had his one good eye on the illicit pornography on his lap, and every so often he'd whistle in shock at the kind of positions high-ranking government officials of advancing years managed to get themselves into. He was well aware how slippery and malleable politicians could be, but some of this material was Olympic-gymnast quality. He came across another photo that he couldn't quite make out, and then, on recognizing the face, placed it hurriedly to the back of the book. Because of the state of his left eye, he didn't notice that Valérie had seen his sleight of hand.

"Who was that?" she asked in a tone that sounded like a customs official snapping their rubber gloves on.

"Oh, no one important. Where do you think these were taken?" he added quickly, trying to change the subject.

"Grosmallard's restaurant in Paris, I suspect. A back room for hire, a secret camera. It's not a new trick." She sounded impatient. "You didn't answer my question."

"Really, in terms of who else we have here, it's someone very much from the bottom shelf."

"I see." She screeched the car around a tight bend. "You mean commissaire Henri LaPierre?" she asked quietly when the noise had died down.

"Yes," he sighed. "Sorry."

She laughed. "Oh, Richard, why? Are you to blame? No. Why else would Henri be posted here if not to protect the interests of more important people? All that nonsense about fishing."

"And he's using us to do the unofficial legwork?"

"Yes. I should have realized sooner."

"How could you, though? We've only just found the book."

"Yes. But you said it yourself: How has Grosmallard financed the restaurant when his value as a chef is so low? The money must come from somewhere. Why was he released so quickly? Why was the evidence lost?"

"Because people want to protect their investment?"

"They want to protect who they've been forced to invest in, yes, and they don't want the famous Sébastien Grosmallard complaining publicly either."

"So this was the book he was moaning about on his arrest, then, not the one we found before?"

"I think so. And it was a warning that I think Henri understood immediately."

"Even so..." Richard wasn't altogether sure where this sentence was going, but he had a vague idea of something that he needed to formulate. "It all seems a bit over the top to me. French politicians normally just shrug off sex scandals, don't they? I've even heard people question some politicians' fitness for public office because they *haven't* got a mistress."

"Male politicians, Richard. Female politicians are judged very differently."

"Oh yes, of course, and I wasn't suggesting..." He let the sentence drift off. "What I'm saying is, three murders to cover up something that would normally just blow over pretty quickly, well, it seems excessive."

"I think it goes back to that commune. Something else must have happened there. More than sex. More than drugs."

"Yes, I see." He looked at some more pictures. "Sex is everywhere, isn't it?"

Valérie smiled at him. "Poor Richard," she said, like a mother wiping her child's grazed knee.

The aforementioned Commissaire LaPierre was waiting for them in the car park at Garçon! Valérie took the opportunity to hide the scrapbook while reaching for her bag, sliding it under Passepartout's bed as he approached. "Madame," the commissaire said with somber formality, before turning to Richard and offering a limp, outstretched hand, which he immediately withdrew after looking him up and down. It was true, Richard couldn't deny it, that being covered in avian fecal matter, and with a weeping, bloodshot, and now yellowing eye, wasn't the image of the suave Englishman he would have liked to portray—a long way from it, in fact. But having just glanced at a photo of a younger commissaire covered head to foot in what looked like motor oil and wearing a tutu while being fanned by a large-breasted woman wearing a false beard, the policeman was in no position to be making snap judgments.

"This way," LaPierre said, unable to take his eyes off Richard. "I will show you through to the kitchen."

The restaurant was dark except for the area near the large windows. A barman was taking notes on stock behind the bar, but he seemed to be the only employee. The rest were made up of police and forensic specialists. Guy Garçon sat at a table alone, looking quite distressed, wiping his finger up and down a chilled bottle of water. He nodded to them briefly as they entered the room, at first not appearing to recognize them and then smiling a weak smile as he did so.

The kitchen, as far as Richard could remember, had exactly the same setup as Grosmallard's. A central working island, washing areas along the wall, and to the rear were the walk-in storage cupboards and enormous chilling units. At the opposite end was the office, where more police were having a look around.

"Is Garçon a suspect?" Richard asked.

"Everyone is a suspect, monsieur," the commissaire replied grandly.

"Really, still? You're not getting very far, then, are you?"

The commissaire stopped and turned, again giving Richard's appearance a sneer of contempt. "He has an alibi for last night. He was dining with Karine Grosmallard."

So that was who Grosmallard was shouting at her about.

"But you can't determine the time of death yet because he's frozen."

"Yes, madame. Frozen solid." He marched them to the largest freezer, where over the double doors a digital display showed the inside temperature as minus twenty-one. He opened the door with an unnecessary flourish like a music hall magician.

The gleaming chrome shelves shone brightly through the icy mist, the stark light inside highlighting their pristine cleanliness. Once the mist had settled, a dark shadow loomed at the back. Poor Auguste Tatillon, a look of frozen self-importance on his face, his eyes looking down as they always seemed to be, was hanging by a butcher's hook between his shoulders, a long knife plunged into his neck. Either side of him hung veal carcasses, and the sneer on the murdered man's face gave the impression that he wasn't impressed at having to share top billing. He would also have been embarrassed about the state of his hair. In the struggle to get him hooked up, his toupee had become dislodged and was sticking up slightly. Now frozen and brittle, it looked like a tame Mohican, which at least matched his sneer, giving off the image of a ubiquitous London punk on a tourist postcard. *Poor man*, thought Richard. *What a way to go. Still, better than the actor Robert Morley's critic, Meredith Merridew in* Theatre of Blood, *who chokes on pies made up of his own poodles.* He sensibly chose to keep this observation to himself.

"Close the door, Henri," Valérie said softly. "There is no need for any more." He did as he was told and then looked from one to the other.

"Well?" He didn't look angry that they might be withholding information—far from it. He looked frustrated, yes, but Richard also had the impression that he was demanding their help. This had gone far enough, and what could they do about it?

"Richard." Valérie put her hand on his arm. "Would you give us a moment or two, please?"

That was fair enough, he thought. She was probably about to tell him all she knew about his involvement and how she knew he was as much a victim of blackmail as anyone further up the food chain. She could also ask him a few searching questions about tutus. He wandered around the kitchen. It was a marvel how they can look like they have never been used at all, such was the effort and necessary work that went into cleaning them. Anything could have gone on in here to get poor Auguste Tatillon into that freezer, yet it looked as clean as a show home.

He made his way slowly into the office, trying not to disturb the two officers seated at Garçon's desk. He wouldn't normally be so bold but he had a hankering to see the photos that would be on the younger chef's wall. He didn't know for sure if there would be any photos, but everything about this kitchen was a mirror image of Garçon's mentor's, so he felt certain there would be. He nodded a *bonjour* to the two plainclothes officers, and put his hands behind his back, falling into film acting shorthand for a higher-ranking officer. They ignored him anyway. There were dozens of framed photographs and certificates on the wall. Guy Garçon was rightly proud of his achievements at such a young age and it was noticeable that the celebrities and politicians were of a different generation to those who adorned Grosmallard's office. They were up-and-comers, whereas Sébastien's were the old establishment. Each collection reflected perfectly the chefs themselves. Apart from Olivia de Havilland, Grosmallard's gallery was all men, too, whereas Garçon attracted a different set. Richard recognized environmental campaigners, current musicians, sports stars. There were one or two politicians but they weren't establishment, at least not yet. The contrast was stark.

There were other memories, too, among the collection. An old picture of Guy and Sébastien in the kitchen, both looking younger. There was a woman in the picture, too, standing between them. Was that Angélique Grosmallard? He put his hand over his bad eye and tried to focus. It must have been Angélique; the resemblance to her daughter, Karine, rather than her son, Antonin, was startling. There was a date on the picture: *2009—Paris—photo by Léopold Royer*. That man again. The longest-serving senator in France, Valérie had said. He made a mental note of this information and turned to see if Valérie and the commissaire had finished. As he turned, he noticed another picture on the wall, hidden slightly by the open office door. It was the famous Grosmallard dessert, inevitably. That one piece of culinary genius seemed to haunt everyone involved. It had an inscription too: *To Guy*, it read. *You have the talent, use this wisely. AG.*

So Angélique had signed her husband's dessert. That seemed to underline Valérie's theory about Madame Grosmallard being the talent in the family. To get a better look, he covered his bad eye again, but it wasn't dated as far as he could tell. With his available hand, he tried to trace the words along the picture to help his focus, but his depth of perception was out by a country mile and he inadvertently knocked the frame. It wobbled and then, mortified, Richard watched it fall to the floor. The officers at the desk looked up at him, bored.

"Sorry," he said nervously and pointing to his eye. "I can't see what I'm doing." They went back to whatever they were doing and Richard bent down to pick up the frame. Thankfully it wasn't smashed, but the back had come away slightly at the bottom, where he noticed a piece of paper sticking out. He slid it out gently. It was a copy of the original recipe! And it was solely in Angélique's hand-writing. He reached in his pocket for his phone to take a picture of the paper, but his phone wasn't there. Cursing quietly and making sure that he wasn't being watched, he pocketed the piece of paper instead and put the picture frame back on the wall.

"Are you ready to go, Richard?" A very serious looking Valérie stuck her head around the door.

"Yes, yes," he replied hurriedly. "Ready when you are."

Back in the open air of the car park, an excited Richard asked how the conversation with the commissaire had gone.

"He is very worried, Richard; he is trying not to show it, but he is."

"Did you tell him that we know he's being blackmailed too?"

She stopped walking. "No. I don't think that would help right now. I told him that we think blackmail is behind all of this, but as far as he is concerned, only that we know his hands are tied."

"Well, I've seen the picture. Having his hands tied is what got him into this mess!"

"Richard, this is no time for jokes. This is very serious."

He cursed his flippancy. "I know," he said. "So what do you think of this, then?"

He gave Valérie the photocopy of the torn-out recipe and told her about the signed picture from Angélique and about the other picture taken by senator Léopold Royer.

"Oh, Richard," she said, her eyes aflame. "That is brilliant!" And she stood on tiptoe to kiss his cheek, her hair digging deep into his weeping, now black, eye and irritating it further.

31

"There's something I don't understand, though." Richard opened the door to the salon back at the *chambre d'hôte* and allowed Valérie to pass through before him. He followed her in and turned to close the door. "Why would Angélique send Garçon the recipe in the first place?" He turned back to face Valérie and nearly jumped out of his skin at the sight—at best half sight—that confronted him.

Alicia and Sly were standing by the breakfast bar, a look of nervous anticipation bordering on horror making their faces almost gargoyle-esque. Madame Tablier was leaning inevitably on a broom in the far corner, looking like an old shepherd who'd lost their flock, found someone else's, and was expecting carnage. The husband-and-husband team of Messieurs Fontaine were mixing cocktails by the open door to the *terrasse*, apparently oblivious to what was about to go down. And at the center of it all sat Clare, an open laptop in front of her, talking—in her phone voice like a 1950s television continuity announcer—about how important her husband is in local police liaisons. She noticed Richard out of the corner of her eye.

"Ah, here he is, Sir Michael, sorry, master. My husband, Richard Ainsworth. Only a few minutes late." She stood up so that he could take the seat at this ad-hoc interview panel. Only then did she notice his appearance and Richard thought she might buckle. "What the hell do you look like? What have you done to your eye? What's that smell?" Each question went up an octave in angry, whispered exasperation. "And I texted you!" she hissed.

Richard tapped his pockets to show he had no idea where his phone was, then sat down quietly and looked at the screen in front of him. Even given the distance that technology afforded, it was still a quite terrifying sight. Three men sat opposite him, all showing varying degrees of impatience at his late arrival.

"Ah, Dr. Ainsworth, I presume?" It was the man sitting in the middle who spoke first. He was an old man, with not unkind features, but he looked so tired. Even allowing for the screen resolution and color, his skin looked sallow, and his forehead had a number of liver spots on it. The eyes, like the rest of his features, drooped, giving him the appearance of an old bloodhound, but he had a full head of gray hair that curled upward like an ice cream. "It is my privilege to be master of this fine old college; I am Sir Michael Sterns." He paused. "Is there something wrong with your eye, Dr. Ainsworth?"

"I, erm, had an accident with the hens."

"Nothing too serious I hope."

"No, master."

"Good. Well, you'll be safe here. We have no hens. Plenty of wolves, no hens." He chuckled to himself. "On my left here is Peter Gwynne, emeritus professor of pedantics."

"Semantics." Peter Gwynne rolled his eyes. "Emeritus professor of semantics."

"Ha!" snorted the master. "Just my little joke. Works every time."

Emeritus professor of semantics Peter Gwynne didn't laugh. In fact, it looked like he hadn't laughed since the last century. Instead his bald head shone, while his long black beard remained static. It gave the impression of a man who had his head on upside down. "These hens, are they large? You look like you've been wrestling them."

Richard looked down at his shirt. The semantics professor had a point.

"Yes, anyway," the master interrupted. "Peter is leaving us to join Harvard." There wasn't a flicker of emotion either way in his voice. "Our loss is their gain and so on." It looked like it had been a struggle to get that the right way round. "Anyway, on my right, well, you two know each other..."

"Richard, how delightful to see you," Sir Stephen Roachford oozed across the internet.

The other two on the call looked steeped in academia; something about them looked cocooned, shielded, even, and comfortable. Sir Stephen Roachford gave off a different energy. Even his clothes looked different—shiny, almost. He looked like he'd gone to the college to sell them double glazing.

"Stephen, how are you?"

"Fine. You look like you've been in the wars, though. Is chicken wrestling a thing over there?"

"We make our own entertainment, Stephen."

"Glad to hear it."

"Sir Stephen has kindly offered to fund your chair, Dr. Ainsworth, and from what he tells us, we'll be very lucky to have you." He saw Stephen Roachford smirk. "This is really just a formality, a get-to-know-you call." The master seemed keen to get on with proceedings, which suited Richard just fine. In the background he could feel Clare relax. And in the camera view of himself he saw Valérie quietly sneak upstairs behind him, Passepartout inevitably in her arms. It was all a formality.

"I'd like to ask a question, if I may?" Peter Gwynne had a look on his face that suggested there was no such thing as a formality and he was determined to prove it. Richard saw the master roll his eyes. Stephen Roachford stuck with his fixed smirk.

"If you must," the master said impatiently.

Peter Gwynne leaned in to the computer camera. He was now so close he looked like he was being seen through a hotel door peephole, his face rounded and aggressive. "In the Max Horkheimer and Theodor Adorno work *The Dialectic of Enlightenment*, the writers pursue the theory that advanced capitalism renders all art as a 'culture industry.' This is truer for cinema than any other media artifact, I would say. So filmgoers are merely consumers, a captive crowd for crass commercialization."

He stopped there and Richard was damned if he knew what the hell to do with that. Was it even a question? Should he take the statement on face value and shout an enthusiastic *yes*, or go with his inner voice and just shout, *Oh, belt up, you old bore. It's a film, it's escapism. Let me just enjoy it!*

"Would you agree or disagree?" The man was relentless.

He was about to try to answer when Valérie once again appeared in the view behind. His bad eye meant that she was slightly out of focus, but the men on the screen were clearly rapt, their eyes bulging. The master even put on his glasses, while the emeritus professor tilted his head like a confused dog. Stephen Roachford's smirk became a death mask as he saw his hard-fought battle to be a knight of the realm and a man of society hanging by a thread. Madame Tablier dropped her broom, Messieurs Fontaine settled in for a show, while Alicia cried, "Oh, Daddy!" and Clare let out a shriek of horror. Richard turned around slowly, holding his hand over the black eye.

Valérie was standing in direct view of the camera, holding up with one hand, and against her white blouse, a red-lace basque of quite demonic detail. Its bra elements were like steel cones, its leather straps beneath like expensive cat collars. She turned it sideways, nearly breaking Sly's jaw, which was somewhere beneath his belt line. In the other hand she held a bullwhip, which had the biggest handle he had ever seen, and then as his eye focused he realized it wasn't a handle at all and he turned quickly back to Clare's laptop, filling as much of the camera as he could. She wasn't done yet, though. In a voice so coquettish it would have made early 1960s Brigitte Bardot sound like a foghorn, she said, "Oh, Reeshar, I zink I peeked oop ze wrong bag at Gennie's 'ouse."

There was, inevitably, a silence so uncomfortable it felt like torture and which lasted nearly a whole minute. Eventually, Richard had a go at breaking it. "Well, professor, to return to your question about 'the industry of culture' and the aesthetics of commercial art."

"Yes, I rather think we've moved on, Dr. Ainsworth; we've all had as much enlightenment as we can take." The master couldn't hide the delight that his afternoon had been brightened up enormously by the proceedings.

"Maybe I am mistaken," Valérie carried on in the background. "I weel try it on. Per'aps it was a present, Reeshar."

"If I could just interrupt at this point, master." Clare leaned in to the camera, practically shoving Richard off his chair. "Currently my husband runs a hotel in France and I think while he was acting in his official role as liaison with the police, they have been having a party." She moved aside, dragging Richard back into view.

"Is that the case, Dr. Ainsworth?" Peter Gwynne asked with heavy skepticism.

"Well..."

"They just don't want him to leave." Clare shot into view again. "They're all terribly upset."

The master was chuckling; the other two were not. "I'm afraid my colleague will want his question answered," he said jovially.

"Well, I guess it is." Richard smiled weakly. "It's like the film *It's Great to Be Young!*, where a schoolteacher, music teacher in, er, in this case, is so popular that when he gets another job, his pupils rebel to undermine the, er, promotion."

"Richard!" Clare had had enough.

"In fact, a very similar idea was used in *Carry on Teacher*, just a couple of years later." He paused for effect. "Interestingly, the ring-leader of the children was the same in each film. Richard O'Sullivan." He smiled like an exhausted MP who's spent the night filibustering. "Yes. Richard O'Sullivan."

"Richard!"

"Monsieur Richard Ainsworth?"

"Yes?" Richard said weakly, turning to his right. The three

interviewees instinctively turned to their left, wondering who the other voice belonged to.

"Monsieur Richard Ainsworth," repeated Commissaire LaPierre. "I arrest you for the murder of Auguste Tatillon!"

Richard looked back at the screen apologetically, where the three men were waiting on tenterhooks. Then he looked wearily up at LaPierre. "Really? But on what grounds?"

"Is this your cell phone, monsieur?"

"Yes. Looks like it."

"It was found near the dead body this morning."

"But I may have dropped it this morning!"

"Or you came back to retrieve it!" He held up a damning finger.

"Is there anything else?" Richard felt so tired all of a sudden.

"Yes, monsieur! Excuse me, messieurs." He nodded as he appeared on camera. "Where were you last night? Around midnight?"

"Er, well. Here!" he shouted. "I was here chatting to my daughter. Wasn't I, Alicia? We were here, weren't we?"

Alicia stepped forward. "No, Daddy." She winked at him and stepped back.

"What?"

"You 'ave no other h'alibi?" Richard wondered why the commissaire was speaking in English.

"No. After that I went to bed."

"Alone, monsieur?"

"Yes!"

Clare sighed in relief, but the men on the screen looked immensely disappointed.

"Wait! No, oh never mind."

"You are better off saying now, monsieur!"

"I was with Passepartout!" Richard was in a state of heavy panic.

"Is that your valet?" the master asked, apparently impressed.

"No, master. He's a small Chihuahua."

Nobody knew quite what to say to that. Valérie chose that moment to re-emerge. She was dressed normally, but still brandishing the bullwhip, which caused Madame Tablier to react like a nervous sentry, waving her broom in retaliation.

"A Chihuahua, eh?" the master said. "We had a chap here once." He shook his head. "Nasty business."

"Monsieur, I must insist you accompany me to ze police station." LaPierre was enjoying himself.

"I must say it's a shame." The master was talking to his colleagues now. "I rather liked him; bit rich for our blood, though, I fancy. Sherry, anyone?"

LaPierre helped Richard to stand, holding his arm. Richard himself—black eye, covered in chicken poo, his forehead laden with sweat, his reputation concerning didactics, wives, and small dogs ruined—had little to add.

"Just one thing, commissaire." His voice was like that of a lost child. "Could I have a cell to myself, please? I could really do with a rest."

He dared not catch Clare's eye as he was marched out.

32

It was something of a stark, uncomfortable realization for an incarcerated Richard that the breakfast he served daily in what he regarded as his high-end B&B was of substantially lower quality and offered less choice than the breakfast served in the cells of the local police station. He was tempted, if he was ever released, to leave a more than favorable review for the place on Tripadvisor. The coffee was excellent and the right side of boiling, and the bread and croissants were still warm, presumably having been rushed over from Jeanine's *boulangerie*. There was a choice of freshly squeezed juices, and he'd even been offered an omelette, something he would never do at his place. Either the criminal classes were a demanding clientele or, as René DuPont had said, the arrival of two Michelin-starred chefs into Saint-Sauver had forced everyone to up their game.

He had slept well, as well as he had done for days, after being offered a portable DVD player by a young policeman and a choice of films. He had chosen the French classic *Monsieur Hulot's Holiday*, the story of a bungling innocent getting into scrapes over which he had no control chiming with his mood. All in all, he had to admit he was quite content to book himself in for a while. There was no bail offered in France, he'd checked that, and no longer any death penalty either, so if this was the standard of incarceration, he was more than happy to take the rap.

Alas, it wasn't Richard's day.

"Monsieur Ainsworth, good morning." The commissaire opened the door to the cell with a weary look on his face and an even wearier malaise in his voice. "I hope you slept well." He looked around the cell, tutting at what he clearly regarded as opulence. "This room is bigger than my own in the police apartment block."

"I slept very well, thank you. And the breakfast was excellent."

The commissaire looked at him with an ennui bordering on disdain.

"I am so pleased," he said, though Richard could tell that he didn't mean it.

"Is there a lunch menu?" It wasn't necessarily in Richard's character to be cheeky to high office, but he felt he should try to lighten the mood. It didn't work.

"For you, no. You are being released."

"Oh, really?" It was Richard's turn to feel the weight of the world.

"Yes."

"Why?"

"Because you have done nothing wrong, monsieur. That would be why." The commissaire was starting to get irritated. "You are only here because I was doing my former wife a favor." Richard had guessed as much.

Without any fanfare, then, he was thrust into the blinding light of the great outdoors. His eye was in much better shape but he had trouble seeing clearly at first in the bright sunshine. As his eyes adjusted, he could make out four figures, and it quickly became clear who they were. Alicia and Sly, Clare, and Valérie. He felt like turning around and begging to be locked back up in the relative safety of police incarceration.

"Daddy!" Alicia cried, and ran forward to hug him.

"You look well, Dick." Sly seemed impressed by Richard's fortitude.

Clare stepped forward and brushed some imaginary dust off his collar. "I've brought you a fresh shirt," she whispered, managing to make it sound like a threat. "And I've brought your girlfriend too."

"She's not..."

"Valérie's car wouldn't start, so we towed it to the garage this morning. Didn't we, Valérie?" Valérie didn't respond. "She's very resourceful, isn't she? I wouldn't have known where to start. You can both easily walk there from here."

"OK, thanks." Richard really didn't know what to say.

"We are going to the airport." Clare had raised her voice, as if it were a protest against deportation. "But, Richard..." She leaned in close again. "This isn't over. You still need to buy me out. And," she added menacingly, "that's assuming I'm willing to sell." She turned smartly on her heel and went back to the rental car. Sly waved his goodbye and got in after her, leaving Alicia to hug Richard once more and tell him she loved him and that she would ring soon.

They left, leaving Richard and Valérie looking at each other, a distance of five meters or so between them.

"There goes Clare." Richard tried to sound upbeat about the situation, but it all felt a bit final.

Valérie smiled apologetically. "Did you sleep well?"

"Ha!" Richard chuckled. "That's the kind of thing I normally ask. Very well, thank you. Though I must say, your methods are a little brutal. Was the black eye planned as well, or was that just a fortunate accident?"

"Planned."

"Yes. Well, like I say, brutal."

"But effective." They began walking the short distance toward the garage to pick her car up, Passepartout on a short lead in front of them.

"I can't deny that! I imagine that not only will I not be leading a course at Cambridge University on film aesthetics, there's probably a court order banning me from the city borders."

"You would have hated it anyway."

And he nodded in reply.

The car was waiting for them when they arrived and the mechanic, dressed exactly as he had been before, overalls stripped to the waist, was inevitably wiping his hands on an oily rag. He took Richard aside.

"You learn quick," he said. "The VT leads in the distributor were unplugged."

Richard looked over at Valérie as she placed Passepartout carefully on the back seat. She looked back at him, and though she couldn't have overheard the mechanic, she guessed what was being said; she shrugged her shoulders and smiled knowingly. Every time Richard felt he couldn't lose any more of his grip on the situation, he did so. He had absolutely no idea what was going on.

"What's going on?" he asked a few moments later as they drove away.

"With the car?" she replied innocently. "I disconnected the VT leads from the distributor cap."

"But why? I don't get it."

"Why not? Sometimes it is good to test people."

Richard thought about this. "Nope," he said. "I still don't get it."

She giggled. "You didn't believe that my car had broken down before, did you?"

"Well..."

"You didn't. Well, it did. It's an old car, these things happen." Richard felt like an old car. "But today I did it myself. I wanted to see if your wife would help me out. She did. I think she's a good woman, really. Not for you maybe, too ambitious. But she has a good heart, and your daughter was excellent yesterday too."

He sighed. "Can I have my phone back, please?"

"It's in my bag."

He reached in and found his phone. That it was underneath a tiny handgun neither surprised him nor made him pause. It was now, it seemed, just a fact of his daily life. "Right, then." He breathed out heavily. "But what is going on?"

Valérie wrinkled her forehead. "I just told you."

"No. What is *going on*? I mean with all this." He spread his arms wide to indicate that his question could very well be an existential one concerning the meaning of life, a general inquiry, or specifically about three murders in a small French town.

"Ah," she replied, "that." She made it sound almost mundane, like a stain on a coffee table.

"Yes, that!" Richard was beginning to get exasperated. "Are we assuming that Sébastien Grosmallard killed Ménard, Tatillon, and his own son, and that we can do absolutely nothing about it?" Valérie didn't say anything. "It's not right."

"I agree, Richard." Though she sounded noncommittal.

"Couldn't you, erm, couldn't you..."

She turned toward him sharply. "No, I could not! What *do* you think I am?"

"Well, I saw the gun in your bag and..."

"That's for self-defense." There was a hint of self-righteousness in her voice.

They carried on in silence for a moment.

"Ha!" Richard snorted. "I couldn't afford to hire you anyway. I can't even afford to buy Clare out of the business!" He looked out of the car window and started whining. "How's it going, Richard? Well, I'm in my mid-fifties, I've just been released from prison, I have chicken poo on my shirt, and I can't even afford to get a divorce!"

"Have you finished?" Valérie asked.

He sighed again. "Yes, sorry. It is very annoying, though."

"The divorce?"

"Well, that as well. No, I meant Grosmallard. A nasty piece of work, highly likely a murderer, but, as he said himself, 'untouchable.' Hang on, though, we've got the stuff everyone's frightened of. The scrapbook we found at Tatillon's: Why don't we try a little blackmail of our own and get Grosmallard arrested?"

She thought about this for a second. "I don't think it would make a difference, Richard."

"Why not, though?" He was genuinely put out.

"Because the people protecting Sébastien Grosmallard don't want any publicity or connection with this at all. What if they were to arrest him? And then he went to trial? Do you think he would do that quietly? He would tell the world who he was blackmailing and why; he is that arrogant, I think. And people would believe him, probably, and then ask why he wasn't arrested sooner but was actually free to kill again. No, it won't do."

Richard slumped in the car seat. "I'm not even sure I know why he's killed anyone. Fabrice because he mucked up the cheese order for the dessert, Antonin because he mucked up the dessert, and Tatillon because he didn't like the dessert? It all seems a bit much for a fancy pudding, even in France. I mean, we're not even sure he created the bloody dessert in the first place. That was Angélique, who killed herself having torn the recipe from his book and sent it to Garçon, who I don't think even knew he had it!"

He opened his wallet and pulled out the recipe.

"Well, there's no butter. It just seems like a bog-standard set of ingredients to me, although there are loads of them. So many different flavors and pinpoint-accurate measurements. You never really think that when you're eating, do you? Maybe there's a secret ingredient that she didn't write down?"

Valérie thought about this for a moment. "You might be right, Richard. Anyway, Sébastien Grosmallard is incapable of recreating that dessert, for whatever reason, and it seems to have driven him mad that he can't."

Richard felt deflated. "There must be something we can do. I mean, *everyone's* protecting him. Right from on high through to the police, probably even the wife of one of his victims!"

"Do you mean Elisabeth?"

"Yes. I don't get her. Her husband is murdered, her son—if he was her son—or lover goes the same way, and she doesn't kick up a fuss. Why not? She even sneaks around his place at night."

"Maybe they needed to talk about Antonin, away from the glare."

"Maybe." Richard wasn't convinced.

"Maybe she didn't like her husband?"

"A cheap divorce, you mean? No. She was there at this commune thing, or camp, or whatever it was—they all were. So she knows everyone. Something else must have gone on there that nobody wants to talk about and I think she's frightened."

"Frightened of what?" It was Valérie's turn to sound skeptical.

"I don't know. Whatever went on there. I don't have any details. I'm working on it."

Valérie parked the car outside the *boulangerie.*

"Can you go in?" he asked. "I don't think Jeanine could stand to see the earl of Grantham covered in hen excrement."

She left him mulling over his thoughts but was back quickly with a baguette.

Richard carried on. "You know, I even thought yesterday that, well, what if Elisabeth Ménard and Angélique Royer were sisters?"

"Sisters?" Valérie looked decidedly skeptical about the suggestion.

"Yes. That they were sisters and they shared everything. Including Grosmallard. That's why she's protecting him: she loves him. He might even be Hugo's father too. Poor Fabrice had a heart condition, sometimes that makes men...well, you know, they can't...they can't function in the trouser department."

"Function in the trouser department?" She looked at him blankly.

"Yes, you know! That he fired blanks."

"What?"

Richard sighed. "That he couldn't have children!"

"Why didn't you just say that?"

"I don't know!" he said very deliberately.

"So Hugo would be Sébastien's son as well."

"Yes. They shared everything. Like sisters."

She thought this over while putting the key in the ignition. "What gave you this idea, Richard?" she asked, offering him some encouragement.

"Well, it was Joan Crawford." He said it as if it were the most obvious thing in the world.

"Your hen?"

"Yes. While you were talking to Clare yesterday, I thought about what you'd said about men, and then the sisterhood and all that. Joan Crawford jumped onto my shoulder and I thought about her and Bette Davis..."

"Bette Davis is a hen?"

"No. The actress. She and Joan Crawford, the actress, not the hen, were in a film together, *What Ever Happened to Baby Jane?*, 1962, Warner Brothers."

"Richard."

"Sorry. Anyway, they played sisters but they hated each other. Bette Davis was especially evil, which is interesting because she wasn't evil in *Hush... Hush, Sweet Charlotte*. Joan Crawford was going to be the evil one in *Hush...Hush, Sweet Charlotte*." Richard noticed the look of deep confusion on Valérie's face and began to lose faith in himself as a result. "Anyway, she pulled out. Olivia de Havilland played the role instead."

"And?"

"And I can't remember. I think I got a bit carried away by Bette Davis swapping roles."

Valérie smiled at him and started the car. "You have slept well, haven't you, Richard?"

33

Richard pushed the fourth and final drawing pin in as far it would go, then stood back to admire his handiwork.

"It doesn't look straight, Richard," Valérie said adamantly, standing even further back.

"It's a printed poster on the town hall noticeboard, not a Da Vinci in the bloody Louvre."

"Yes, but if a job is worth doing..."

"I think madame is correct, Richard," Noel Mabit oozed from a safe distance.

"Maybe you didn't print them straight, Noel!"

The truth was that Richard was not on top form. He had barely seen Valérie since their chat about Bette Davis, Sébastien Grosmallard, Joan Crawford, and firing blanks. Thirty-six hours later, she had re-emerged with "a plan." That plan was now in the early stages of operation, and although ostensibly on the organizing and execution committee, he was none the wiser. And frankly he objected to Noel Mabit apparently being kept informed before he was, in his role as keyholder for the town hall photocopier.

Richard stood back and looked at his handiwork.

Food Festival!
Can you beat the Michelin stars?
Enter the Saint-Sauver Dessert Competition
Saturday 16h45, Salle Polyvalente Victor Hugo

He shook his head. "I think it's a terrible idea," he said emphatically.

"Ooh, can I have a go?" Jeanine had appeared at his side, a little closer than was necessary.

Richard tutted. "Shouldn't you be in the *boulangerie*?" he asked in exasperation. "It's market day, I thought you'd be run off your feet."

"I saw you and wondered what you were up to."

"Jeanine, could you put one of these up in the *boulangerie*, please?" Valérie handed her an A3-sized poster. "And of course, you should enter. We need to show these men a thing or two!"

Jeanine giggled as she took the poster. "That, Valérie, is a very good idea!"

Richard had no idea when first-name terms had been adopted, but Valérie was, all of a sudden, "in society," which was swift work on her part, especially being that most disliked creature, a Parisian in rural France.

"Valérie?" Not Mabit too, surely? "Could I take one for the tourist office, please?"

"Yes, Monsieur Mabit, there you go." This short exchange bucked Richard up immensely, and he smiled as a wounded Mabit took his poster sullenly.

"You know, by rights you should have checked with the committee before putting any of these things up."

"Who is on the committee?" Valérie asked, showing remarkable patience.

"I am." Mabit mumbled his reply.

"Well, Noel." Valérie spoke as if to a naughty five-year-old. "Can I put my posters up?"

He looked at the ground. "Yes, Valérie."

"Thank you. Now, Richard. Where shall we put our next one?"

Richard puffed out his cheeks. "René's place, I suppose."

"Yes, but we'll do that last otherwise I'll never get you out again."

It was a fair point. "What about the *salle polyvalente* itself, then?"

They walked the short distance to where, on Saturday evening, the action would take place. Richard still couldn't work out the thinking behind the scheme, though, and there must be some thinking rather than just Valérie's competitive muscle needing to be flexed.

"You are struggling with this, aren't you, Richard?" she asked as they walked.

He wasn't surprised that she knew what he was thinking; he'd come to expect it.

"Yes, yes, I am. I don't know what the aim of the exercise is. How will this help us nail Grosmallard in a way that can't be ignored by the authorities? I don't get it."

"It's very simple: in my experience of men"—Richard wisely chose not to comment—"they are above all childishly competitive. As great chefs, even more so."

He waited for some further explanation, which didn't appear. "No, I'm still lost, I'm afraid."

"Richard. If there were a competition on film knowledge and you lost because a competitor cheated..."

"IMDB'd it, you mean?"

"Yes, how would you feel?"

"I'd be bloody furious."

"Precisely."

"But as far as I can tell Grosmallard is always bloody furious—what will be different about this time?" He unraveled a poster and started to attach Blu-Tack to the corners.

"Ah, leave that to me, but the intention is to confront him with his crimes..."

"Via dessert and patisserie?" Richard was skeptical.

"Yes, Richard, via dessert and patisserie, so that he will lose—how do you say in English?—it, he will lose it."

"Ah, send him over the edge, you mean? Right." He attached the poster to the glass door. "Well, I don't know, but it's all we have." They turned and walked back toward the town center. "How can you be sure that he'll even enter the competition, though?"

"As I said, the childish competitive instinct. He'll enter because Guy Garçon has entered."

"And how can you be sure that Guy Garçon will enter?"

"Because I'll tell him that Sébastien Grosmallard has entered."

Richard chewed this over. "It's a very dangerous game you're playing, Valérie."

She stopped and turned to face him. "*We're* playing, Richard, it's a dangerous game *we're* playing. We are a team now."

He had absolutely no idea what to make of this statement, but his normal English reticence and reserved caution were at that moment internally being torn into tiny pieces and scattered on the ground. He hadn't felt this important in years. And, confidence-boosting aside, it was also quite scary.

"What will you cook, then?" he asked.

"Why me?" she snapped, her "team" heroics forgotten. "Because I'm a woman?"

He started to stutter in reply, "N-no, I-I didn't for...no."

She broke out into a huge smile. "I am joking, Richard." He nearly buckled. "I do not know yet. You? A spotted dick." The way she pronounced "a spotted dick" could probably have made her a fortune in cell phone notification downloads, and he nearly buckled again.

"I don't think so," he said, recovering some poise. "I'd never hear the end of it from Martin if I did so. Same with any kind of tart, arctic roll, cobbler, or Eve's pudding."

Valérie winced. "They all sound so heavy."

"Yes, they are. I might go for an Eton mess, or bread-and-butter pudding. Or a flies' graveyard." She looked pained by the list. "And you? You know, assuming that you want to, you don't have to of course, just because, you know?"

She smiled at him. "I'll need to borrow Angélique's recipe from you, please."

"Don't let anyone tell you you're not ambitious!"

They'd reached the Café des Tasses Cassées, which was heaving as usual on market day, and René was growling his way through customer service outside on the *terrasse.*

"René, can we put a poster up in the window, please?" Valérie asked as if they'd known each other for years.

"Yeah, go ahead, Val. Rosé, Richard?"

Richard sat down at a recently vacated table. It was remarkable just how quickly Valérie had fitted into town life. She hadn't even bought a house yet, if that was even still her intention. He watched her put the poster up on the inside of the main window. She may be settling into rural French life, he thought, but the excitement of the chase with Grosmallard was certainly the thing that fired her up at her core. There was a quite serious element of danger if Grosmallard suspected he was being hunted, but if anything, she seemed to thrive on it. When all this had died down, then, and the bucolic pace of life returned, would she still be so happy to be here? Sadly, he couldn't see it. *But*, he told himself in a rare effort to be positive, *enjoy the ride while it lasts, for once.*

René placed a glass of rosé in front of him and left a small bottle of Perrier for Valérie, who appeared behind him.

"I take it you'll be entering the competition on Saturday, René?"

"Eh? What competition?" He looked at the poster in the window, and nodded before turning back to the two of them. "That's a dangerous game, if you ask me," he said quietly. "These highly strung chef types can go right off the rails if they're pushed, you know?" Valérie dismissed his concerns with a wave of her hand. "But yes, I'm in."

"What will you cook, René?" Richard asked, genuinely fascinated as to what this bull of a man had in mind.

"Well, my tarte tatin was famous in A block at La Santé." He seemed almost wistful at the memory.

"La Santé?" Richard asked.

"It's a large prison in Paris," Valérie said.

"It sounds like a health retreat. Hang on, you could cook your own meals?"

"Well, sometimes, yes. We had to. If we were rioting and they shut the block off, you still had to eat."

It made perfect sense. "So you'll be going with tarte tatin, then?"

"Maybe. Or I might go with a lemon-berry savarin. I'll have a think."

"Monsieur!" A customer a few tables away was trying to get his attention.

"In a minute, I'm thinking! Bloody customers." And he rolled off menacingly.

Richard took a sip of his wine while Valérie poured some Perrier for Passepartout. It struck Richard that he barely noticed Passepartout these days. The little dog was so much a part of Valérie as to be almost inseparable from her. He'd even started to tolerate Richard, though still kept a jaundiced eye on him from time to time, obviously.

They sat in silence for a while. Valérie had her head tilted up toward the sun, while Richard soaked up the pure Frenchness of the scene. The sun shone, glasses clinked, there were cries of recognition as old couples bumped into other old couples and went through a loud greeting ceremony as if they hadn't seen each other for years, when the truth was that they had met at exactly the same spot and time just a week earlier. The comfort that Richard found in a world that rarely changed was one of the reasons why he loved the place and had moved here.

"Another one, Richard?"

And that was another reason. He closed his eyes too, soaking it all up.

"Richard, it is so peaceful here."

"It is," he sighed happily. "Apart from murder, wife-swapping, destroyed culinary reputations, and corruption."

"Well, you can't have it all," she replied dreamily.

"Madame, monsieur?" In their reverie they had completely failed to notice Karine Grosmallard standing nervously at their table. "Can I talk with you, please?"

"Yes, of course," Valérie said, sitting up straight. "Richard, find a chair for Karine, would you? I can call you Karine?"

"Yes, madame."

"Then you must call me Valérie. And, of course, this is Richard."

Richard appeared at that moment with a chair, which he placed discreetly behind Karine. "Can I order you something?" he asked as he sat back down.

"No, no thank you." She was obviously unsettled by something. She played with the locket on her necklace, a prayer box locket if Richard wasn't mistaken, which she handled as if it gave her strength. She looked younger close up than he'd thought she was. Tired, drained even, having had to grow up too quickly, perhaps. The poor girl couldn't have it easy working for her father, but as she herself had said, she was determined to put him back at the top where he belonged. What she didn't know was that her table companions were trying to put her father where they thought he belonged: in prison.

"What's up, my dear?" Valérie had a marvelous gift for sounding like a favorite aunt at times.

"I have seen your posters, madame…"

"Valérie."

"Valérie. I have seen your posters and I am worried for my father. I don't think he will want to do it."

"Oh, I see." Valérie shot Richard a quick glance, which he interpreted as his cue to come in.

"That is a shame," he said, toying with his glass. "And totally understandable, obviously." He paused. "Of course, it does rather play into Monsieur Garçon's hands..." He saw Valérie suppress a smile.

"Monsieur Garçon has entered the competition?" She looked surprised.

"Well, it was rather his idea if you remember?" It wasn't, but it was worth stretching the point. "I felt at the time it was more like the calling of a duel. You know, whisks at dawn, that kind of thing."

Valérie now looked at him as if to say, "Don't overdo it."

"I would have thought, Karine, that your father would relish the idea. It is a chance for him to recreate his famous *parfait de fromage de chèvre de Grosmallard.*" She said it with a flourish, hopefully tempting the mousey Karine into seeing the possibilities.

"That is if everything goes well, Valérie. If it does not..." She left the sentence hanging, allowing them to draw their own conclusions.

"It could push him over the edge?" Richard said it as gently as he could, and Karine didn't reply; she just nodded.

"Well," Valérie said, sounding suddenly quite breezy. "I'm sure the judge of the competition wouldn't allow that!"

This was news to Richard. He hadn't actually given any thought as to who might be the judge, though he'd half expected Noel Mabit to wheedle his way onto any panel.

"Who is judging, madame?" Karine asked nervously.

"Yes, who is judging?" Richard couldn't help himself.

34

In certain parts of the Loire Valley, there are rules about punctuality. In the Touraine, for instance, and certainly in Tours itself,
it's almost rude to be on time. Nobody is on time; if you're on
time then you're up to something and probably trying to catch the
party you are meeting up to something too. Of course, Louis XVIII
regarded punctuality as the "politeness of kings," but he was post–
French Revolution and a constitutional monarch; it was probably
some career-politician's idea and it didn't catch on. Fifteen minutes
late is the acceptable norm for arrival time in the Loire Valley, and
the same rule, give or take a few minutes, had been applied in the
Follet Valley since as long as anyone could remember. The poster
for the dessert competition said that it would start at 16.45, which
is just about when people would drift in. Everyone except Richard
and Valérie, that is.

Richard had worked out that everyone else applied the fifteen-
minute rule, so that in this instance proceedings could begin at five,
and Valérie had her own fifteen-minute rule on top of that so that
she could make the grand entrance and be the center of attention.

It also meant that she would have complete control of the room, which, especially on this occasion, she was determined to have so that her plan—of which Richard still knew very little—could be carried out effectively. Everyone gave in their desserts, carried in anonymous white boxes as per the rules, to staff at the door, who took them downstairs to the fridges, and then they entered the main room itself. Everyone was there, and the atmosphere was tense. The atmosphere would have been tense anyway; this was a cookery competition, which, thanks to television, have become absurdly competitive. It was also a cooking competition in France, so there was national pride at stake. It was a cookery competition that pitted talented, and not so talented, amateurs against the greats of French cuisine. Michelin stars were involved, and it was a cookery competition whose principal aim—although not everyone was aware of this yet—was to publicly unmask a killer. Saint-Sauver had rarely seen the like.

Noel Mabit fussed around like a housefly banging up against a window, his anxiety double its usual level because he knew he wasn't in control. His wife was there too, sitting next to Madame Tablier, who held a large feather duster. They watched from chairs in the corner, contempt for the man chiseled on their faces. Martin and Gennie were chatting happily with Jeanine. Commissaire LaPierre stood by the door looking like a nightclub bouncer; he also appeared stressed, knowing that this was mainly in the hands of Valérie and he had no idea which way it would go. Richard's guests, the Fontaines, were by the large windows, in beautiful matching cream suits, like guests at a wedding. Guy Garçon and René DuPont stood by a table at the back. Garçon had that boyish, relaxed smile that television loved so much, whereas René wore the kind of stony-faced scowl that made him the talk of A block and the scourge of customer service. Elisabeth and Hugo Ménard were on one side of the room, Elisabeth sitting down while Hugo had his hand stiffly on her shoulder, and on the other side, as far away as possible as though to communicate to the room that they had all never actually known each other, were Karine and Sébastien Grosmallard. She leaned against the window, looking out while he paced up and down, a monstrous energy about him like a dam about to burst. Even the Liebowitz brothers were there, though Richard couldn't understand why, wearing their usual garish shirts and bickering like the Three Stooges.

Richard felt a surge of excitement. He may not have had a clue what Valérie really had in mind, but she knew how to pull in a crowd, that was for sure. Noel Mabit, now on the stage, banged his gavel unnecessarily to get everyone's attention. It was unnecessary because there was so much tension in the room that nobody was making enough noise to be talked over, but he did it all the same, then Valérie appeared at his side, which surprised Richard, as he hadn't noticed her slip away.

"Ladies and gentlemen, er, thank you for coming. Quite the turn-out. Erm, well, this was all Valérie's, Madame d'Orçay's idea, so I'll let madame explain the rules."

Valérie stepped forward, her floral-print summer dress swishing just above her knees as she did so, and Mabit bowed absurdly into the background.

"Thank you all so much for coming!" Valérie gushed, a warm smile on her face. "I know we all take these things terribly seriously, but let's remember it *is* just a bit of fun. So please keep smiling. There is a photographer from the press who will be milling around; we shall put Saint-Sauver firmly on France's culinary map!" She nodded to the corner of the stage where smartly dressed waiting staff had appeared, each holding a tray covered with a silver dome cloche. There were eleven in total and they brought them solemnly forward, placing them on chilled trays on a long trestle table just below the stage. "Each dessert will be tasted anonymously—that is, no one knows who has made what. At the end our judge will decide the winner." Richard still had no idea who the judge would be. Valérie had remained very coy about that.

"Mabit's not the judge, is he?" René shouted from the back. "He still owes me for an unpaid bar bill!"

The weak laughter died down. "No, monsieur." Valérie smiled. "Ladies and gentlemen, please welcome your judge for the first ever Saint-Sauver Prix des Desserts, senator Léopold Royer!"

Karine gasped and Sébastien sat down on the nearest chair, stunned. Elisabeth looked mortified as well, and the rest of the room just stared at each other, it dawning on some of them that this was way more than a mere cookery competition.

"Hang on!" It was René again. "Much as I have great respect for high authority, he's Sébastien Grosmallard's father-in-law. That's hardly fair, is it?"

Richard turned back to the stage rather than catch René's eye. He acknowledged that the man had a point in terms of strict adherence to the rules of justice, but having eaten many times at his restaurant, he really couldn't see it having a great deal of impact on where he finished.

"Well, it's not, is it?" René continued, starting a murmur in the room.

Grosmallard stood up. "You have absolutely nothing to fear, monsieur," he said dramatically, "the man hates my guts. Isn't that right, Papi?" He gave the last word as much sarcasm as possible.

Senator Royer had walked slowly to the front of the stage during all this, and now stood next to Valérie. They had the air of a royal couple, the aged king and his younger consort. He wore an immaculate blue suit, with an impeccable tie that matched perfectly. In fact, it almost matched the blue hue of his thin, combed-back hair as well, the kind of violet gray hair that old men have. Tall and with an aristocratic bearing, he was slightly stooped at the shoulders, his neck a little further forward than looked comfortable. He looked like a wetland bird, dipping for water. He held his hands up, a politician's appeal for calm, though there was absolutely no need.

"It is a pleasure to be asked here this evening," he said. "And to put your mind at ease, monsieur, I can guarantee complete impartiality. I think my record on fair play speaks for itself." Nobody believed a word of that, and if it was self-deprecation, it was lost behind what Richard thought were cold and hollow eyes. "And anyway, all the dishes will be blind tasted." There was silence as the crowd tensed up again, impatient for the thing to get underway, and Mabit filled the silence by leading a round of applause as the senator gingerly made his way off the stage.

Valérie came and stood next to Richard. She seemed very calm. "Everything is going to plan," she whispered.

"I wouldn't know," he replied a trifle tartly.

"Oh, Richard." She smiled. "Why not ask the staff to start serving the wine?"

He did as he was asked and made sure that everyone had a glass before the competition started, then they all expectantly crowded around the first cloche. The young waitress raised the dome smartly, revealing a magnificent sculpture of the nearby Moulin de Follet made entirely of macarons, its bright, vivid colors making it look like a three-dimensional watercolour.

"Well now," Senator Royer said, "as far as I'm concerned, this competition is over! My weakness is the humble macaron."

What's humble about a macaron? Richard wondered. There's nothing humble about a macaron. Senator Royer had a touch of the Marie Antoinette about him, besides which, he didn't fancy his chances if Valérie's carefully laid plans were scuppered just because Royer had a hankering for meringue-style sandwich cookies.

"It tastes sublime," he continued, "and looks magnificent as well."

Everyone turned to Jeanine, knowing her macarons were famous in the area, and she blushed, happy with her work.

The second cloche came off and it was fair to say that, early days though it was, Jeanine was still out in front. A white ramekin dish held what everyone assumed to have been a soufflé. Unfortunately, it had punctured and reminded Richard more of a window cleaner's chamois leather cloth instead: wrinkled, muddy brown, utterly deflated. Not unlike Mabit himself, whose cry of anguish figured him as the guilty party.

"I told him to make a tarte tatin," said his wife in the corner, finding hearty agreement from Madame Tablier.

"Number three?" said the senator, eager to move on.

It was perfectly obvious, certainly to Richard, who knew him well, that the creative force behind number three was Martin Thompson. It was the inevitable spotted dick, but shaped roughly like a Christmas log. If, that is, the aforementioned Christmas log had been made by a pervert for a bakery at the rougher end of the red-light district in Pigalle. Royer, seasoned politician that he was, knew full well the pitfalls of a photo with that kind of thing and moved on smartly. Richard caught Martin's eye.

"I got carried away, old man, what can I say?"

The next two desserts were safer territory, but neither challenged Jeanine's lead. There was a lemon-berry savarin, which René had said he was going to make, and a clafoutis that the Fontaines had brought. Richard knew it was the Fontaines because they had asked to use the kitchen and left it cleaner than they had found it. Not that that stopped Madame Tablier going over it again anyway.

Next up was Richard's effort. He had initially attempted a red fruit pavlova but had gotten distracted along the way while watching *La Grande Bouffe*, a film about a group of friends trying to eat themselves to death. It nearly put him off food for life, so he took his eyes off what he was doing and in the end just hit the thing with a toffee hammer and created his own Eton mess. He assumed that this was exactly how the dish was invented anyway: high ideals ruined by distracted incompetence. Anyway, it was passable and Valérie gave him an encouraging smile, but it was noticeable to Richard that none of the desserts of the big players, and the real reason they were there, had been unveiled yet.

"Number seven!" Mabit announced, recovering from his soufflé nightmare and keen to get back involved. The metal lid came away to reveal a dark brown cake ring; nobody seemed to know what to do with it.

"It's a tzimmes cake." Morty Liebowitz stepped forward.

"Hey, it's supposed to be anonymous!" Abe hissed at him.

"Like they ain't gonna guess," Morty replied. "It's actually a stew, a traditional Jewish stew, that someone made up a recipe for a sweet cake out of."

Richard translated for the senator, who didn't seem at all keen, but, with an eye on international relations, he tried some anyway.

"I told you we shoulda gone with the rugelach," Abe said.

"No, I said the rugelach, you said the babka," Hymie countered.

"Ah." Morty shrugged his shoulders. "What does it matter anyways?"

There were only four entrants left and Richard was beginning to suspect that the order of presentation hadn't been as random as was advertised. In fact, he just noticed Valérie stiffen up a little as Mabit grandly declared, "Number eight!"

The silver dome was lifted swiftly, and those who remembered Grosmallard's opening night gasped. There was the raspberry tart, the egg-shaped parfait, and the startling red handprint. It didn't look quite as neat as he'd remembered it; the handprint was slightly smudged and the pastry on the tart was coming apart. He noticed Grosmallard and Garçon take a keen interest in the plate as Royer took a spoonful.

"It's the vegan cheese again," spat Grosmallard. "You see, these dishes are on chilled trays, but still the parfait texture is wilting."

"Now you see it!" Garçon joked, then stepped back in case Grosmallard took a swing at him.

"I think it improves it," Hugo said haughtily. "And plenty of Paris restaurants have ordered my cheese already."

"Number nine!" Mabit decided it was best to move on.

"That's more like it!" Garçon hailed the new dessert. A raspberry tart with goat's cheese parfait on a blood-red hand. The crowd started to mutter among themselves, and Richard noticed Valérie nod toward the commissaire at the back. "Proper goat's cheese," Garçon added, unaware of the muttering behind him. "Oh, no offense," he added, aiming this at the Ménards. Royer took a clean spoon and ate a piece of the parfait, nodding, impressed, as he did so.

Grosmallard leaned in. "I see you changed the nasturtiums to violas. Unnecessary!" he declared.

Senator Royer was beginning, finally, to get a sense of something bigger than just a cooking competition. He had been sold this trip as a good PR exercise for rural votes, a free meal, and an opportunity to take a swipe at his son-in-law's infernal egotism. He now had the look of a man who really wanted to get away, and get away quickly.

"Next!" he said, not waiting for Mabit. The cloche came off. "Is this a joke?" he asked as the revealed plate contained a raspberry tart, a parfait of goat's cheese, and a blood-red hand, but this time with nasturtium leaves.

"No!" Grosmallard shouted, practically frothing at the mouth. "It is not a joke! This is my dessert. This is my recipe. I am the original." He looked around the room. "These people are all, in their way, imposters!" As a way to ingratiate yourself with the locals, it left something to be desired.

Royer looked pained as well and put down his spoon, almost mournfully. "This tastes beautiful," he said sadly.

"Was it ever in doubt?" Grosmallard was triumphant and he was not the kind to hide it.

"Well, we still have one more to try." Mabit was a stickler for rules, and though everyone felt the competition was over, he had a duty to see it through. "Number eleven," he said with little enthusiasm.

The waitress pulled up the cloche and the crowd gasped. A perfect raspberry and beetroot tart, delicately adorned with nasturtium flowers, sat next to a glistening, marble-like goat's cheese parfait, the texture of which still remained despite the wait. And underneath was a blood-red handprint. But it was different from the other handprints. The others were bolder, aggressive even, masculine. This handprint was more delicate, elegant too, feminine.

Everyone was silent. Grosmallard was as white as his chef's tunic and Karine, in deep shock herself, had to almost hold him up. Royer looked like he might weep and asked for a chair. "Madame d'Orçay. I think you have won." He sounded defeated, and he hadn't even tasted it.

"No," Valérie said quietly. "Not I." And she opened up the envelope sitting next to the final plate. Taking out the card inside, she held it up for all to see who had made the dessert.

Angélique Royer, it said, and Sébastien Grosmallard broke down, sobbing.

35

Karine looked torn between who to comfort: the sobbing, incoherent Sébastien slumped on a chair, or the more dignified old man, Royer, who in his way looked just as broken. It was interesting, Richard noted, that she chose the latter. Nobody else dared move, let alone leave, and nobody said a word either. Richard had a feeling that though Valérie's plan seemed to have had the desired effect on the mighty chef—breaking him, that is—he looked too far gone for any sort of lucid admission of guilt. Of course, it might have been an act, but he didn't think it was.

Madame Mabit was the first to make a move. Having decided enough was enough and that nothing seemed to be happening, she reached into her enormous handbag and pulled out her knitting. There was no sense wasting an opportunity; it wasn't in her nature. Valérie herself was very calm about everything.

"I apologize for the theatrics," she began, knowing she had everyone's attention as soon as she opened her mouth.

"Was it absolutely necessary?" There was fire in Karine's eyes as she spoke, and Richard couldn't make up his mind whether she had a point or not. She was sitting in among the wreckage of her family, two men broken, somehow, by a high-class dessert, and also coming on top of the murder of her brother and the previous suicide of her mother. She wasn't the luckiest of young women, Richard concluded, far from it.

"I'm afraid I saw no other way. You yourself were worried about the effect it would have on your father...so the ends justified the means."

"You are an evil woman!" Karine shouted, causing Madame Mabit to miss a stitch and curse.

"We'll see," was the enigmatic reply.

Senator Royer put his head back and took in a deep breath; he closed his eyes slowly. "How long have you known about it, madame?" He spoke softly.

"Ah." Valérie's eyes widened playfully. "But that depends what you mean by 'it.'"

"Must we have more games?" asked the old man wearily.

"I'm not playing games, Monsieur le Sénateur, far from it." She turned and smiled at Richard for some reason, which had the unnerving effect of making him think he should know a bit more about what was going on than he did. "The games have gone on long enough, too long," she continued. "That is why we have three, possibly four, murders."

"Four murders?" Richard immediately regretted asking this as a question, and repeated it straight away more as a statement. "Four murders."

Everybody started talking at once. Noel Mabit went white as a sheet, and to show just how upset he was about the whole thing, he even sat down next to his wife. She concentrated on her knitting, while Madame Tablier, sitting the other side, nodded sagely as if she'd known all along. The Fontaines had a look on their faces that suggested four murders must be very messy, the Liebowitz brothers chewed gum, this kind of carry-on presumably being just an ordinary day in New Jersey, and René DuPont shrugged his shoulders. Guy Garçon lost his cheeky chappie persona for an instant, the Ménards looked pained as usual, and the commissaire caught Richard's eye with a questioning look that seemed to be asking if Valérie was on to something, had flipped her cog, or had just miscounted. Martin and Gennie had a very English fixed smile on each of their faces until Martin said, not unreasonably, "There's never a dull day around here, is there?"

The only person, apart from Valérie, who didn't seem surprised by this bombshell was Senator Royer. His son-in-law was still wrestling with some inner torment and didn't look, on the face of it, like he would ever recover. Karine stared at the floor, and she looked heartbroken.

"Again, madame," the senator said eventually, "I ask how long you have known."

She came and stood next to Richard. "I can't take all the credit. Richard was the first to point out your son-in-law's, for want of a better word, disability." Everyone looked at Richard.

"I was," he said, not sounding entirely convinced, or convincing.

"What disability?" It was a frustrated-sounding commissaire, who, to Richard's relief, seemed to know even less than he did.

"Sébastien Grosmallard has some form of olfactory disorder. He cannot smell or detect taste," she declared. "He hasn't been able to for years." Grosmallard finally looked up on hearing his name, but offered nothing else. "It was one of the reasons he could never recreate the dessert that made *his* name; that complicated blend of delicate, mellow flavors was utterly beyond him."

"And the others?"

"What?" Valérie was a little annoyed by the interruption.

"You said *one* of the reasons; there were others?"

"Oh yes. One other main reason." She paused for effect. "He simply didn't have the talent."

The room was stunned. Richard, however, saw this as his opportunity to at least chip in with some of the stuff he did know.

"It wasn't his dessert," he said simply. "Angélique invented the dessert that made his name; it said as much in his recipe book thing. *Dessert par Angélique*—he was trying to recreate it. It was never his in the first place, but being a man"—he nodded at Valérie—"and in a man's world, he took the credit. It became synonymous with his great success." Valérie smiled at him encouragingly. "Poor Angélique," he continued, "couldn't live with his arrogance and took her own life, but before doing so she tore the original recipe out of the notebook, making it even harder for him personally to recreate. I think it's why he's so tormented now. It's driven him insane."

"And the murders, then?" The commissaire had a skeptical look on his face, which had the effect of taking some of the wind out of Richard's sails.

"Well, it's obvious," Richard blustered. "Fabrice Ménard and Antonin mucked up the dessert on the opening night and Auguste Tatillon was very publicly going after his reputation. Grosmallard really did think he was untouchable."

Everyone stared at him, a range of expressions on their faces from awe and worship on the part of Jeanine, through rank indifference from the New Jersey contingent, to bewildered surprise from Valérie. Richard sat down in triumph, then immediately shot back up again to add to his explanations. "And the blackmail," he said grandly, "financed all of his restaurants. Not cheap, these restaurants." He sat down again.

"Blackmail," the senator repeated knowingly. "Who, may I ask, is in possession of those documents now?"

Richard preferred not to say, as this question seemed to reawaken the Liebowitz brothers.

"Those documents are in a safe-deposit box in Paris." Valérie was calmness personified. "The deposit box is not in my name, and it will not be touched"—Royer went to interrupt her—"just so long as justice is done." She looked at Grosmallard.

Senator Royer nodded his head slowly. "You have my word," he said quietly, and looked with contempt at Sébastien Grosmallard, who was still rocking on a chair and muttering to himself, "though I fear he can only be judged by a higher power now."

"Ha!" Richard couldn't help himself. "John Gielgud, *Murder by Decree*, 1978!" he said, receiving an evil look from the senator, which left him in little doubt that he had ruined the politician's big exit.

"Commissaire LaPierre, you must take him away," Royer said, standing stiffly. "Come, my child." He motioned his hand toward Karine.

Richard felt a pat on his shoulder as Martin stood behind him. "Well done, old man, that was quite the performance!"

"You were so brave!" Jeanine and Gennie both gushed.

"Oh well, you know..."

"Senator?" It was Valérie, standing by the door. "You have agreed that justice will be done."

"I have, madame," he said tetchily, not used to his word being questioned. "I made a promise." Richard didn't know where Valérie was going with this, but he did know that a promise from a politician was like an ice pop in summer, and you'd better make the most of it quickly before it disappears.

"Then we aren't finished here yet, are we?"

The old man's face dropped. "Do we need to do this, madame?" He nodded toward Sébastien. "Is it really necessary?"

"Yes, it is." Richard had never heard her voice sound so solemn.

Everybody sat back down, and Valérie took the floor, walking down the aisle as she spoke.

"As I said, it was Richard who broke the first clue," she said, smiling at him, and leading him to feel once again that for all the pats on the back, he didn't *really* know what was going on.

"Richard told me how he and his lovely family went to eat at Les Gens Qui Mangent, where Monsieur Grosmallard flirted with Richard's wife, even complimenting her on her perfume. But..."

"But she wasn't wearing any!" Richard said excitedly.

"Precisely. That struck me as odd."

"Well, it gives her a rash."

"Oh, I get that," Gennie added.

"No." There was the slightest hint of impatience from Valérie. "That he would make it up. Most women wear perfume; it is a simple lie to make. But why do it? Unless you were covering up that you have no sense of smell."

"Hence he couldn't get the dessert right without my poor Angélique, and why he missed the vegan goat's cheese substitute. We have been through this, madame. The olfactory disorder, yes."

"Not entirely, senator. Sébastien Grosmallard arranged for the goat's cheese substitute himself!"

Again there was no reaction from the chef, but everyone began muttering their surprise.

"Why, madame, it makes no sense!" It was the commissaire.

"Because it was the wisest course of action. He thought that if he could not make the dessert perfectly, he would make it deliberately badly and cover up his failings by blaming saboteurs."

"Why make the dessert at all, then?" Guy Garçon made a fair point, after sitting silently for most of the evening.

"Auguste Tatillon, that is why. In her efforts to build her father up once more, Karine wanted as much publicity as possible. It meant Tatillon and it meant his signature dish. He had no choice."

"I arranged it for him," Karine said softly, a look of pity on her face.

"If he arranged the goat's cheese, why kill Ménard? They were in it together!" The commissaire had struck a chord with the group and everyone again started talking at once.

"My father was not in anything with anyone!" Hugo Ménard stood angrily while Elisabeth tugged on his sleeve with a look of "What does it matter?" on her face.

Valérie let things die down a bit. "No, he wasn't, monsieur. You supplied the cheese, as per Monsieur Grosmallard's order. The vegan cheese." Hugo sat down. "Your father warned you not to get involved with Monsieur Grosmallard's plan, but you saw a chance to make a name for the new Ménard brand."

"My father was old-fashioned." He shook his head. "I thought it would make him proud of me."

"So..." The commissaire sounded weary. "I don't understand. Are you saying that the first victim, Fabrice Ménard, was killed by Sébastien Grosmallard because he *didn't* supply the vegan cheese, even though his son did? That makes no sense."

"Ah, but, commissaire, the first victim was not Fabrice Ménard. The first victim was Angélique Royer."

36

It took a while for the hubbub to die down, and as an uneasy silence fell on the room, it was Karine who spoke. "My mother killed herself," she hissed, like a serpent about to strike.

"Murder, suicide. They can be much the same thing, you know?" Valérie's blasé reply had possibly struck the wrong chord with the room, its cold, matter-of-fact tone not taking into account the feelings of the group, and Richard felt the need to offer a palate cleanser.

"I think what Madame d'Orçay means is the same as Alec Guinness in *Murder by Death*, 1976, and I'm paraphrasing: 'She murdered herself, it wasn't suicide, she hated herself.'" It had the desired effect of taking the spotlight off Valérie's apparent coldness, if only because everyone now looked at Richard and wondered if he was as gaga as the now blithering Sébastien Grosmallard.

"No, Richard. I did not mean that," Valérie said.

"Oh."

"I mean that your mother may have committed suicide, or she may have been murdered. But if one is driven to suicide by others it is murder, no?"

Commissaire LaPierre, who still hadn't taken his eyes off Richard after his last film knowledge intervention, was close to exploding. "So, now you are saying that Sébastien Grosmallard killed his wife, or maybe not. The law demands a little more precision than that, madame."

Richard noticed a cold smile on the face of Senator Royer as Valérie appeared to be losing a grip on proceedings.

"I agree, Commissaire LaPierre," she countered him with the same formality he had shown her. *It must have been a very odd marriage*, Richard thought. "To do that we have to go further back. Twenty-five or so years back, to the Lac des Petites Îles." She paused for effect. Royer's skin tone never changed but there was a definite tension in the jaw. Elisabeth Ménard started crying quietly, but rather than react angrily, as was his way, Hugo sat next to her and put his arm around her. "I understand your pain, Madame Ménard. I am truly sorry that it must be brought to light."

"What are they talking about now?" Madame Mabit asked impatiently over the clicking of her knitting needles.

"The Lac des Petites Îles," was Madame Tablier's response, in a tone suggesting things were about to get even juicier.

"Sodom *and* Gomorrah!" was her friend's high-voiced reply.

"Madame, I really think we should stick with the present..."

"No offense, senator, but you would say that," said Valérie.

The man's eyes burned at her words.

"The camp or commune or whatever it was reached almost mythical status around here. They had never seen its kind of thing before, or since. But what was it?"

"Sodom!" shouted Madame Mabit.

"And Gomorrah!" Madame Tablier completed the biblical title.

"Where you there, though, *mesdames*?" She waited for a reply, which didn't come. "No. It was what these things usually are. A place for young people to feel free, yes, to overindulge, yes, to probably break a little law. But be free before *life*, real adult life, takes over." It was obvious to Richard that this was clearly a subject she felt passionate about. "What harm do they do *usually*? Not much. This one did, though." She knelt by Elisabeth Ménard. "Didn't it, madame?"

She responded by nodding silently.

"Forgetting who else was there, for us there were two young couples. Fabrice Ménard and his young wife, Elisabeth, and Sébastien Grosmallard with Angélique Royer. Angélique was different to the others: she came from a wealthy background and had money, an allowance, which they all lived off. And they did what young people do. They had fun. Then both women became pregnant."

Elisabeth sobbed louder.

"Both by Sébastien Grosmallard."

Hugo bowed his head and hugged his mother tighter.

"Fabrice Ménard had a congenital heart condition and was unable to have children. Again, it was Richard who worked this out."

"Fired blanks?" Martin leaned in behind Richard, but Richard just rolled his eyes.

"An ambitious politician, Léopold Royer could not accept the damage this would cause to his career and privately visited the camp, demanding it be shut down. What was worse was that while his daughter Angélique had given birth to a daughter, the other woman, Elisabeth, had twin boys."

Royer buried his head in his hands.

"A terrible, terrible deal was struck that night. One that I believe we are paying the price for now."

The room let all of this sink in for a moment, and Valérie theatrically allowed them to do so. It also gave Richard a chance to feel rather satisfied with himself as he realized that his witterings about Bette Davis and Joan Crawford swapping roles, being sisters and so on, may just have been the key that unlocked this for Valérie.

"In exchange for the money to set up their business, Royer took one of the boys from Fabrice and Elisabeth, the eldest of the two boys, and forced him on his daughter and son-in-law. All because he wanted a boy, a grandson, a future protégé, because a girl wouldn't be good enough!" She took a breath to calm down. "Neither Elisabeth nor Angélique ever really recovered. The camp was broken up, the money used to forge a glittering career on the back of Sébastien's apparent genius, and the seeds were sown for a family disaster."

"But why kill Angélique Royer?" The commissaire sounded less skeptical now.

"Because she was trying to kill him." She pointed at Grosmallard. "This anosmia, the loss of smell or taste, or whatever he has, it came gradually. She poisoned him. Presumably some heavy metal substance like cadmium or thallium; they have side effects like that. Eventually it would lead to death. But when she realized that it took any culinary skills he had away from him, and did it slowly... it became a preferred, tortuous method of destruction. She came up with the idea of the recipe, used her father's connections and Tatillon to promote it, and a glittering future for Grosmallard was assured. If—if—Angélique was there on hand with her culinary talent."

Grosmallard continued to whimper in the corner. It was difficult to tell if any of this had gone in or not, and nobody wanted to get close enough to really investigate either.

"I do not know," Valérie continued slowly, "if Angélique was driven to suicide or whether Sébastien found out and forced her own poison on her, or even whether Senator Royer killed his own daughter for ruining the Grosmallard business."

"Madame!" Senator Royer sprung to his feet. "That is enough. That I would kill my own daughter because she was bringing to an end her husband's restaurant is vile. It is absurd. You go too far!"

"Oh no, senator," Valérie shot back and the crowd responded like spectators at a tennis match and turned their heads to the other side of the room. "Because she was ruining the very lucrative sideline: blackmail!"

The senator sat down again.

"The Grosmallard restaurant became very fashionable and very popular, not just for the food. But for the back room, or was it an upstairs room? It doesn't matter. People of power would use it, and you, senator, would subsequently use them. You made it look like Grosmallard was the blackmailer, but it was you. I do not know if you killed Angélique; maybe she was planning to reveal what you were, but you used her for sure."

The old man looked around the room. If he was expecting sympathy or even a vestige of respect for his exalted position, there was none. "You have no evidence, madame."

"For Angélique's death, no. But I know where the blackmail dossier is, and you do not want me to approach the other names in it, do you?"

The commissaire coughed nervously. "I can only go with the

evidence, madame, which means for now I must arrest Sébastien Grosmallard."

Nobody really knew what to do at that point. Was it over, even? Richard was trying hard to bite his lip and not blurt out that hiring a room for higher-ups to indulge in extra marital relationships was similar to the Billy Wilder comedy *The Apartment*, but that Jack Lemmon was too nice a guy to take pictures. He decided to draw a line under the thing instead. "So really, we're back where we were. Grosmallard killed Fabrice and Antonin for ruining his dessert, even though he ruined the dessert, knowing that he wouldn't be touched for it. And he killed Tatillon because he was about to break the story wide open."

Most people seemed satisfied with that conclusion and they began to stand up and stretch their limbs, all except for Grosmallard and Royer.

Richard still had questions, though. "But how did Tatillon get his hands on the blackmail dossier?" Everyone stopped shuffling about and pondered this line of inquiry.

"Ah," Valérie began, and everybody began to sit down again. "Because Grosmallard gave it to him."

The reaction was immediate. It was like the end of a horse race when everyone is shouting at once, but most of them shouting different things. The commissaire tried to calm the mob down; Noel Mabit even banged his gavel on the wall, but to no great effect.

"That makes no sense, madame!" It was the commissaire who got his question in first. "Why give him this dossier, then kill him and not retrieve the dossier?"

"He's got a point there," Martin said. "Unless there's a plea of insanity and stupidity in France."

Valérie smiled, but it was Richard who spoke. "Because Sébastien Grosmallard did not kill Auguste Tatillon," he said.

Pandemonium broke loose again. But this time Madame Mabit grabbed her husband's gavel and banged it harder, immediately getting the room into order. The commissaire sat down, shaking his head.

"The problem is that we have all presumed that the motive is Sébastien Grosmallard's monstrous ego. Fabrice, murdered. Antonin, murdered. Why? Because he needed scapegoats to hide his lack of talent. Tatillon, murdered. Why? Because he dared question the talent of the great Grosmallard." Some people turned to look at the man; now there was no ego left, just an enormous husk. "I agree, the man's ego was monstrous, it was destructive. A man must be the genius chef, a man must have a son—he agreed with Royer on that."

"Typical," Madame Tablier threw in.

"I agree, Madame Tablier. But this, no, this was woman's work. A mother gives up her child; that child is a constant reminder of that pain. Someone else is close to finding this out..."

All eyes turned on Elisabeth Ménard, who suddenly looked terrified. "No!" shouted her son, holding her even tighter.

"Do not move!" The words were said calmly, but loudly enough to again silence the room. All eyes turned to the speaker, who had an arm around Valérie's neck and one of Madame Mabit's knitting needles jabbed sharply at her throat. "I will not hesitate to kill you. I think you know that by now." Karine Grosmallard most definitely meant what she said.

The room was rapt by the sight and realization that it was Karine who had been behind all of this. That this apparently devoted daughter, the staunch defender of the Grosmallard brand, was behind its spectacular, explosive downfall. Richard, though on the same wavelength as everybody else, was also wondering how Valérie, as stealthy as a leopard and as in control as a film auteur, had allowed Karine to sneak up on her like that.

"Hey, that's my knitting needle!" cried an outraged Madame Mabit. "You"—she nudged her husband—"go and get it back."

"Stay where you are!" Karine shouted, and Mabit, never having seriously considered the alternative, did as he was told. He even put his hands up, throwing a ball of wool away as he did so, as though it were a primed explosive. The wool landed at Richard's feet across the aisle of chairs where he had sat down, wondering what to do next.

"Karine, please." Senator Royer stood, his arms open and pleading to his granddaughter. "No more."

She laughed at him malevolently. "Look how weak you are, all of you. My father, broken. You, begging. You all ruined my life! The weak Ménard gave up a son to take *my* place. A weak little boy who never grew up. Auguste Tatillon, another weak, vain man. And all of you controlled and haunted by my mother, the only powerful one in the family." She laughed a hollow laugh once more. "And it even took a woman to work it out too!"

"I could not have done it without Richard's help."

Richard was usually keen to be thrown a few crumbs of praise but this didn't feel like the right time, so he avoided eye contact with either of them and picked up the ball of wool from the floor instead.

Valérie still looked relaxed, though. "It was all very clever, Karine," she continued, as though it were a conversation over a coffee. "You persuade your father to build up the business with blackmail money and contacts. The intention was to put the name Grosmallard back at the top of the culinary tree, was it not? And then you shake the tree, and watch him fall from an even greater height than before. You kill Ménard first to throw suspicion on your father, a half-hearted suicide note in your father's forged writing, just in case. And the tree starts to shake. Then you kill Antonin while pretending to be in Paris, and the tree should shake some more, but it does not. The body has been removed. The investors have paid for people to protect their investment and the dossier from being revealed. *Bonsoir*, gentlemen."

The Liebowitz brothers all gave her a muted response; presumably they wanted to bicker about how their cover had been blown but felt this wasn't the time. "Ma'am," was all Morty offered.

Valérie continued. "They removed the body, assuming that it was Grosmallard, their clients' investment, who had killed him. You had left out a notebook detailing payments also, but Richard found that. Oh, take that look off your face, commissaire." She turned back to Karine. "You then killed Tatillon and planted the blackmail dossier where you knew it would be found."

Karine didn't deny any of this but looked like she was going through a mental checklist to ensure nothing was left out.

"Have I missed anything? No. I would guess that Guy Garçon was next on your list. The rather obvious menu choices, which again the male ego didn't see. The frog legs, like Ménard and ironically like Antonin, but that was just luck, as that was how the Liebowitzs dumped the body when they realized it wasn't their client's doing. The crown of thorns, the dessert. Always, the dessert."

"Karine." It was the senator, still standing. "I cannot protect you anymore. This must stop now."

"You never did protect her, monsieur. I even have a feeling that you knew all along."

The senator moved threateningly forward and at surprising speed, taking aim for Valérie with a murderous look in his eyes. Richard jumped to stand in his way, and as he did so he pulled on the ball of wool trapped around the chair legs. The senator tripped into Richard's arms as Valérie, using the distraction to move the knitting needle away from her neck, grabbed Karine's necklace and collar and used them to throw her over her shoulder, knocking the old man and Richard down in the process like bowling pins. Valérie held the broken necklace and immediately opened up the prayer locket. She unrolled a small piece of paper. It was the original *dessert pour Sébastien.*

The doors crashed open, surprising the Liebowitzs and Commissaire LaPierre, who were still in shock and in position. The crowd all turned around with a "What now?" look on their faces.

"Have you lot not finished yet?" Monsieur Clavet was beside himself, even for a caretaker. "I've got a Zumba group in twenty minutes."

37

Richard and Valérie sat as if in a bubble at a corner table on the terrace of the Café de Tasses Cassées. They were both exhausted by the evening's events, Valérie especially, who had conducted the whole thing like a circus ringmaster or an orchestra conductor. The plan, not that she'd let anyone else entirely into it, seemed to have gone without a hitch, and now she had her eyes closed and was enjoying the last of the warm evening sun, reunited with her beloved Passepartout. The commissaire and his men were dealing with the fallout of Karine's confession and Royer's involvement. Both of them, and Grosmallard, had been taken away. The Liebowitz brothers had vanished into thin air. Guy Garçon was now calling his restaurant a "pop-up," which meant he had no intention of sticking around. Jeanine had preparation to do for the Sunday trade. And the Ménards, Elisabeth and Hugo, had gone quietly home to deal with their grief and vegan dairy products.

"I mean, I get it." Martin was taking a small spoon to what was left of the raspberry and beetroot tart on the table in front of them,

Gennie sipping a gin and tonic next to him. "It's nice, but is it four-murders nice? Seems a bit of overkill to me."

"Oh, Martin!"

"What? Oh! Ha! No pun intended."

Richard smiled and looked at the smeared plate. "I don't think it's what it is as such, but what it represented. Power and place and all that."

"Ah, right." Martin still didn't sound sure. "Well, I've had some expensive tarts in my time—"

"That's enough, Martin," Gennie interrupted firmly, putting a stop to whatever innuendo barrage Martin had in mind. "Did you really make this, Valérie? You've missed your calling..."

Valérie sat up and had a sip of her drink. "Oh, no. I had it delivered from a patisserie in Montmartre. They are excellent and I knew they could do it."

"Well, you see that's the thing for me." Martin had more points to clear up. "If it's so easily copied, what was all the fuss about?"

Richard decided to explain. "It was that Grosmallard couldn't do it, firstly, that he was a fraud from the start. Almost a front, if you like, for Royer's blackmail, and then when he was poisoned as well, it added to his lack of talent. It drove him mad." He paused for a second. "And in a sense Karine was carrying on her mother's work, torment-ing the man who had killed, in one way or another, her mother."

"And just tasting it set him off?"

"Oh no," Richard said. "It was the touch that all the other chefs missed. They had always put their own handprint on the plate. But it was a woman who invented the recipe; the first time Grosmallard saw it, it would have been a woman's hand, with the wedding ring imprint. That's how, I believe, Angélique first presented the dish to him. Now the handprints are manufactured, I suppose, but the first was with, and by, her hand. That's what broke him."

"You are clever, you two! You should become detectives." Gennie beamed.

Valérie smiled at Richard. It was a tempting idea, was his feeling on the subject. Valérie would be the brain and the brawn, while he, like an idiot savant, would produce odd flashes of gibbering, cinema-related brilliance and develop a cramp-based martial art.

"And presumably they'll get the book thrown at them. No more friends in high places."

Something clicked with Richard, and he made a mental note to ask Valérie about it later.

"OK, *mesdames et messieurs*, here's some champagne!" René popped the cork on a bottle and poured out five glasses. "*Santé*," he said, raising his glass.

"This is good stuff, René, where did you get it?" Richard asked, recognizing the taste.

"Ah." René smiled. "The same place as I got a full restaurant of customers tonight." The others looked blankly at him. "Grosmallard's place. I drove up there after we finished earlier and put a notice on the door. 'Closed for good. Your reservations will be honored at the Café des Tasses Cassées.' And I borrowed some stock, too." He finished his glass. "Well, he's not going to need it, is he? Right, I'd better crack on. I've never been so busy; that Mabit bloke is helping Remi in the kitchen while Mesdames Mabit and Tablier are helping me serve." He dashed off.

"I'm not sure the concept of customer service could survive a three-pronged attack like that." Richard was thinking aloud. "A lot of those people are expecting Michelin stars and silver service. Instead they're getting Remi's omelettes served with menaces."

"Look, if you're not eating, you'll have to go." Madame Tablier had appeared and was as ever taking her role seriously.

They got up to leave, said their goodbyes, and Richard, Valérie, and Passepartout walked slowly back across the square to her car.

"What do you think, Richard?"

He waited a second before answering. "I think you put the hooks into *Friends in High Places* Potineaux," he said. "That's why you went to Paris. Somehow you knew he was involved. Now, how would you know?"

She turned to face him. "Richard, a journalist never reveals their sources."

"You're not a journalist."

"I am sometimes, if a cover is needed. Anyway, that's not what I asked. I was asking about what Gennie said."

"About becoming detectives? What, private eyes?"

"Yes."

"Answer me this first. Did you really know Olivia de Havilland? You didn't seem to recognize her in Grosmallard's photo."

They'd reached the car and she bent down to put Passepartout in the back seat, then she looked at him. "You won't like the answer, Richard."

He looked crestfallen; he'd known it all along. That she'd lied to him. "Oh well," he said, not able to hide his disappointment.

"The answer, Richard, is yes. I did know her. I didn't really look at the picture, and she was glamorous, I think there, for the press? I knew her as a neighbor."

He perked up immediately. "Really?"

"Yes." Then she looked guilty. "But I didn't know *who* she was; she was just a little old lady, that was all."

He thought about this for a second and decided it was more charming that way. "Well in that case, I don't have a choice, do I? I have to join your detective agency just to plug the shocking gaps in your knowledge." She smiled and kissed him on the cheek. "Oh, hang on. How can I? I'm probably going to have to sell up anyway. I'll need to pay for a divorce."

"Oh, don't worry about that, Richard," she said breezily. "The new regime of South Sudeliland have proved to be very fast payers."

They both got in the car. "I thought that was you. Good old general Winston Cash, eh? I'll raise a glass to him." Though in truth he was uneasy as to whether he was really up to this line of work or, especially, Valérie's dangerous lifestyle. She turned the key in the ignition. There was nothing. "You may have to buy a new car too," he said as she tried again, with the same result. She kept trying but still it wouldn't start.

"It's no good, Richard, you'll have to get out and push."

"Push, me?"

"Well, I cannot do it in these heels!"

He got out petulantly, slamming the door behind him, now having serious doubts about any future joint venture. After a hefty shove and some under-the-breath expletives, the car stuttered and jumped into life and kangarooed along the road.

A puffing Richard fell into the passenger seat. "Fasten your seatbelt, Richard," Valérie said, a thrill in her voice, "it's going to be a bumpy ride."

It was close enough for him; he was in.

Acknowledgments

Once again, my sincere thanks go to my family, Natalie, Samuel, Maurice, and Thérence, who ride this rollercoaster with white knuckles most of the time. We laugh and love, and there's not much more you need in the world than that.

To all the people who make this dream a reality, I say a hearty thanks—to my agent, Bill Goodall, and to all at Farrago Books: Pete Duncan, Rob Wilding, and Matt Casbourne and to Abbie Headon, for always being there. A *grand merci* to Christelle Couchoux, who helped with French-language specifics when I was too embarrassed to approach my family.

None of this would have been possible without the above, and none of it would have even been thinkable without the glorious goats cheese producers here in the Loire Valley. As Monty Python once said, "Blessed are the cheesemakers."

About the Author

Ian Moore is a leading stand-up comedian, known for his sharp, entertaining punditry. He has performed all over the world, on every continent except South America. A TV/radio regular, he stars in Dave's satirical TV show *Unspun* and Channel 5's topical *Comedy Bigmouths*.

Credit: © Richard Wood

Ian lives in rural France and commutes back to the UK every week. In his spare time, he makes mean chutneys and jams.

He is also the author of two memoirs on life in France contrasting with life on the road in the UK. *À la Mod: My So-Called Tranquil Family Life in Rural France* and *C'est Modnifique: Adventures of an English Grump in Rural France.*

Death at the Chateau

(A FOLLET VALLEY MYSTERY 3)

R ichard Ainsworth and Valérie d'Orçay have set up their detective agency, and after eschewing all "marital work," to avoid being ostracized by French society, they now have their first assignment. They are to protect beautiful actress Lionel Margaux as she works on a Franco-American film production in the nearby Chateau de Valençay.

Richard's first day on the job starts badly when a Resistance hero dies on set, and despite all the evidence pointing to natural causes, Richard tries to convince a skeptical Valérie otherwise. But when major American film star Reed Turnbull also dies in mysterious circumstances, they both know there's definitely a murderer in the crew.

COMING SOON